The Body in the Wardrobe

The Body in the Wardrobe

A Faith Fairchild Mystery

Katherine Hall Page

An Imprint of HarperCollinsPublishers

Grateful acknowledgment is made by the publisher for permission to reprint
"The Queens Came Late" by Norma Farber. Copyright © by Thomas
Farber. Used by permission. Thanks to Dr. Daniel Pinkham, Director of
Music, King's Chapel, Boston, for providing me with the information about
the poem, originally a choral lyric.

HarperCollins books may be purchased for educational, business, or
sales promotional use. For information please e-mail the Special Markets
Department at SPsales@harpercollins.com.

FIRST HARPERLUXE EDITION

ISBN: 978-0-06-246629-7

HarperLuxe™ is a trademark of HarperCollins Publishers.

Library of Congress Cataloging-in-Publication Data is available upon
request.

16 17 18 19 20 ID/RRD 10 9 8 7 6 5 4 3 2 1

For Meg Katz, Sandy Kay, and Valerie Wolzien
My Savannah Trio

All shall be done, but it may be harder than you think.

—C. S. LEWIS, *The Lion, the Witch and the Wardrobe*

Acknowledgments

Many thanks to the following for help from a broad area of expertises: Faith Hamlin, Ed Maxwell, Dr. Robert DeMartino, Luci Hansson Zahray (The Poison Lady), Katherine Nintzel, Danielle Bartlett, Maria Silva, Marguerite Weisman, Jean Fogelberg, Michael Epstein, Ann Walker, and Savannah chef extraordinaire Joe Randall.

Some liberty has been taken with the geography of the city of Savannah as well as with what may or may not be underground in this work of fiction.

Chapter 1

When Sophie Maxwell became engaged to Will Tarkington Maxwell (the surnames a happy coincidence), she assumed she would be acquiring a number of new kin, but during her first visit to Savannah, Will's hometown, she was startled to discover she was soon to be related to roughly half the population of Georgia. Introductions such as "My mother's cousin Jack's sister-in-law" and "Aunt Nancy's son's second wife" spilled from Will's lips with bewildering speed at an equally bewildering number of gatherings—Savannahians liked a party. Rather than even begin to try to remember everyone, Sophie smiled—and smiled again.

She had met Will the previous summer on Sanpere Island in Maine's Penobscot Bay. Will had accompanied his great-uncle, Paul McAllister, to Paul's late wife Priscilla's "cottage," The Birches—said cottage more like those of a similar name in Bar Harbor and Newport. Priscilla had been Sophie's great-aunt. It was Paul's difficult job to decide which of his wife's nieces and nephews should inherit the valuable property.

It was far from love at first sight for Sophie and Will. He assumed she was as money grubbing and devious as the rest of the contenders. She found him arrogant and crude. They sniped at each other incessantly and, of course, fell madly in love. After Will saved Sophie from the clutches of a murderer, their troth was definitely plighted. And, having come through such danger, they didn't want to wait too long for their happily-ever-after. At the end of the summer Will, a private investigator, had to return south to his practice. Sophie went from Sanpere to her childhood home in Connecticut to plan the fall wedding. She'd grown up in a large beautifully restored Victorian overlooking Long Island Sound. The restoration had been accomplished over many years, and many husbands, by her mother, Babs. Sophie thought her mother had finally found a keeper in Ed Harrington, who was a sweetheart. Since he played a great deal of golf in many locations, the marriage was succeeding. Babs liked her space and was of the "For Better or Worse, but Not for Lunch" School.

Sophie had assumed Babs would want a lavish wedding for her only child. Plus Babs had a wealth of experience planning trips down the aisle to draw upon. Resolved to agree to whatever her mother wanted, mentally drawing a line, however, at the release of a flock of white doves, Sophie was surprised, when they sat down to talk, to find that her mother was proposing exactly what Sophie herself had envisioned.

"Smallish," Babs had said. "About a hundred total? And the ceremony outdoors with the double parlor's doors opened up to create an indoor room as backup. A best man for Will and some sort of maid or matron—really, these labels are so archaic—for you. Delicious food, that goes without saying, and plenty to drink. The reception and dancing in the barn. So glad we redid it for Ed's birthday party last year. And a Jenny Packham dress for you, love? Something Pre-Raphaelite, but beaded. We can run over to London, choose, and they'll send a toile. Time is short, but they'll rise to the occasion."

Sophie had shuddered at the last suggestion. Less than a year ago she had given up her corner office in a prestigious Manhattan law firm for what she mistakenly thought was the real thing, moving to London to be with her English beau.

Babs had picked up on the reaction immediately. "Oh, darling, you can't rule out the UK forever just because of one rotten banger in the mash. No matter. Such fun to go to the bridal salon at Bergdorf's instead. My first and third."

"It sounds perfect, Mother. Exactly what Will and I have talked about. We hoped the wedding could be at Sanpere, but impossible at this time of year. Are you sure this is what you'll be happy with, too? Something simple? I thought you'd want to go the whole nine yards. I only intend to do this once." Realizing that could be interpreted as a dig, she'd clapped her hand over her mouth and muttered, "Sorry!"

Babs had laughed. "I was an old-fashioned girl if you can believe it. I married them. Not like the young nowadays. All this hooking up."

It had been Sophie's turn to laugh at her mother's easy use of the slang phrase. And her mother was like a younger woman in other ways, particularly her appearance. Babs was not yet fifty, or not admitting it, and looked forty—late thirties on a good day—thanks to discreet vacations at a Costa Rica resort-cum-clinic.

"Thank you. It will be everything I've ever dreamed of," Sophie had said, kissing her mother. "Do you think we can shoot for a date in early November?"

"Darling girl, I could pull this whole thing together for next Saturday. Call Will and let's get going!"

It was only later that Sophie realized one of her mother's reasons for the small guest list was to limit the invitations for the groom's family. Georgia was a good-size state.

And so it was that on November 8, a brilliantly sunny Saturday, Sophie and Will exchanged vows with the glistening waters of the Sound as a backdrop. Uncle Paul gave Sophie away, Will's stepbrother, Randall, was Will's best man, and Sophie's cousin Autumn Proctor was her self-styled "best woman." There were no doves, but there were other white birds: terns and seagulls circled overhead, their cries reminding Sophie of Maine—and the way Will and she had met. She'd squeezed her husband's arm as they were showered with rose petals, making their way across the broad front lawn to the reception. In her other hand, Sophie clutched the nosegay bouquet Babs had designed: soft peach roses, mock orange, stephanotis, and shiny deep-green magnolia leaves. The only beading she wore was a Juliet cap of seed pearls on her dark hair. The long-sleeved ivory satin gown ended in filmy lace cuffs, its sole adornment. Will's preferred attire was casual veering toward grunge, but he wore a tux today and had even agreed to socks. What was it with Southern men and bare feet? Sophie had wondered throughout her Savannah visit. Not a bad look for most, but still . . .

Firmly rejecting her friend and caterer Faith Fairchild's offer to provide the comestibles—insisting she be a guest—Sophie *had* accepted the offer from the Reverend Thomas Fairchild, Faith's husband, to perform the ceremony, which he had done so beautifully most eyes were moist. As a teen on Sanpere Sophie had babysat for the Fairchild children, Ben and Amy, now teens themselves. The dramatic events of last summer had forged the friendship into a lifelong bond, one especially tight between Sophie and Faith.

A week later Sophie Maxwell Maxwell was again walking side by side with her beloved—on Georgia's Tybee Island beach at dusk, marveling that it was November and she didn't need a jacket. She'd be getting out the down coat designed by a Michelin Man were she still up north.

It was the last night of their honeymoon. Having taken the whole summer off, Will needed to catch up on work and suggested Tybee, a short thirty-minute commute from downtown, as an alternative to somewhere far away. Sophie had readily agreed. They had their whole lives for trips farther afield. And it had been a magical week. She fell in love with Tybee the moment she drove across the bridge past the shrimp boats and long marshes surrounding the tidal inlets. The feeling grew as Will drove by the island's brightly colored houses, lush tropical yards filled with eclectic artwork—and cars never besmirched by salted icy roads. Will had eagerly pointed out favorite spots and kept up a running commentary on the island's history, starting with his grandparents' stories of how they used to take the train out for dances at the old pavilion on the beach.

"Tybee is synonymous with a way of life around here. I guess it's a lot like the good part of the 1960s. Tybee people march to a different drummer. Always have and I hope always will."

Uncle Paul had given them his treasured vintage sports car, a 1973 Triumph Stag. It had supplied the occasion for their first meeting and it was only fitting that this should be the honeymoon car now. They hadn't had to put the top up once since Will had steered them into the driveway of one of the island's raised cottages. It looked like a house on stilts, something out of a folktale, Sophie thought.

While her new husband went into work, Sophie spent her days exploring, but first, at Will's insistence, sharing an early breakfast at The Breakfast Club on Butler Avenue, Tybee's main drag. Each morning Will tried to entice his bride into trying his favorite, "Helen's Solidarity AKA The Grill Cleaner's Special": diced potatoes, house-made Polish sausage, green peppers, and onions tossed on the hot griddle; two scrambled eggs, topped with melted Monterey Jack and American cheese; grits; and toast. Sophie had opted for other choices, twice the French toast made from the kitchen's own cinnamon raisin challah bread. Will had had to finish her helpings, even after his plate was clean. He was what was known as a "big, hungry boy" and never seemed to put an ounce on his tall, lanky frame.

Will had taken today off, their last day before heading back to the start of married life for real. They'd slept in, then not slept in, finally getting out of bed to lounge on the screened-in porch that overlooked the yard and was surrounded by live oaks dripping with Spanish moss. Sophie thought it was the most romantic plant she had ever seen, soft cascades like veils—maybe more Miss Havisham's than the Duchess of Cambridge's and even more mysterious at night filtering the moonlight. The moss was an "air plant" Will told her: it fed itself and wasn't a parasite like kudzu, or bittersweet in New England. When she had started to gather some to bring inside to arrange in a basket, he'd laughed and told her while harmless itself, it could harbor spiders, mice, and other critters Sophie might not want around.

Reluctantly leaving the house that had become home in a short period of time, they'd spent the rest of the day at the black-and-white-striped Tybee Lighthouse, towering far, far above the palm trees, and at the nearby Tybee Museum at Fort Screven—both things Will had planned for them to do that they hadn't gotten around to so far. After Lucile's Fish Po' Boys at Sting Ray's, another item on his list, they headed back and packed a basket for the beach. By the time they got there, the late afternoon sun was waning and the tide was turning. They kicked off their flip-flops and walked across the sand toward the incoming waves. By Maine standards the water was balmy, but Savannahians weren't swimming much this late in the year, and they had the beach to themselves.

"Happy, darling?" Will asked, pulling Sophie close.

She kissed him in reply, marveling at how comfortable she felt with this man—and safe. She kissed him harder and ran her hands up the back of the loose linen shirt he was wearing. His skin was warm. She felt her body respond, embracing him even closer, wanting to melt into him. He lifted her into his arms and ran back to the blanket they had spread out in a sheltered part of the beach. In the growing darkness, neither needed to say a word. Later, as she reached for her hastily discarded clothes, Sophie said, "In answer to that question of yours, *very* happy, darling."

Will popped the champagne they'd brought and they watched the moon begin to rise.

"I wish we could stay longer," Sophie said. "Somewhere in the neighborhood of forever. I love the house in the treetops."

"We can come back soon. There are more pretty cottages we can use when they're not rented. Gloria's late husband's family was very savvy when it came to real estate and got in early out here and in town."

Sophie knew this and was grateful. Gloria was Will's stepmother, and a cousin of hers had offered the Tybee house they were using. Further, until the newlyweds found their own place, they'd be living in a house near the river in the historic district that Gloria herself owned and was renovating for resale.

Will hadn't wanted to tie themselves down with a rental lease. He wanted his bride to get to know the area before deciding where they should live. "Doesn't have to be in the heart of town," he'd said. "Maybe out on Skidaway Island. I kind of like the notion of crossing the Moon River to get home." He'd hummed a few bars of the Johnny Mercer classic and Sophie thought how much luckier she was than Holly Golightly. Forget breakfast at Tiffany's; grits and eggs at The Breakfast Club was what she preferred. Breakfast anywhere—just so long as it was with Will.

Faith Fairchild had read somewhere that as you got older time seemed to pass faster, which didn't make sense—wouldn't time slow down as *you* did? But as she approached a milestone birthday (happily still not until spring) time *did* seem to be passing more quickly. For instance, what happened to fall? There were still things in the ironing basket from the summer on Sanpere. And—to be absolutely truthful—at the bottom, there were kids' things in the basket that only her future grandchildren would be able to fit into, as well as several damask tablecloths and napkins that she kept meaning to get to. Now, with the autumn months almost over, the Fairchilds were once again lurching into the holidays. This was always a tough time for clerical families, as Faith well remembered from her own childhood. Like her father, the Reverend Lawrence Sibley, Tom was in constant demand, not only for all those extra services that went with the gig, but also to tend to the members of his flock suffering from depression and loneliness, intensified by the jollity of the season.

Have Faith, Faith's catering firm, was also busy, swamped with jobs. In addition to her longtime partner, Niki Theodopoulos, Faith had hired her part-time assistant Tricia Phelan to work full-time until January.

Thanksgiving was still a week away, but they were busy making hors d'oeuvres that froze well, like phyllo triangles with various fillings, bite-size crab cakes, and both veggie and nonveggie pot stickers. As for Turkey Day, that was a meal Faith always loved to cook, and this year with her mother-in-law, Marian, fully recovered from heart surgery, Faith would be offering up more than her usual hearty thanks for the blessings in her life as she passed around her chestnut stuffing, giblet gravy, mashed potatoes, and the brussels sprouts with toasted walnuts that she had managed to convince her father-in-law to eat by not telling him what they were. "Love these cute little cabbage things," he'd announced after his first taste of the much-maligned vegetable. In addition to the Fairchild clan, neighbors Patsy and Will Avery with their children, Kianna and Devon, had been joining them for the last several years. Besides the excellent company they provided, Patsy brought her sweet potato pie (see recipe, page 234), which was everyone's favorite dessert, trumping apple and pumpkin. Patsy had had to bring two last year, along with plenty of her special family recipe for the caramel pecan sauce to pour on top.

As she worked in the catering kitchen alongside the others, Faith was nagged by the thought that although it had been a good fall for the rest of the family, it hadn't been for her daughter, Amy.

A moment later, Niki seemed to have read her partner's mind. "Are things going better for Amy at school?"

Faith sighed. "Not really. She's still clinging to her old friends and we've had to limit her Skype time with Daisy out in California—the Proctor girl she made friends with last summer." The Fairchilds had been given sound advice when son Ben was Amy's age to move computers to public spaces like the kitchen. An adult presence made kids pause before hitting the button that would send something into cyberspace— and possibly all over the globe.

"I may be the mother of a toddler," Niki said, "and a toddler that is adding years to my own every day— Sofia swallowed a paper clip Sunday, and the books do *not* tell you what to do about that; you just wait, by the way—but I am not so far removed from adolescence that I don't recall what hell it was. Even my mother, who as you know is the queen of clichés, didn't dare say they were the best years of my life. We have a no-brainer here. Clinging to her old friends means Amy's surrounded by people who don't want to be her new ones. You know what I'm saying—Mean Girls!"

Faith nodded. "Unfortunately too true. I'm still so mad at the superintendent I don't trust myself to take the shortcut home through the school department parking lot. Her car has a vanity plate that says 'super,' and I've always got keys in my pocketbook."

At the end of August the Fairchilds had been notified that due to redistricting, Amy would be going to the other middle school in town, not the one where all the kids she'd been with since kindergarten through sixth grade would be attending. Assuming it was a mistake, as Amy was one of the only ones being transferred, and the only girl, Faith had called the school department. She'd gotten nowhere with anyone—"No exceptions." Unable to stand her daughter's tears, she'd made an appointment to meet with the superintendent, driving the five hours down to Aleford from Sanpere, sure that she would be able to make the educator see what this kind of change would mean for an almost thirteen-year-old. The superintendent didn't, and Faith grew even angrier when it was pointed out that Amy should have been going to a different school, as should Ben, all these years. The school district boundary ran through the old graveyard between the parsonage and the church. Faith had started to lose her temper at the super's recalcitrance, suggesting pointedly that maybe they should move Amy's bedroom to a spot among the tombstones, which fell in her old district, so she could stay where she was. The superintendent was as firm as the granite markers. "We can't bend the rules for anyone. Amy will get over it. This is a perfect opportunity for your daughter to broaden her friendship pool," were her parting words. Faith's were muttered out of earshot in the hallway.

The "friendship pool" had proved to be filled with piranhas. Niki was right. "Mean" didn't come close. One day Amy had stormed into the kitchen after school, grabbed her laptop from a shelf, and deleted something on her Facebook timeline. Faith hadn't seen what had been posted, but Ben said it was pretty bad. Stuff about watching Amy salute the flag during assembly, how maybe she needed to move her hand farther up toward her shoulder.

"The worst part," Faith continued, "is that there isn't anything I can do about it. Thank goodness for Girl Scouts. Most of the troop is from her old school."

" 'Mean Girls' tend to be interested in things other than merit badges and selling cookies," Niki said. "Things like stealing each other's boyfriends, shoplifting expensive cosmetics, and nowadays doing as much damage as possible to their prey with social media."

Tricia joined them after finishing a tray of ham and cheese puff pastry squares. "Do you know who the girls are? Usually there's one queen bee and the others do what she says so they won't end up targets. I'm not suggesting you call their parents—that would be the kiss of death. But Scott has friends who would be more than happy to help out—nothing extreme, but say a whiff of death?"

It was a welcome touch of humor, and Faith found it an extremely attractive notion for a few seconds. Tricia's husband, Scott, Faith's longtime friend and the person who helped her solve a murder many years ago, owned a body shop in Byford, the next town.

"I'll keep it in mind but will get on your other suggestion—finding out who the ringleader is—right away. Aleford's a small town. And I have my methods."

Niki shook her head slowly back and forth. "She's screwed until high school. Two more years. Sorry, Faith. Think you might want to go for the graveyard idea you told me about. An igloo is a legal dwelling, right?"

Sophie's father-in-law, Anson, had kept the family law firm's name, Maxwell & Maxwell, after his father died, expecting that Will, who was finishing up at Duke's law school at the time, would be joining him. The firm was good-size, and its excellent reputation was not limited to Savannah and Chatham County. Anson gave his son time, waiting while Will went into the Peace Corps, even bragging on him—"Every family needs a do-gooder." But when Will came back and announced he was going to be a private investigator, his father was not so understanding. He made his disappointment clear, but as the years went by he'd gotten over it. "Wouldn't have worked out anyway. Too much alike—independent cusses."

Eventually, Anson's stepson, Randall, joined the firm fresh out of UGA's law school. Randall's reason for choosing the university—undergrad as well—largely centered on being close to the Bulldogs, the school's beloved football team. When he married Carlene, a former cheerleader, no one was surprised at his choice of a red dress shirt under his tux or her bouquet of red roses as big as pom-poms. Team spirit prevailed down to the favors: china replicas of Uga, the team mascot, with BULLDOGS, RANDY, AND CARLENE FOREVER baked into the glaze of the distinctive white English breed.

When Will brought Sophie to meet her future in-laws, Anson had been delighted to learn that she had specialized in intellectual property when she was practicing in New York. He'd placed her on his right at the family dinner to welcome her, which took place at Gloria's family home, Bells Mills, a short drive west of the city. Bells Mills looked to Sophie like something straight from the pages of *Gone with the Wind*, complete with pillars, verandas, and Spanish moss so thick it created a canopy above the long drive leading to the house. The house itself was all that was left of what had been a rice plantation, and although, Will had explained in private, Gloria would have you believe the first bit of tabby—the oyster shell, lime, sand, and water building material—was laid by an ancestor who sailed with Oglethorpe on the *Anne* in 1733, the place dated only to the late 1800s.

Sophie had loved it all. She had reveled in the easy back and forth of conversation around the table and the sense of kinship, something she had never had. And she would try to get used to sweet tea. Will's accent had become noticeably thicker than it had been in Maine, and his endearments were peppered with "shug" and "darlin'" now.

Over dessert (the best banana pudding Sophie had ever tasted) Anson announced that he had double-checked what he'd hoped—that Sophie's New York license to practice law was good in Georgia—and offered her a job. "You'd be doing me a favor—and Gloria. We're spending more time out here and less in town. And the firm really would be Maxwell and Maxwell again."

Will had warned her that his father had been thinking about all this, so Sophie'd had time to think, too. She knew she wanted to get back to work—she'd missed it—and this seemed ideal. Maxwell & Maxwell didn't currently have anyone with her expertise, so she wouldn't be treading on any toes. She'd said yes.

When they returned from Tybee, Sophie found herself settling into married life with an ease she didn't know she possessed. She knew she'd always miss parts of her Big Apple life and she'd enjoy going back to see her mother. Yet she didn't miss the pressure, the crazy hours, or the crowded subway. The house they were staying in was a short walk to the law firm's offices on Chippewa Square, and both were close to the office Will rented on Drayton Street staffed with a part-time secretary, Coralee Jones. Walking past the houses in the historic district with many plants still blooming, thanks to Savannah's ten-month growing season, was a much better way to start the workday than the litter and cold gray skies that had typically greeted her in New York this time of year.

Sophie was a coffee, yogurt, and fruit quick-breakfast person, so Will returned to his habit of stopping by Clary's for his more ample, leisurely fare. In addition, he said, time spent there was a necessity in his line of work. If they weren't talking about it at the venerable café on Abercorn, it hadn't happened yet. After work, the two met in the middle of Chippewa by Oglethorpe's statue, which Sophie pointed out was the work of New Englander Daniel Chester French, before going to dinner at the Sapphire Grill, the Olde Pink House, the 17Hundred90 Inn and Restaurant, or out of town to Pearl's for hush puppies and seafood. Will had insisted they consider the whole month, or more, a honeymoon.

"I know you're a good cook," he'd said when Sophie protested, saying she could make dinner for them. "I don't think I've ever eaten as well as I did last summer when you were in charge of The Birches's kitchen. But eating out is part of your initiation into our way of life here."

Sophie stopped objecting and vowed instead to start running off the biscuit-and-honey, fried-green-tomato-type calories she was happily consuming. Besides, she enjoyed being outside. The whole city was especially festive, decked out for the holidays. Will had been telling her about the Savannah Boat Parade of Lights since the summer. When the Saturday after Thanksgiving finally arrived and Sophie saw the fifty or so boats trimmed with lights go up and down the river, nautical jewels against the dark night, she oohed and aahed louder than everyone—especially when the sky exploded in fireworks. Savannah was a party every day, all year long.

Most weeks they went out to Bells Mills for Sunday dinner, getting to know yet more relatives, including Will's stepsister Patty Sue. She had left just after the wedding for a long visit to her Agnes Scott roommate. "I'm not sure she would have married Jeff if she'd have known he'd up and take a job so far from home!" she'd told Sophie. "She's perishing, so of course I had to go cheer her up. We had the best time ever at the beach."

When Sophie asked her where her friend lived, expecting something like San Diego, she was surprised— and not surprised—to learn the place of exile was Jacksonville, about two hours south.

Patty Sue worked at a local art gallery, an employer that seemed extremely lenient when it came to time off, as well as long lunch hours, as Sophie discovered when Patty Sue asked her to meet her "for a bite" at The Collins Quarter. She'd greeted Sophie on the appointed day and led her to a large communal table at the back of the restaurant, which was new and already famed for its Australian coffee. Sophie assumed it was like Mrs. Wilkes Dining Room, where you shared a table with other diners. In fact the choice was to make room for all of Patty Sue's friends who soon drifted in. The "bite" was moving well into the second hour when Sophie left to go back to work. The food had been excellent—Sophie had ordered the smashed avocado on toast with feta, cherry tomatoes, sesame seeds, and see-through radish slices, all of it in a presentation almost too pretty to eat. Nobody else was leaving, drinking more coffee and, in some cases, wine. Patty Sue had been gracious about introducing Sophie, but it was the one place so far where she had distinctly felt like the outsider she was. Judging from their gossip, all the other women had known one another forever, either starting in kindergarten at St. Vincent's or Country Day and moving on to make their debuts at the Christmas Cotillion. It wasn't that they were rude; they just ignored her.

They were certainly a well-heeled bunch, Sophie observed. Their clothes did not resemble their New York counterparts—not black, for one thing—except in what they had cost. Patty Sue's salary at the gallery surely would not have covered her Longchamp leather bag, or the Tory Burch flats she was wearing. She was living in the carriage house behind her parents' house near Monterey Square, so no worries about rent, but even so she must be getting a nice allowance—or have a very lucrative paper route. Sophie hadn't seen the carriage house, or the main house, but she was sure both were as beautifully decorated as Bells Mills. Gloria definitely had a talent for decor, although she had explained to Sophie that "most of my treasures are family heirlooms." Anson had overheard the remark and teased her—"Conveniently stored in Mr. Raskin's shop on Bull Street, I believe."

Sophie was very happy living in Gloria's current project. It would be perfect for them, but they would be looking for something way less expensive. She secretly hoped it would take Gloria many more months to finish the house and put it on the market.

On her way out of the restaurant, she passed a woman who had entered and was waving at the table Sophie had just left. They exchanged smiles—another thing not like New York that Sophie had come to like.

The woman moved quickly toward the short stairs leading to the dining area in the rear. She was beautiful. Her pale blond hair was smoothed back from her flawless ivory skin in a French twist, and she looked like Grace Kelly. Her chic white linen suit didn't have a single wrinkle. The only note of color was a turquoise choker, the beads a perfect match for her eyes.

Sophie stepped aside to let a party of four through the door and heard someone at the table greet the new arrival.

"Hey, Miss Laura, y'all just missed the Yankee who stole your man!"

Patty Sue called that night. Sophie's first thought upon hearing her sister-in-law's voice was that Patty Sue had somehow realized Sophie had overheard the remark in the restaurant, but that wasn't why she was calling.

"Have y'all got a dress for the shindig Mom and Dad are giving for you?"

Since so many friends and relatives had not attended the wedding, the Maxwells had planned a reception at their house in town to celebrate the nuptials. Once she saw the engraved invitations that went out, Sophie realized this was not going to be a simple meet and greet with cups of Savannah's signature cocktail—Chatham Artillery Punch, concocted first in the late 1700s, a truly lethal combination of rum, brandy, rye whiskey, gin, Benedictine, green tea, oranges, lemons, Catawba wine, brown sugar, and maraschino cherries all allowed to ferment for weeks before champagne was added and the whole thing poured over ice in a large punch bowl—with or without a pinch of gunpowder!

No, Anson and Gloria were throwing a party in keeping with Savannah's nickname, "The Hostess City"—and they didn't mean Twinkies.

"I thought I'd wear the dress I wore for my rehearsal dinner. You may remember—it's a pretty, deep-rose-colored satin sheath. Since the party is during the holidays I thought it would work." She wanted to add that Will loved her in it so much he never left it on for long. So there, "Miss Laura."

"Oh, honey, I *do* recall that dress. It was pretty." Patty Sue's emphasis on the word spoke volumes—deadly dull ones. "I have a suggestion. It's part of an old tradition we have here for dos like this, perfect for your introduction to Savannah society."

Good Lord, Sophie thought, was she going to have to wear a sash and long white kid gloves. "What is it?" she asked. "I know the party's important."

"Important! Might could be the most important of your life here. And everybody's talking about it, especially the people Mama didn't invite. Meet me tomorrow at the house—I don't think you've been there unless Will has given you a tour and you should see it before the big day in any case. We'll look at all the portraits and our little dressmaker can copy one of the gowns. There are a few brides. That would be perfect if one strikes you!"

"So the tradition is to dress up as one of your ancestresses? Or one by marriage in my case."

"I knew you'd get it. Obviously *your* mama didn't raise any stupid children!" Patty Sue gave a laugh that sounded partly like a snort. Sophie had heard it before, especially at lunch today.

"Well, my mama only raised me, so I don't know about how she would have done with any others.

Anyway she's coming to the party, and this dress idea is just the kind of thing she loves," Sophie said.

"Shhh," Patty Sue cautioned. Sophie was positive she was putting her finger to her lips. "We want to surprise everybody. It's going to be so much fun!"

She agreed to meet Patty Sue the next day at the house, which Will *hadn't* had a chance to show her yet, forgoing lunch. As she hung up, Sophie felt more excited than she had previously about the party. Adopting the tradition would give her a kind of armor and maybe the attendees would forget Sherman's March for the duration of the evening.

"What was all that about?" Will asked. "It was my sister, right?"

"Nothing much. Just some details about the party."

His face lit up. "Your first Savannah party and you'll finally get a taste of what I've been talking about! I guarantee it's a night you'll remember for the rest of your life."

Sophie grinned. Indeed, one of the first things Will had shared with her about the place he loved was the saying "In Charleston when they meet you they ask who your people are. In Savannah we ask what you'll have to drink." He'd also explained what he pointed out was a very civilized tradition that actually kept public drinking from getting out of hand—the "to-go cup." If you were over twenty-one, you could walk the streets of downtown sipping your favorite potable from an open no-more-than-sixteen-ounce Styrofoam or plastic cup. "No broken glass, metal cans on the streets," he'd said. "No one trying to drink from a paper bag from a much larger bottle." It did make a certain kind of sense, Sophie thought, and explained the stack of cups she saw at the end of the city's bars, convenient for people to grab—and go. To be a Savannahian meant an innate ability to make merry.

"You'll be the belle of the ball," Will said, sweeping her into his arms and twirling her around the room for an impromptu waltz.

Thanksgiving had been a warm and wonderful time for Faith, except for the perennial thorn in her side that was her daughter. When they went around the table, each saying briefly what they were thankful for—a tradition started by the Averys the year they adopted their children—Amy sat mute, finally mumbling that she was thankful she didn't have school the next day.

Faith had consulted her neighbor Pix Miller, who was her guide in all things parental, as well as Alefordian. She thought of her dear friend much as Lewis and Clark must have regarded Sacajawea. Pix had been as furious with the superintendent as Faith but told her that Aleford administrators had a long history of never ceding to a parent's demands for a student to be moved to another school or class. "It's the fear of opening the floodgates, and I'm sorry to say they're probably right." Having been shocked at her first parent night when Ben was in kindergarten by a parent's request for the name of a spelling tutor for her child, Faith was forced to agree. Aleford parents were a tough bunch with high expectations.

Faith had pried the name of the ringleader from Amy—Cassie Arnold—but it wasn't a family she or Pix knew. Eventually her own work demands and the impending holidays forced her to shelve the matter, counting herself lucky that she was able to get Amy out of bed and to school each day, an increasingly difficult task.

Ben had informed them that he did not want anything for Christmas except cash or a check and to please tell all his relatives the same. His French class was going to spend ten days after Christmas with families in Aleford's twin town outside Paris—Faith was having trouble envisioning such a place, but her French friends were all crazy for what they called "mapple syrup," so perhaps such a twin did exist—and the students were required to raise some of the money for the trip themselves in another one of those life lessons that adults think kids need. Faith wasn't against the principle but the timing. Although she was forgoing such holiday tasks as making a replica of Chartres in gingerbread, she, and all the other mothers she knew, were stretched to the limit without having to dream up fundraising schemes for their offspring. She readily fell in with Ben's plan but said he had to write the letters—snail not e-mail—and explain this sudden mercenary streak.

Sophie Maxwell had sent Tom and Faith an invitation to a formal party her in-laws were giving for the newlyweds with a note saying she knew the Fairchilds couldn't come but she wanted them to feel included. Since she'd moved to Savannah, Sophie had been in touch by text and e-mail, with the occasional phone call, and Faith was delighted that the young woman was finding happiness in her new home. She was reminded of the huge adjustment she'd had to make when she left her native Manhattan for Aleford. The quiet at night with only a cricket or bullfrog breaking the stillness had driven her mad at first. She'd grown up lulled to sleep by the sounds of sirens, horns, and sometimes shouts on the Upper East Side that were even louder when she got her own apartment on the other side of the park. Plus it was New England—they definitely did things differently there. After all these years, though, the place had grown on her like the mosses on the proverbial old manse. She could but hope that Sophie would find similar joy in all those garlands of Spanish moss where she was now.

Sophie was. The Maxwells' house in town looked spectacular. The crystal chandeliers seemed to be made of diamonds, not glass, and enormous holiday flower arrangements filled the rooms with a heavenly fragrance. Bells Mills had supplied the mistletoe, holly, and other greens. No tree yet, in order to make room for the guests, but shiny gold and silver ornaments trimmed the mantels.

Gloria had handed Sophie a flute of champagne and sent her upstairs to dress an hour earlier and now she was ready. She could hear the guests gathered in the enormous foyer at the bottom of the long curved staircase, a happy murmur that rose and fell. A pianist was playing Johnny Mercer songs—of course.

The portrait Patty Sue had particularly pointed out was the one Sophie had been drawn to as well. It was of a very beautiful early twentieth-century bride, and Sophie thought the painter might have been a student of John Singer Sargent. The loose brushstrokes and color that seemed to glow from within looked like his work. Whoever she was—Patty Sue didn't know—was standing tall and looked both happy and a bit shy. The dress seemed to be made of white satin or silk and had a small train with sleeves fashionably puffed to the elbow that showed off the woman's graceful arms. The bodice was covered with a bib of what Sophie recognized as openwork lace, an elegant kind of tatting that may have been the bride's own work. Her hair was dressed like a Gibson girl's, and Sophie, who had kept her own very similar dark locks shoulder length, thought she could imitate the style. But where could she get the lace? The rest of the dress would not be difficult to copy.

When she mentioned the dilemma to Patty Sue, her sister-in-law had a ready answer. "Oh, there's boxes of that stuff in the attic. Anson's family has lived here forever and never throws anything away. You might have to bleach it, but I'm sure you can find something. I have to run back to work, but I'll show you how to get into the attic—stairs, no ladder and nothing spooky, don't worry. The boxes should be labeled 'linens and lace trim.' "

Will had never mentioned that this was his family home, Sophie realized. His mother had died when he was fifteen, and soon after, his father married Gloria, who had lost her husband the year before. The two couples had been friends.

After Patty Sue reassured her several times that it was "just fine" to poke around the attic and take some lace, she'd left. Sophie located the boxes stacked next to the door with ease and found a large piece that would work perfectly.

The seamstress took the photo Sophie had snapped of the portrait, and the trim, promising the dress in time for the party. Now, looking at herself in the cheval glass in the bedroom, Sophie wasn't sure whether she was looking at herself or the woman in the portrait. The seamstress had worked magic. She was clasping her wedding pearls—a gift from Babs and Ed—around her neck, the final touch, when Will walked in.

"Shug, people are getting restless even with liquor flowing like the Savannah River in flood season."

Smiling in expectation as she moved toward him, Sophie thought she had never felt more beautiful, or more in love.

What happened next remained a blur for many days. First Will froze, his face drained of color. Then the blood rushed back in, turning his expression into an angry mask. He crossed the distance between them in two rapid steps and began pulling at the gown.

"What the hell are you playing at?" he said in a voice she had never heard. "Get this off!"

Sophie's necklace snapped and pearls rolled to the floor.

"What's wrong?" she shrieked. "The dress? What is it?"

Will was trying in vain to find a zipper, but the dress was done up the back with tiny satin-covered buttons. She felt and heard the fabric rip.

"Hush! Do you want the whole city to hear you? I'll go stall. Find something, anything else to wear!"

"But, Will!" Sophie was sobbing now. "What is it? What did I do?"

"You're wearing my grandmother's wedding dress. Quite a trick, since after a horrific battle with the Grim Reaper, she was laid to rest in Bonaventure Cemetery wearing it."

Chapter 2

Sophie collapsed onto the floor, the gown a tattered mess beneath her. Will had left the door open, and she could hear him addressing the group below.

"Have another round, everyone. My Yankee bride has already adopted our Savannah habit of never being on time. She's doing some last-minute primping. Y'all know how women are."

Again, Sophie had never heard her husband use that tone of voice. It was as if some sort of alien had snatched her Will, replacing him with someone she didn't know—or much like. She did know one thing, however. There was no way she was going to appear at the party.

"What the hell is going on? What are you doing on the floor?"

It was Mother.

Babs closed the door behind her and crouched down next to her daughter. "Are you ill? And what on earth are you wearing?"

Sophie started crying again. She supposed she had been in shock before, unable to move or make a sound. Now it was as if she was reliving the scene over and over.

"Stop that crying! You're obviously not sick. I didn't hear what Will was saying just now, but when you were taking so long to make your grand entrance I knew something must be wrong, so I came up the back stairs. And that's the way I'm going to leave as soon as we get you dressed in, well, anything else."

"She said it was a custom here!" Sophie wailed. "And Will was so angry!"

"You can tell me all about it later. You have a party to attend, remember?"

"I'm not going! Wild horses wouldn't drag me down those stairs."

Wild horses may not have been able to drag Sophie Maxwell down to the throng of eagerly waiting party-goers, but Babs was more than up to the task.

"Wash your face and redo your makeup. And take your hair down. It looks ridiculous. Did you think it was a costume party? No, not now," she fumed as

Sophie seemed about to speak again. "We're lucky I'm staying here with Gloria and Anson. I'll get a more appropriate outfit. Fortunately I remembered they don't wear black down here unless they're art students, so you won't give them that to talk about. Seems like there's enough to fuel the gossip mill as it is. And, daughter dearest, if you blow this off it will be the end of you so far as Savannah is concerned. You'll have to move, possibly to another continent." She yanked Sophie to her feet and pushed her toward the bathroom.

Sophie removed the dress, which had started to feel like a shroud. Her mother was back soon with a flask and a Chanel turquoise silk sheath. The two women were the same size, although Sophie was a few inches taller. Babs had maintained her girlish figure with the help of Canyon Ranch and Pilates.

"Drink this. If nothing else, it will put some roses in your cheeks."

Sophie tilted the flask and almost choked as straight bourbon filled her mouth.

"Here." Babs fastened the diamond necklace she had been wearing around her daughter's neck. "And you might as well have this, too." She fastened the matching bracelet around Sophie's slim wrist. "At least they'll see you have good jewelry. Mind you, I want it back after tonight. Now, I'll go get Will. And Sophie, take it from me—whatever happened between you two tonight isn't going to get straightened out here. You love him dearly and he loves you, so take his arm, walk down that absurdly Southern movie set staircase, and smile for the camera."

"Give me another shot of that bourbon first," Sophie said.

"Don't they make a fine couple!" Anson Maxwell said, holding his glass high. "Please join me in a toast to the bride and groom." He gave Sophie a big kiss and added, "I couldn't be more tickled. Gained a daughter-in-law *and* a partner-in-law!" He laughed at his own pun as Sophie was engulfed by well-wishers.

Will hadn't said a word as he took her arm before descending the staircase. She kept her own mouth shut, too. The bourbon, or maybe a heavy dose of righteous indignation, had swept all of her hesitation about the party firmly away. Damn it, she would hold her head high and show everyone that this Yankee bride knew how to party. If her husband was suddenly going to talk like a "good ol' boy," then she'd play along.

Thank goodness for Mother's bling, she thought. As she moved among the crowd she heard several not too sotto voce comments about the plainness of her dress—"You'd think she'd wear something fancier. It looks like an outfit my mother would wear" was just one remark she picked up. Compared with what the other women were wearing, she was like a wren among peacocks. She also picked up several remarks about how late she had been—"What all could have been keeping her? I was beginning to think we had a Runaway Bride!"

Inevitably she came face-to-face with Patty Sue, who air kissed her cheek. "Such a sweet color on you, darlin'," Patty Sue said. She was wearing red, the exact same hue that Sophie's previously maligned rehearsal dress had been, except this number was cut almost to the navel in front and cinched tight at the waist before billowing out in a bouffant three-quarters-length skirt. She'd been hitting the Chatham Artillery Punch, Sophie suspected; her face was flushed and her speech ever so slightly slurred.

They were standing in front of the portrait of the woman Sophie now knew was Will's grandmother and, she realized, Uncle Paul McAllister's sister. She so wished he was here, for protection, and even more for information. Unfortunately Paul was on an extended trip to British friends living in Singapore, and since they'd planned to go on from there to other parts of Asia, he would be impossible to reach for weeks.

She'd let Patty Sue steer her toward the portrait, knowing it was no accident. "Beautiful. I wonder who she is?" Sophie commented coolly.

"Aurora McAllister Maxwell. Will's grandmother. She came to this house as a bride." Patty Sue's memory had come back it seemed. "You do recall when we were here a couple of weeks ago looking at it, how I told you about the tradition of wearing your bridal gown for formal events the first year after the wedding? Not too many do nowadays, but it's a nice custom."

"I'm sure it is." Sophie tried not to choke on her words. The desire to grab her sister-in-law by the neck and strangle her was almost overwhelming. "I wanted something new for this wonderful party, though."

A waiter approached with an assortment of drinks on a silver tray and Sophie took a glass of champagne, avoiding the punch. She'd had enough hard liquor for one night and wanted to keep her head clear.

Patty Sue slipped off and Sophie sipped the cold bubbly, watching the scene in front of her. Everyone seemed to be having a marvelous time. A few couples were dancing, including Anson and Gloria, whose exuberant steps to "Something's Gotta Give" rivaled Ginger and Fred's. Sophie had seen Johnny Mercer's statue in Ellis Square but had yet to make a visit to his grave site and the bench in Bonaventure Cemetery. The cemetery! She wouldn't be going there anytime soon, if ever.

What had happened at his grandmother's death to make Will flare up as he had? She tried not to think about the inevitable scene with her husband that awaited. From the way the party was going, they wouldn't be leaving until the very wee hours of the morning. As the guests of honor they'd have to stay until the last person departed. And tomorrow afternoon the Maxwells were hosting a somewhat smaller gathering out at Bells Mills—a Lowcountry boil—to cap off the celebratory weekend.

Patty Sue had been diabolically clever. Easy to deny everything. She had been alone with Sophie and didn't go into the attic with her. Those boxes, so conveniently placed! Sophie was willing to bet if she went up now, she'd find them tucked away where they were stored before. What a stoopnagle she had been! (And where did *that* word come from, but it was perfect.) A chump, an imbecile, a fool, above all an idiot.

She realized she'd drained her glass. She'd had nothing to eat since breakfast and needed food to sop up the alcohol, champagne on top of Maker's Mark. There was a lavish spread laid out on the dining room table, one large enough to seat twelve comfortably without its leaves. She'd heard Gloria talking about the menu—crab in many forms from she-crab soup to deviled crab stuffed back in the shell and crab cakes. Country ham, turkey with oyster dressing, seafood gumbo, Savannah red rice, biscuits, and all kinds of desserts! Her mouth was watering as she made her way to the door, slowed down by new friends and more new relatives introducing themselves. Sophie's face was beginning to hurt from smiling. She looked back over her shoulder, and as suddenly as her appetite had come, it vanished.

Will and the exquisite blond "Miss Laura" were in deep conversation. From the way they were looking at each other, the notion that both might be regretting a certain Northerner's stealing Will Tarkington Maxwell away was not at all far-fetched.

She now knew what one of her father-in-law's favorite expressions—"Rode hard and put away wet"—felt like, Sophie thought, closing her eyes against the morning glare coming in through the bedroom window. She opened them again. Part of her was happy to see that her husband was very sound asleep next to her; part wanted to slap him awake and demand some answers. Her attempt at conversation as they walked back from the party earlier this morning had been firmly rebuffed. "I'm tired; you're tired. This is no time to talk," Will had said. What he did not say was when or even *if* they would talk about the evening. He'd dropped his clothes in a heap on the floor, gone into the bathroom, and then headed straight to bed. He'd been asleep before she had hung Babs's dress in the wardrobe, an enormous armoire. These old houses didn't run to closets, and though Gloria was converting a small bedroom, perhaps a nursery, into a huge walk-in, the armoire was serving as Sophie's closet for the present. Babs had told Sophie to keep the dress and be sure to wear it again soon, but had indeed reclaimed her jewels.

Sophie looked at the clock. It was not even eight. They were due at Bells Mills at one o'clock. It would take at least thirty minutes to drive, still plenty of time to get some more sleep, but she knew she wouldn't. Slipping out of bed, she started to head for a shower and then changed course, grabbing her phone from the nightstand before heading downstairs to the kitchen.

In a house this vintage the kitchen would have been on the ground level and a historic renovation would have had to leave it there, but Gloria had received permission to move it to the main floor, since the house wasn't on the Historic Register or significant architecturally. She'd had a beautiful modern kitchen installed—more convenient for the twenty-first century yet still with heart-of-pine floors and glass-fronted period cabinets, all from an architectural salvage place. Afterward, Gloria had turned to the empty ground level, creating an up-to-date entertainment area closed off from a spacious nineteenth-century-type garden room with doors opening to the brick walled enclosure behind the house. So far the yard had been filled with building materials, but when the project was completed it would be a lush garden with a small screened-in gazebo.

Aside from the pounding headache, one thought had been filling Sophie's head since she'd awoken—the same thought that had filled it until she had finally sunk into sleep. What had happened around Will's grandmother's death to provoke his over-the-top response? Clearly she was not going to find out from him anytime soon. And there weren't going to be any answers from Patty Sue.

Patty Sue. What was the quote? "Keep your friends close, but your enemies closer"? Sophie had always thought it was Shakespeare, or an early Roman, but when she'd finally looked it up, it turned out to be Sun Tzu, a Chinese general from around 400 BC. It was certainly apt advice at the moment. She was glad that her sister-in-law had revealed herself so early, she told herself.

Glad. No, she had to admit—not glad at all. It wasn't supposed to be like this.

She started grinding beans to make her usual French press coffee, then decided today was not the day to fuss and instead stuck a mug with several spoons of instant in the microwave. A minute later she was sipping the noxious brew and hitting Faith Fairchild's number on her Favorites list. Faith answered as Sophie was realizing Sunday morning might not be the best time to call.

"Faith, it's Sophie. I'm sorry to bother you when you must be getting ready for church. I'll be quick—or I can call back later."

"The kids are still sleeping, and once I located a clean collar, Tom took off, presumably to think divine thoughts but more likely to put finishing touches on his sermon. Is everything all right? And why are you whispering?"

Even with two closed doors and a floor between her and Will, Sophie had still instinctively lowered her voice. She spoke up now. "Everything's fine. No, it isn't, but it's too long to go into. I was hoping you could do me a favor."

"Anything, you know that."

"Uncle Paul is in Singapore visiting some British ex-pat friends and may already have headed off with them—Mongolia, I believe—otherwise I could ask him and the whole thing would be clear, or clearer. Then I thought that Ursula might know. Maybe you could ask her? She is so close to him, and was to Aunt Priscilla. She might have heard them discussing it."

"Happy to help, but Sophie"—Faith gave a little laugh—"what is it I'm supposed to ask Ursula about?"

"Oh dear. I have got to snap to. More coffee, much more. Last night Will got terribly annoyed about something I stupidly did that reminded him of his grandmother's death. She was Paul's sister, remember? Her name was Aurora. Could you ask Ursula if she's ever heard anything about the circumstances surrounding Aurora's death? *Anything*. How she died? Where?"

"I'll stop by later this afternoon. The holidays are so hectic that I haven't been to see her lately, so I'm happy to have this excuse. But why can't you ask Will?"

A few moments of silence stretched out before Sophie replied, her voice lowered again, "I just can't. Not right now."

"Oh, sweetie, your first quarrel? I remember ours. I was sure we were headed for divorce and it was too late for an annulment. I know it doesn't help to tell you it will be fine, but I will anyway. And if you're lucky you'll have plenty more. You only have what sounds like a really serious argument with the person you love most—and that's Will."

Sophie snuffled audibly. Faith added, "How about asking someone in his family? Southern families worship their ancestors as much as New England ones—and love talking about them. Start a generation or so before and work your way to the more recent kin like Aurora."

Taking a deep breath, Sophie cleared her throat. "The only person I'd feel comfortable asking would be Will's dad. Aurora was his mother. Maybe I will, but not today. The chance that it would upset him is not one I want to take. We're all gathering at Bells Mills, Gloria's family plantation house, for a Lowcountry boil."

"Oh I wish I could jump on a plane and get down there! I'm assuming you have never had one. You're in for a rare treat! When I serve up our pot roast Sunday dinner, my thoughts will be with all the shrimp, sausage, and other yummy things you'll be eating instead. A boil is a little like a clambake, but the seasoning—Old Bay is best—adds way more kick. This could sum up the difference between the two regions in a nutshell, or I should say stockpot."

"I'd better let you go and I should start to get ready, too," Sophie said. What she really wanted to do was talk some more, with a real cup of coffee, unburdening herself to Faith about all the events of the previous evening. Faith would have some juicy words to describe Patty Sue. Sophie sighed, and it must have been audible.

"Put on a pretty outfit, Sophie Maxwell, and get yourself out there. Babs is still in Savannah, right? You two make a fine pair, just as you and Will do. Where is he now?"

"Upstairs asleep. The party wasn't over until after three."

"Then go wake him up with a kiss and more."

It was after two o'clock by the time Faith walked toward Meredith Hill, where Ursula lived, carrying a basket with lemon squares and gingerbread, both Ursula's favorites. She felt a bit as if she should be wearing a hooded little red cape. After she crossed the Green from the parsonage, she walked swiftly past Millicent Revere McKinley's small white house, strategically located so the bow window in the parlor afforded a view straight down Main Street and over most of the town's historic Green. The town clerk had let slip to Faith that Millicent—admitting to seventy—was well past eighty. The octogenarian spent most of her days perched behind the sheer muslin curtains, keeping an eye on Aleford. She'd know that Faith was going to Ursula's as soon as Faith turned up Meredith Street and she'd guess what was in the basket. She wouldn't know why, though, and Faith didn't want to be stopped. Millicent had a knack for creating spur-of-the-moment errands that placed her directly in her quarry's path. Yet, the slight figure of the older woman did not come bolting from the front door and Faith kept walking. Perversely she began to worry why Millicent *hadn't* stopped her. She was grateful to avoid the interruption, but now she was worried that Miss (not Ms., thank you very much) McKinley's sight was not as sharp as it had been. She'd pack another basket with corn muffins and anadama rolls—no sweets, thank you very much—and visit Millicent tomorrow.

The large homes in this part of town were already discreetly decked out for Christmas with wreaths and occasionally some pine roping around the lamp-post. Nary an inflatable Santa nor LED reindeer, and, heavens above, no tacky lighting festooned across the center-entrance Colonial facades.

She'd called Ursula to make sure she'd be home—and alone. The door opened before Faith could ring the bell.

"This is a delight," Ursula said. "Come in. I have the kettle on."

Faith followed her into the kitchen at the rear of the large Victorian house and put the basket on the round table by the windows across the back, which the Rowes had put in many years ago to take advantage of the view toward the river at the bottom of the garden. Faith knew that Ursula and her husband had moved into the house after their marriage, Arnold Rowe dying much too young many years ago. They'd raised son Arnie and daughter Pix here. It was a house that had always been filled with people—grandchildren and the prospect of a great-grandchild, now that the Millers' oldest son was married.

"You spoil me, Faith," Ursula said. "I doubt the basket you are carrying is the latest handbag fashion, although one never knows." She emptied some of the boiling water she'd used to warm the teapot into the sink and added the tea leaves before pouring in the rest of the water. "Lapsang souchong, so I think no lemon, all right?"

"Perfect," Faith agreed.

They let the tea steep a few minutes while they talked of various parish and Aleford matters and then Ursula filled the cups. Her hands with their long slender fingers were steady, but Faith noticed that the skin was becoming as translucent as the fine bone china Ursula had put out.

"Pix wants me to take in a lodger, or move to one of those assisted living places," Ursula said. She had followed her visitor's glance and correctly interpreted the look of concern that Faith had not been able to keep from her face. "I suppose that's why you're here. She wants you to talk to me about it."

"Oh no, absolutely not. I would have said so on the phone. In any case it's not my business. Maybe Tom's." One thing Faith had learned very much the hard way was that New Englanders, particularly Ursula's generation, were extremely private people.

Ursula startled her by laughing. "Don't be upset. I *have* talked to the reverend—a number of times. Why don't you tell me what you think? I know it's a big house for one old lady. You must have an opinion."

Faith did. She'd had this conversation with Pix with increasing frequency over the last years, and especially after Ursula's serious bout with pneumonia two winters ago.

"I don't think you would be happy living anywhere else," she said. "Of course Pix, and all of us, worry about your being here alone. What do *you* think about a lodger? Just to have someone else in the house."

"It depends on who it is. Nobody too chatty. I wouldn't have minded that girl from Sanpere who needed a place to stay—she was a quiet little thing— but she is going to finish her senior year on the island and live with the Hamiltons."

"Maybe start with just a few changes. Like wearing one of those medical alert devices around your neck or on your wrist."

Ursula smiled. "Tom's idea, too, and I've said yes. He put it nicely. Told me it was for all your sakes not mine."

It certainly would have been simpler if her husband had shared these conversations with her, Faith thought, but he was scrupulously tight-lipped about what amounted to the secrets of the confessional. This time it was only mildly irritating; others were much more so.

"What else did he suggest?"

"He thinks I should move my bedroom to this floor and remodel the half bath into a full accessible one. We measured my bed and it would fit nicely in the library, along with most of the rest of the furniture from my room. He said we could move my father's big desk out into the living room below the bay window facing the street. He measured that, too."

Her husband was quite the Boy Scout, Faith thought. It looked like a done deal. Pix would be very happy.

"I intend to tell Pix and Sam when they come back from Charleston," Ursula added. "Who would have thought they'd become such good friends with their in-laws so soon?"

It wasn't her story to tell, but Faith wished she could let Ursula in on her daughter's secret—that Pix had known (in the biblical sense!) the father of the bride in college, meeting in complete surprise after the intervening years at the wedding.

"Now, enough about me. I know that look, Faith Sibley Fairchild. You came here with something on your mind other than gingerbread and lemon squares."

Faith accepted some more tea and quickly related her telephone conversation with Sophie.

"Paul and his older sister, Aurora, were very close," Ursula said. "I think there were only the two of them. His marriage to Priscilla was a first for him and a second for her. Priscilla and Aurora hit it off immediately, which must have pleased Paul. I remember Priscilla talking about how much she loved their trips to Savannah. Aurora was one of those determined women who got together to form the Historic Savannah Foundation and literally saved the downtown. It was all going to be strip malls and office buildings. Now I believe it's the largest historic district in the country."

"Never underestimate the power of women," Faith said, looking forward to telling Sophie about Aurora's role in transforming what Britain's Lady Astor called the city in 1946—"a pretty woman with a dirty face."

"As I recall," Ursula continued, "Paul's brother-in-law was a good bit older than his wife. He had a heart attack and died when she was about forty. That's all I know about him. I'm sorry not to be more help, but I've forgotten a lot of what Priscilla probably told me. You know how she loved a good chat."

A good gossip, Faith thought to herself. Priscilla Proctor had not been a mean gossip—if she had been Ursula wouldn't have been her friend.

"Paul wanted his sister to come to Sanpere for a visit, but she was always busy down there with one cause or another, especially after her husband died and then her goddaughter—now what was her name?—married Aurora's son: Will's mother and father. She was thrilled. Gave them the big house and moved into the carriage house behind it. Priscilla and Paul went to the party for the baptism after Will was born. Priscilla couldn't get over it—how many people there were, with tons of food and drink, starting the day before and going on into the day after."

"They know how to party in the South," Faith said, ruefully thinking of all the staid postbaptismal gatherings she'd attended where thimble-size glasses filled with very dry sherry and small platters with very dry tea sandwiches were the standard fare.

"I do know Will's mother died when he was a teenager after battling breast cancer for years. It must have been devastating for all of them. Paul is the one who told me how hard his sister was taking it. Amanda—I thought her name would come back to me—was like a daughter to Aurora, something about Amanda's losing her own mother young and Aurora stepping in."

"This all sounds very tragic, but what about Aurora's death?" Faith asked.

Ursula looked stricken. "That was tragic, too, my dear, even more tragic. She died only a few months later, a suicide. Losing Amanda had caused a breakdown of some kind. Paul and Priscilla raced down to Savannah—it happened during the summer, when they were on Sanpere—but weren't in time. Whatever she had taken or done left her alive for more than a day, but there was no hope. Horrible for her family. I do remember being surprised when I heard. She'd always been portrayed as a very strong woman, plus she still had her son and grandson, whom she adored."

What news to bring Sophie, Faith thought, as she sat in silence with Ursula. Poor Will. To lose the two most important women in his life, both so close together and both such cruel deaths. Amanda must have been quite young.

Ursula patted Faith's hand—the New England equivalent of a bear hug. "This will help clear things up between the newlyweds, even if it is a sad story. Sophie needs to know what her husband has suffered, and must be suffering still."

Faith brought the dishes to the sink and obeyed Ursula's quick response to leave everything for her to do. They'd been down this road before.

Walking home, she started to shiver and wished she'd worn a warmer jacket. It had been a glorious fall, the foliage more brilliant than she had ever remembered. Mother Nature's ruse to ease everyone into the bleakness of winter. They'd already had a substantial snowfall, gone now, but there was little doubt that more was waiting in the wings. She would call Sophie in the morning and deliver the unwelcome news.

She was surprised to find Tom at home sitting in a darkened living room. She sat down on the couch next to him, but before she could say anything, he did. The phrase no one ever wants to hear:

"We need to talk."

"We're purists when it comes to our boil," Randy said, slipping his arm through Sophie's and leading her over to three big stockpots simmering on an outdoor grill. "That means no vegetables except corn on the cob and potatoes—new ones, the kind with red skins. And shrimp with the shell on, no crab. Lots and lots of shrimp. Lots of smoked sausage, too. And only Old Bay for seasoning. I don't think you have that up north. Looks like we're close to adding the shrimp. Come take a look."

Sophie was glad her brother-in-law had taken her under his wing, a role he'd adopted at the office, too. He was funny and smart with charm to burn. They worked on different floors, but he often swooped into her office and insisted she go for coffee, where he regaled her with highly entertaining stories of Savannah, past and present.

"I do know what Old Bay is. My friend Faith Fairchild in Massachusetts uses it in her crab cakes. She told me it has just about everything in the spice cabinet from paprika to cardamom."

Randy looked a little skeptical at the idea of Bay State crab cakes with Old Bay. He grabbed a pot holder and lifted the lid. "Just breathe that in, sugar."

The aroma was heavenly, and Sophie said so. It seemed like a simple recipe—everything went into a pot of boiling water at various times, potatoes first—but Randy assured her the proportions had to be just right.

"Across the river in South Carolina, they call this Frogmore Stew, being as the guy who invented it back in the day was from Frogmore. The town is called Saint

Helena now, but you'll still see 'Frogmore' on some menus. It's always been called a Lowcountry boil here. Better get you plenty of paper napkins, maybe a bib, or you'll get your nice little dress messed up good."

After talking to Faith, Sophie had waited awhile, then taken her advice and kissed her husband to wake him up. He'd started to respond sleepily before leaping from the bed, exclaiming they were going to be late and why hadn't she roused him earlier? She'd been tempted to say he'd been sleeping so soundly it would have been almost impossible, but kept her mouth shut and went on to don a pretty outfit as also suggested. Deceptively demure, the jade green sundress with pink ribbon spaghetti straps and more ribbon around the waist was cut low in back. But Will had not seemed to notice what she was wearing, saying little on the drive out to Bells Mills in the sports car. Conversation would have been difficult the way Will was driving. Sophie wondered if he was speeding on purpose.

Anson was waiting for them. Sophie gave her father-in-law a kiss and whispered a big thank-you for the party in his ear. He was taking Babs and Ed out for a short ride in his Grady-White powerboat and wanted the newlyweds to come along, too. "Tide's right and we'll probably see dolphins." Windblown and still reeling a bit from the drive, Sophie declined, noting with a sinking feeling how Will leaped on board with alacrity. She headed into the house to freshen up, or down—her hair was sticking straight out—passing Patty Sue. Her sister-in-law raised an eyebrow, but neither woman spoke. As she made her way to the elegant main floor powder room, Sophie tried to think of ways to avoid speaking to the woman for the rest of both their natural lives.

When she came back outside, the party had already kicked in to high gear. She was grateful when Randy headed her way. Everyone looked familiar—and friendly—but en masse she found them daunting. At other gatherings, Will had shepherded her around. Sophie knew she would never be a true Savannahian—like an old Maine saying, "A cat can have kittens in the oven, but that doesn't make them biscuits"—yet, would she always feel like such an outsider?

When the boating group returned, the contents of the pots were dumped out on long picnic tables covered with newspaper—no plates needed—and everyone dug in. Randy, joined by his wife, Carlene, flanked Sophie. "We'll teach you how we do it," Carlene said. "You eat with your fingers like a kid. See? The oil from the sausage makes the shell slide off the shrimp easy. They peel themselves. Kind of like you when you're in the mood," she added slyly, looking at her husband. He shot back, "More like when *you're* in the mood," and she reached across Sophie to throw a corncob in his lap.

Babs passed by. "Smile, sweetie, and start looking like you're having the time of your life," she hissed in Sophie's ear. "This isn't a wake." Sophie found the food helped and soon she *was* enjoying herself. Like all Savannah parties, everyone had come determined to have a good time. As the empty beer bottles mounted and crusty loaves of garlic bread turned into crumbs, all that was left of the boil itself was stripped corncobs and shrimp shells. For a moment she let herself enjoy the cadence of conversation flowing around her—the soft accents, gentle teasing, joke after joke, and stories.

Will had been sitting at another table with his father and Gloria. He came over and took Sophie's hand.

"From the look of it, I'd say you've been enjoying yourself." He picked a piece of shell from her chin and rubbed his thumb over the spot. "Let's go for a walk. It's close to sunset, and they're always special on boil nights. Must be the steam doing something to the atmosphere."

Sophie jumped up and squeezed his hand.

As they passed a group gathered around a fire pit, Randy called out, "If you're not here by morning, we'll send out a search party—or maybe you'd rather we didn't." Sophie laughed with the rest and squeezed

Will's hand even harder. They walked out on the long dock to the small enclosure set at the end, screened in with benches along three sides. Will opened the door and Sophie was glad to go in, away from the tiny gnats ever present near the water. There was still a great view of the sun, now a molten red ball sending purple streamers along the horizon.

They sat down, and she realized she was very, very tired. She put her head on Will's shoulder. That so familiar shoulder, the perfect height for her to lean on.

"I've been offered a case in Atlanta that I can't afford to turn down," Will said.

Sophie sat up. "But that's wonderful. Congratulations."

"It will mean staying up there during the week."

She wasn't sure what she was supposed to say—or feel. She knew that Will's work would take him away on occasion. He specialized in white-collar crime and had told her he never wanted to be the kind of PI that was hired to get the goods on a cheating spouse. "Give me an old-fashioned embezzler any day."

"Okay. I mean, fine. I'll be fine here."

He nodded. "Besides the office, you'll be busy looking at houses. Gloria doesn't know when she'll be finished with the one we're in, but we need to be ready to move sooner than later. I've been in touch with a Realtor we know and she'll be giving you a call once she's lined up some places. I told her we were open—downtown, Ardsley Park, Skidaway Island."

He sounded very businesslike. Sophie pushed away her feelings of regret and disappointment, seeking the same tone in return. "I'm sorry you won't be looking with me, but if there's anything I think we should consider, I can e-mail you the information."

Will nodded. "Sounds like a plan." Sophie began to relax again. She loved to look at other people's houses, especially knowing one of them might turn out to be theirs.

The sky was midnight blue. The sun had vanished into the water and the moon hadn't risen. She had that "The Only Two People in the World" feeling as the night closed in.

"I'll be leaving early tomorrow morning."

"Tomorrow!"

"Sorry."

She wished she could believe him. He didn't sound sorry at all.

Will did go early the next morning.

"I hate to leave you without a car. We'll get one next weekend. Should have before this."

They'd joked out on Tybee about "Mommy cars," a monster Hummer or other SUV. Sophie had something along the lines of a small Subaru in mind.

"I don't really need a car, and if I do there are Zip cars."

Will had been preoccupied, almost as if he hadn't heard her, and just shook his head before giving her a kiss good-bye. It wasn't the worst kiss she'd ever received, but it left a great deal to be desired. He was gone before she could return it with more feeling.

As it turned out, the days passed quickly. Tuesday night Randy and Carlene appeared at Sophie's office door at six and told her she was working way too hard.

"Don't want you making me look bad with the old man," Randy said. "We're kidnapping you, you poor lonely baby."

Sophie smiled. "Am I allowed to know where?"

"Let's surprise her, honey," Carlene said.

They walked down Bull Street and crossed over to River Street. Sophie decided Carlene was a much, much better sister-in-law than she whose name must not be said. Carlene was still in great shape, like the cheerleader she had been, and while her streaked blond hair wasn't big hair, it was close. It was Sophie's impression that although the couple had known each other "since Noah," Carlene said, they had been married only two or three years. No children yet, "But we're practicing." She'd laughed when she related this to Sophie.

They were easy to be with, and when Sophie stepped out onto the Top Deck Bar on the roof of the Cotton Sail Hotel, she was very glad she'd been kidnapped. The view of the river and the Talmadge Bridge was spectacular. Soon she was sipping a mojito, perched on a high stool, staring at one of the container ships plying the waters, so close it seemed she could reach out and touch it. A behemoth that looked like a floating horizontal skyscraper.

"People don't realize we're the fourth largest port in the country," Randy said. He'd ordered an assortment of food from the bar menu, and Sophie was enjoying smoked salmon and capers on flatbread and eyeing the shrimp and crab spring rolls. She nodded. Her mouth was full.

Randy continued, "And as fast as we can build storage and distribution facilities, companies are filling them up. We've already got Walmart, Target, and Home Depot. Ikea too. Hell, we've got them all and more coming. You wouldn't think something happening in another part of the world—the expansion of the Panama and Suez canals—would affect little bitty Savannah, but it means bigger ships can get here, and faster. I'm boring you, aren't I, darlin'? You need another drink!" He motioned for the server.

Sophie started to protest, then decided why not? She was a few short blocks from the house.

"No, you're not boring me at all. I don't know much about the city, and definitely very little about the port."

Randy opened his mouth to speak, but Carlene interrupted. "He'll go on all night. Now, *I* want to hear about living in New York City. I mean to go there someday and see all those shops."

They insisted on walking Sophie home. They lived on East Jones Street. Sophie hadn't been inside the mid-nineteenth-century house yet, but Will had pointed it out during one of their walks. It was exactly the kind of house she wanted, she'd told him—the long windows of the first floor told her the ceilings were high, and the exterior was a warm golden brick with a decorative iron railing on the steep front steps that was a possible indication of more on the balconies and veranda in the back.

That night, when she'd turned the key to go in, the thought of the empty house awaiting undid all that the mojitos and company had produced. She had trouble sleeping, and it seemed that when she did close her eyes a creak or a groan from the old house would immediately jolt her awake.

Wednesday night was worse. The wind had picked up and whistled down the chimneys, moaning. It seemed a forest of branches was hitting the house and falling to the street below.

By Thursday night she was determined to get some rest. Will would be home the next day. She needed sleep to do something about the deep circles under her eyes. Faith had called Monday to report on what Ursula had said about both Will's grandmother and mother. It helped explain his reaction to the dress somewhat, but the response had been so extreme she was sure more must be involved. She had years to find out and comfort her husband, she thought happily. He'd been communicating by e-mail. Brief, almost impersonal notes. No phone calls. He was very busy. This would change once they were face-to-face.

She made sure the house was locked up tight. Will had been amused by this. He didn't see the need when the house was occupied, particularly the back door. "Have to be a pretty determined burglar to climb over those high walls and then there's the glass shards studded in the concrete on top to deal with."

Gloria was having an alarm system installed but was waiting until other electrical work was completed, she'd explained. "People want them. Personally ours is a nuisance. Anson is always setting it off by accident so we never use it."

After work, Sophie had stopped to buy the DVD of John Berendt's *Midnight in the Garden of Good and Evil*, or "The Book" as Will explained it was known in the city itself. "We get down on our knees and thank him—most of us anyway. Put us on the map for tourists." She'd read the book years ago but had never seen the film and thought it would be fun. It would no doubt show places she now knew, plus she liked both Kevin Spacey and John Cusack.

She ate dinner standing up at the kitchen counter—a salad she'd picked up at Parker's market on Drayton—and took a big bowl of rice pudding, her comfort food, down to the ground-level entertainment room. She tended to get sleepy at the movies, and Gloria had furnished the room with tasteful comfy recliners that had Sophie's eyelids feeling heavy even before she started the film.

She'd barely watched half of it when she realized she had fallen sound asleep. Turning off the set, she climbed the two flights of stairs, took pajamas from the drawer, and went to hang the skirt she'd been wearing in the wardrobe. The door gave its usual creak—they really must oil the hinges—as she flung it wide open.

A very large, very dead man tumbled out, crashing to the floor facedown at her feet. Sophie knew he was dead because there was a very large knife sticking out from his back.

Besides, he wasn't moving.

Chapter 3

Not moving at all.

And neither was Sophie. Her limbs were frozen in place as she stared down at the man, a dark shape against the rich colors of the Oriental carpet on the floor. It was impossible to believe. A body in the wardrobe?

She opened her mouth, took a deep breath, but couldn't make a sound. And then as if a starter's gun had gone off, she tore down the stairs and found herself in the kitchen, staring at a door she knew was locked. Just as all the doors were.

Her phone! She looked down at her bare legs. The phone was in the bedroom. She'd taken it out of her skirt. The skirt she was about to hang in the wardrobe. The wardrobe where the dead man had been. Waiting for her to open the door.

Think, Sophie, think! She snatched the landline receiver from the counter, punching in 9-1-1, turned the lock, and wrenched the door open, stumbling into the cool night air. Relief started to flood over her until she realized the killer could be hiding behind the stacks of lumber and bags of cement that filled that garden at the back of the house. Quickly she darted to the path surrounding the house and the gate beyond. She pushed down on the handle; it opened easily.

There was no front yard, only a small patch of ivy with a cast iron planter at the foot of the stairs leading to the front door. Gloria had filled the urn with red cyclamen, evergreens, and pinecones. Sophie moved across to the square and stood under a streetlight. No cars were passing and no one was on the sidewalks, although lights were on in most of the houses.

Her call was picked up. Listening to the voice on the other end saying "this call is being recorded," Sophie struggled to clear her throat, finally gasping out, "There's a dead man in my bedroom. He's been stabbed."

The remarkably calm-sounding woman on the line responded by asking Sophie's name, the address, and if she was still inside the house. Sophie answered, her voice getting stronger. Her heart began to slow and her mind began to clear.

"Can you confirm the identity of the dead man?"

"No, I don't know." Her thoughts swirled again. Who was he? One of the crew working on the house? She was almost positive she had never seen him before, yet it had all happened so fast she hadn't gotten more than a glimpse of his face.

"There is a squad car in your area and will be with you immediately," the dispatcher said. "Are you alone?"

"Yes," Sophie answered. "I'm alone." *Very alone.*

But not for long.

Two police cars, lights flashing, pulled up. Officers wasted no time rushing into the house—through the back when Sophie told them she thought the front was locked. A female officer took Sophie into one of the cars and put a blanket around her. Sophie hadn't realized she was shivering until she felt the warmth. She was able to answer questions—her name again and a description of the deceased—"At least six feet tall. Heavyset. Long dark hair. Greasy. Dark clothing. Maybe jeans." She closed her eyes, trying to see it again. Not wanting to see it again.

"Can you describe the weapon?" The officer was busy taking notes.

"A knife with a long, thick black handle. I couldn't see the blade. It was . . ." Sophie felt her throat close and stopped.

"That's fine. You're doing just fine, honey. Is there someone we can call? Family?"

Sophie almost laughed. An hysterical sort of laugh. Her accent had betrayed her. The question mark after "family" could have been drawn in the air with neon it was so vivid. She wasn't from here.

"My husband is in Atlanta working. This is my mother-in-law's house."

Neighbors had gathered a safe distance away from the action. Sophie could see them in small knots speculating on what piece of Savannah news was unfolding. She was overwhelmed with fatigue. The fatigue that had haunted her since the night of the party. She wanted Will. Will, her husband, her beloved. And she wanted him now. Tears gathered in the corners of her eye and blurred the surreal scene outside the squad car window.

The door opened and the officer who had been the first to take off for the house slid next to Sophie.

"Mrs. Maxwell?"

Sophie wiped her eyes with her hand and sat up straight, clutching the blanket around her. "Yes?"

"You did say that the man fell out of the wardrobe in the bedroom at the top of the stairs in the front of the house?"

"Yes, I was putting my clothes away and he . . ." Her voice gave out again for a moment, but she regained it.

"He came tumbling right out and I could see he was dead."

The officer's voice softened. "There's no one in the house, dead or alive, darlin'."

"Please, you *have* to believe me. There was a man, a very large man, in the wardrobe and he was dead! He fell out when I opened the door to hang up my skirt! He wasn't moving!" Sophie realized she was shouting and lowered her voice. *Rational. Stay rational!* "Somebody else must have been in the house. No, it had to be more than one person to carry him. They must have taken him out the back way when I was here in the front!"

"We've checked the yard. Without a ladder or some other equipment I'm afraid there was no way a body could be transported over those walls. The only exit to the front is that gate." He pointed out the window. "Did you see anyone come through it?" He was being very, very patient with her.

Sophie shook her head. "No," she said softly. This was fast becoming even more of a nightmare than it had been to start. "*I* came that way, out the kitchen door. But they could be hiding with him someplace else in the house!" The female officer started patting Sophie's hand.

"We've gone over every room, every possible space of concealment, top to bottom, and we are doing it again now."

There was a knock on the car window. Sophie recognized an older woman she saw walking her dog most days.

"I don't want to interrupt y'all, but we know Mrs. Maxwell's husband is away, so I took the liberty of calling her brother-in-law, Randall. He should be here any minute."

The glance the two cops exchanged said it all: *Phew, now we can hand this nutcase off.*

Sophie closed her eyes and waited. For what she knew not.

Silently blessing the neighbor who had called him, and noting that although Sophie herself knew nothing about anyone in the neighborhood, they all apparently knew everything about her, she tried to tell Randy what had happened on the short drive to his house.

"Hush now. Let's get you a drink. I'm betting you didn't have much dinner, either. Rabbit food when your husband's away, most likely. Least it is for Carlene. Thinks she can go down a size before I get back."

It was wonderful to let them take over. Carlene settled Sophie on the couch with a soft mohair throw.

The living room was just as Sophie had imagined, looking at it from outside. High ceilings and walls the color of Meyer lemons. A tray was waiting for her on the coffee table with a plate of sandwiches—"I didn't know what you'd have a taste for, so there's a little bit of everything: pimento cheese, chicken salad, roast beef."

Randy put a tumbler in her hand. "Bourbon and branch. Drink up. Let me get one. I'm sure Carlene is set." He winked at his wife, who was indeed sipping what appeared to be the whiskey-and-water combination.

"Now," he said, once he returned with a drink for himself, "what's all this about a corpse in my mama's wardrobe?"

Reflecting that she was consuming more bourbon lately than she had in her entire life, Sophie described what had happened, appreciative of the serious expressions on Randy's and Carlene's faces, as well as Carlene's occasional sympathetic gasps.

Randy shook his head slowly. "You say you were watching the movie about The Book?"

"Yes," Sophie answered, swallowing a mouthful of the best chicken salad she'd ever had. "But why would that have anything to do with the murder?"

Randy got up and sat next to her. Carlene had been on her other side. For a moment Sophie was transported back to the boil, when they'd flanked her as well. A different kind of protection.

"Don't you think you might could have been thinking of what you saw on the screen and carried the image with you? You said you were almost asleep, right?"

"Yes, but I wasn't imagining what I saw. And heard! A figment wouldn't make the sound he did when he crashed to the floor."

"Did you touch him?" Carlene asked. "I mean, did you happen to maybe poke him with your foot?"

Sophie shuddered. "No, I did not, and if I had my toe would not have gone straight through him!"

"Oh, Sophie, sweetheart, Savannah isn't known as the most haunted city in the country for no reason," Randy said. "You most certainly saw some kind of manifestation. Mama will be pleased. She'll be checking to see who lived there, and more important, who died there in order to add a few grand to the price."

Carlene's cheeks were flushed. "Will took you to the Olde Pink House for dinner, didn't he? I know lots of people who have seen those ghosts, especially James. And now we kinda have our own!"

Will had taken Sophie to the famous restaurant on Reynolds Square and told her about the sightings of the Revolutionary War hero James Habersham Jr., as well as of an unidentified female, who occasionally appeared sobbing on an upper floor. Habersham, he'd told her, was a genial spirit who tended to stay in what was now a ground-level tavern where he welcomed guests, ever the hospitable host. Sophie had laughed and later teased her husband about his apparent lack of skepticism. He'd quoted Mark Twain in answer, "'I do not believe in ghosts, but I am afraid of them.'"

She thought of the conversation now. The body she'd discovered tonight was not a ghost, but she was very much afraid of him.

"It's late, shug," Randy said. "We need to get you to bed. We'll talk more in the morning. Maybe it was some sort of prank the workmen were pulling. I'll go speak to the contractor tomorrow in any case."

Carlene wasn't letting the ghost theory go. "And I personally have seen tears on the cheeks of poor little six-year-old Gracie Watson's statue in Bonaventure when there hasn't been a cloud in the sky. And what about the Gordons? Willie and Nellie—they were Juliette Gordon Low's parents; you must have been a Girl Scout, Sophie. She founded them right here. Anyway those two had a real love match and people see them in the garden or the foyer all the time. Sometimes Nellie plays the piano for Willie. Not even death could keep them apart."

"So I suppose I'm going to have to listen to you belting out UGA's fight song after we're gone?" Randy said, putting his arm through Sophie's and pulling her to her feet. "Now, Carlene is going to tuck you in and I'll bring you some cocoa. You might want it if whatever you saw tonight starts to keep you awake."

Upstairs Carlene handed Sophie a nightgown and showed her where the bathroom was. "We're down the hall. Give a yell if you want anything—or see anything."

Somehow Sophie was finding Carlene's insistence on the paranormal comforting—"Y'all have to think why *wouldn't* a ghost want to live in Savannah?" It didn't diminish what she knew had happened, but it was most certainly taking her mind off the event.

An event that came crowding back the moment her head sank into the down pillows. She closed her eyes and watched it all again, as if pushing rewind on a remote. Rewinding further to all the nights she'd spent alone in the house this week. The noises she'd heard. Not ghosts, but now she was certain, very much alive human beings.

Giving up, she drank the cocoa, and slipped into oblivion.

All week long Faith had been going over her conversation with Tom on Sunday night—"We need to talk"—to the point where she could almost describe it in picture-perfect detail. The problem being that the recollection wasn't helping her understand, or come any closer to terms with what he'd said.

The first thing she'd done was switch on a light. It was so not Tom to sit in the dark. "What's wrong? What do we need to talk about?"

He'd run his fingers through his rusty brown hair causing it to stick straight up, a gesture when he was agitated or worried, but he hadn't responded right away. She'd filled the silence.

"This is such a hard time of year for you, so much holiday joy; so many sad people . . ." Suddenly she'd realized why he must be depressed. "Have we lost someone?" Several parishioners were close to death, and Tom had been called to these bedsides with greater frequency in the last few days.

"Not yet, but I've been expecting to hear from Charles Frawley's family soon. No, it's not the parish. Or rather it *is* the parish—and another one as well."

At that point, Faith had been thoroughly mystified. "Another one? Here?" Aleford's clerical community was remarkably congenial and had not engaged in the turf wars that had been known to occur among religious institutions in other places—no turning of cheeks there.

Tom had started to raise his hand to his hair again but lowered it, taking his wife's instead. "The search committee from a church on the South Shore has been in touch with me several times lately, urging me to throw my collar in the ring."

This happened with some frequency, and Faith was never surprised. Of course her husband would be in demand.

"That's always wonderful for you, darling," she'd said and turned her thoughts to dinner. Sunday nights meant a simple supper. Describing the Lowcountry boil to Sophie had turned Faith's appetite south. Maybe grilled pimento cheese sandwiches with a big salad.

"I'm thinking of taking it."

Faith had immediately tuned back in. "You mean moving?"

Tom nodded. "At least I'll go talk to them and guest preach—get a feel for the congregation."

There had been so many questions on the tip of Faith's tongue that she didn't know which to give voice to first. Uppermost was the notion that Tom had been thinking about something so major for God only knew how long (and of course must), without this representative on earth telling his nearest and dearest. They didn't have that kind of marriage—the kind where one spouse kept things from the other. Maybe Faith had on occasion for Tom's own good, but *he* wasn't supposed to follow suit. She'd tried to keep her voice calm.

"I thought after the sabbatical in Cambridge, you had decided to stay in Aleford."

"I decided to stay in a parish ministry, but I never said I would always be in Aleford."

Faith had noted that it was the kind of semantics she would have expected from her teenage son, not her grown-up husband.

Tom had continued, "I've been thinking about how long I've been in Aleford for some time. I was here for a year before we were married, remember. I'm not sure it's the best thing for the life of a church to have one minister so embedded. What First Parish needs is new blood. Rattle the pews maybe."

Ignoring the wildly mixed metaphors, Faith had said, "Well, they do that on their own." First Parish dated back to the eighteenth century, and not only were the benches hard, but the pews also had doors that closed from the aisle—the better for a captive audience? Over time the hinges had loosened and were apt to emit audible creaks as the congregation stood up and sat down.

"The new parish would be near Norwell. After last summer, I think we should be closer to my parents."

Marian and Dick Fairchild were a forty-minute drive away, less without traffic. Tom's sister, Betsey, lived in the neighboring town. Faith had also been shaken by Marian's cardiac surgery in July, but her mother-in-law had made a full recovery and was talking about a trip to Cuba.

Faith thought back to her own next words, chosen carefully. "Both good reasons, but how about a third? Maybe it's you who need the change?"

Tom managed a slightly lopsided smile. "Maybe." He'd pulled her in for a hug. "They have an interim, so the job wouldn't start until June, maybe the end of the summer. We'd have time in Maine together. And from what the two people who have contacted me have said, it's a church that is struggling. An older congregation, although it's a town that has seen an influx of young families in recent years."

"Ripe for the picking," Faith had said as she reflected on the problem that was facing all denominations. Dwindling numbers. Even the arrival of young families didn't mean an increase in a congregation. Weekends for families meant precious break time, a respite from the work and school week, which kept families on such different schedules that few ate dinner, or even breakfast, together. Saturday and Sunday meant a somewhat slower pace—soccer and other activities to attend, but it was together time—a different kind of together from attendance at services. So far First Parish had a very active Sunday school, and the congregation was diverse in age and other respects.

"So, what do you say? Should I go for it? I know it's a big change," Tom had said.

What she saw then was as clear now. Her husband's face—somewhat like that of a kid who has found a new bike from Santa under the tree. Faith had replied, "Yes, and they'd be lucky to get you, darling."

Tom had left the house to go to his office at the church, where he had the phone number of the search committee head, to arrange to preach in January, and Faith had headed for comfort in the kitchen. This was all happening fast. Too fast, she thought. Could it be that after all these years, Aleford had well and truly become her home? She was filled with a deep reluctance to leave. Well, not the parsonage itself. It dated back almost as far as the church, and coping with the uneven floors, small windows that let in precious little light, plus a Vestry that funded only basic repairs made Faith appreciate the smaller house on Sanpere that at least was completely theirs. She could paint it bright pink if she wanted. The parsonage's clapboard had always been white, and its interior walls had always been neutral colors—world without end. After dinner she'd resolved to Google the South Shore church. Maybe their home page had a photo of the parsonage. Or maybe, with luck, there wasn't one and Faith could go house hunting. She'd stopped dead still, a lump of cheddar in one hand, a grater in the other. *House hunting! Moving!*

The outside kitchen door had opened and the tall handsome stranger with the deep voice that her son had so quickly, and alarmingly, become strode into the room, dropped his knapsack, grabbed an apple from the bowl on the table, and said, "What's for supper, Mom?"

"And yes, I'm fine thank you. Toasted pimento cheese [see recipe, page 231] sandwiches, salad, and fruit kebabs for dessert." Faith had discovered that her family would consume much more fruit if she cut it into chunks and put it on a wooden skewer like an hors d'oeuvre with some sort of yogurt dipping sauce than if she simply put it in a bowl or cup.

"What's pimento cheese? Aren't pimentos those weird little red things in olives?"

"Those 'weird little red things' are diced cherry peppers and when you combine them with grated cheddar, mayo, and one or two other ingredients you get what some people call 'the caviar of the South.' It makes great grilled cheese among other dishes."

Ben made a face. "You know I don't like fish eggs."

"Not yet anyway. But you'll like this. If you had grown up in Georgia or South Carolina you'd have had pimento cheese sandwiches in your lunch box instead of peanut butter."

"Whatever," Ben had said and loped out of the room. He was now taller than Tom. He didn't slouch but still managed to move as if he were one of those folding yardsticks not fully extended.

Since then, Faith had continued to think about what taking this position would mean for the Fairchild family. Ben would definitely not be happy to leave his friends, especially with only two years left until graduation. And she predicted just as the movers were packing boxes, Amy would have found a terrific group of new friends and have to be dragged kicking and screaming out of Aleford. What about Faith herself? She'd moved her catering business once, from Manhattan, and could do it again; but she had a firm client base here. She'd have to start from scratch, and would Niki be willing to commute to wherever the new site was? She lived in Watertown, conveniently close, now. And the other part-time employees?

Yet the worst would be leaving Pix—and Ursula. Yes, she'd see Pix in the summer and Ursula, too. But in Ursula's case for how long? Faith couldn't go there. Couldn't picture a world without Ursula Rowe in it.

What happened next on what was fast seeming a momentous Sunday night was taking a backseat to Tom's declaration, but not by much.

"Mom," Ben was back and standing next to her. She hadn't heard him come in and startled, dropped the knife she was using to slice radicchio for the salad. "Mom," he'd repeated. "I don't want to rat her out, but you may need to hear what Amy is saying to Daisy. They're Skyping."

He'd slipped away again and Faith picked the knife up off the floor, putting it in the sink. She'd given Amy permission to Skype with Daisy in her room for privacy. Hard to go back on that, but Ben wasn't a tattletale. The opposite in fact, often to Faith's dismay. He seemed to inherit his secret-keeping capacity from his father and he wasn't ordained.

Sighing, she'd gone to the bottom of the stairs, slipped her shoes off, and walked up to the hallway. Amy's door was open and Faith could hear both girls clearly.

"It really works," Daisy was saying. "You distract her somehow. Like tell her you're going to throw up and while she's getting a bucket or something, you hold the thermometer near the light. But not too near or it will be crazy high."

"Okay, got it. Gym tomorrow and I can't say I've got my period again so soon."

"I wish you could come out here and go to school with me. Everyone would love you and the teachers are so nice."

"I wish I could, too. Well, I gotta finish an essay for English. Really stupid. We have to write about something that changed our life. I mean, I'm only thirteen. Nothing has happened yet."

"I wouldn't have a problem with it," Daisy said, and both girls laughed, although the reference to what had happened the summer before to Daisy's family hadn't been a laughing matter at the time.

"At least everything is okay now," Amy said. "I could write about how changing school changed my life for the worse, but Miss Stolfi reads some out loud and it would be just my luck to have her pick mine. See what I mean? Nothing at school is safe."

Faith had quietly crept away. She'd hoped things were getting better at school for Amy, but it sounded as if they were the same or worse. The old thermometer trick. She and Hope had tried it more than once on their mother and she'd never been fooled. Faith wouldn't be, either, and even though it was tearing at her heart, she'd send her daughter off to school in the morning, off to the wolves. At least she'd try to introduce the topic of gym. Find out what was going on—in the locker room, most probably. Would that all those middle school female wiles could be harnessed for good instead of evil. It would solve a whole lot of world problems. An army of thirteen-year-old Mean Girls would be formidable.

The pimento grilled cheese had been a big hit and there was enough of the spread left over so Faith could stuff celery with it for lunches. It had been Amy's turn to clear the table and help clean up the kitchen. Faith had tried to steer the conversation to school, particularly gym, but her daughter kept steadily directing it to other topics, finally the one Faith now knew Amy had to write about.

"So, Mom, what would you say was an event that changed your life?"

Pick one, any one! Faith thought, realizing that the kinds of things on her list weren't ones Amy could write about.

"Now or when I was your age?"

"My age, I guess."

"Hmmm. That's hard." She honestly couldn't think of any. "What would you say?" It wasn't playing fair, but Amy *was* the one who had to write the paper.

"I'd say nothing. Like I haven't had anything happen to me yet. Getting Daisy as a best friend, but I can't put that in an essay. It would sound lame."

"Why not write just that? Nothing has happened that is life changing so far. And maybe that's a good thing?"

Amy had given her mother a big hug. "That's a great idea! I can even write about how sick Granny was last summer, and if she had died that would have changed my life, but she didn't so it stayed the same, which is a *very* good thing."

She'd dashed out of the kitchen.

Faith sat down. Child rearing was exhausting. Which brought her back to Pix again—Pix, her guide and mentor for all things familial. They'd talk on the phone and meet for lunch in town; but it wouldn't be the same as having her Sacajawea right next door.

Oh, Tom!

It had been a busy morning at the catering kitchen on Monday, but Faith squeezed in the baking she wanted to do for Millicent. She'd also had to squeeze her mouth shut. She and Tom had agreed that until things were definite, they wouldn't mention a possible move to anyone. Faith kept looking at Niki, and Tricia, who lived farther west than Niki did and would not be able to make a commute to the South Shore. She also kept looking at the facility itself. When the kids were little she'd created a play space well away from the main part of the kitchen so that she could keep them with her when they weren't in school. The bonus was that as both grew up, each had learned some simple cooking techniques. Future spouses would thank Faith. Now Niki's young daughter was enjoying the play area, making it possible for her mother to be with her, plus saving the young parents child care costs. Faith made a mental note to include this provision on the list when she started searching for spots where she could relocate her business.

"All morning you've been looking as if you just lost your best friend," Niki said. "What's up?"

Make that plural and you'd be on the money, Faith thought.

"Oh, the holidays. Feeling kind of stressed. And Amy." Faith had the feeling that if it hadn't been a gym day, Amy would have saved the trick for another time. Good old locker room bullying. "She tried to convince me she had a temperature and couldn't go to school this morning."

"My friends used to do that," Niki said. "If I had tried it, I'd still be grounded. You can imagine what my mother was like when I was a teen."

Faith could. She loved Niki's mother, and the whole Greek American family, but Mrs. Constantine was a force of nature.

"Keep an eye on her," Tricia said. "I never tried any tricks with my mother. Just got dressed, grabbed my books, and skipped. Nobody seemed to care, and I was very good at forging her signature on the absentee notes and report cards."

Faith knew Tricia had dropped out as soon as she had turned sixteen, which made it all the more admirable that the young woman had gone on to get a GED and an associate's degree in culinary arts from the local community college. Again she felt a pang. Tricia and Scott's kids were in elementary school now, which had meant Tricia could be at Have Faith both as an intern and working part-time. Would she be able to find a similar position if Faith moved?

"I'm going to head out. I want to drop these off at Millicent's," Faith said.

"Oh *that* will really cheer you up," Niki said. "Why don't you just bang your head against a wall? It will be something like she noticed poor Tom had two different-colored socks on the last time she saw him or your poor neglected children were hanging out in the center with undesirable companions." These were two of many items in Millicent's litany regarding Faith's shortcomings.

"I could only wish Amy had undesirable companions, and as for Ben, he's so intent on raising money for his trip that I doubt he's loitering. His class is badgering all the local businesses for items for an auction now.

See you both tomorrow—and don't forget we have the Uppity Women Luncheon Club's holiday party next week. Remind me to call Sandra Katz. It's at her house."

The Uppity Women were a small group of Aleford women—professionals, stay-at-home moms, and all sorts of variations. Years ago one of them had given a luncheon for friends of hers she thought should get to know one another. Thus the informal club was born; now it met at members' homes several times a year. The Uppities used their own china and cutlery, and supplied the wine; but they hired Faith to cook for them so the hostess could be free to enjoy herself. One of them was always on some sort of diet—Atkins, Paleo, no carbs—so Faith wanted to check to see what it was this time. And if one was following the 5:2 diet, she'd have to forgo a fasting day!

She left her car at the parsonage and once more set out across the Green, but this time she turned into Millicent's front walk, being sure to shut the gate in the white picket fence securely behind her. She'd been chastised before.

Millicent Revere McKinley was the great-great-great-granddaughter of a distant cousin of Paul Revere. It was this relative, Ezekiel Revere, who had cast the bell that hung in Aleford's old belfry atop Belfry

Hill overlooking the Green. When she was relatively new to Aleford, Faith had climbed the hill with baby Benjamin strapped close in his Snugli and discovered the still warm dead body of a parishioner in the small, dark structure. She had stood up, grasped the rope, and rung the bell repeatedly before racing down the hill to safety. Suffice it to say that in the days that followed, the murder was overshadowed by the controversy over the bell ringing—a bell, as Millicent was the first to point out, rung only in April, on Patriots' Day; for the death of a president; and for the death of a descendent of the brave force who faced the British on that famous day and year. Faith's explanation that the murderer might still have been lurking nearby and therefore an imme-diate alarm was called for met with a curl of Millicent's lip. There were still people in Aleford who referred to Faith as "that New Yorker who rang the bell."

Millicent was not a member of First Parish, but considered herself one ex officio, as well as of all the other houses of worship in Aleford. She also belonged to virtually every club in town, the D.A.R. at the top of the list. Faith liked to think the two of them had made peace with each other lo these many years and there was also the fact that Millicent had saved Faith's life not once, but twice. Baked goods hardly evened the score.

The brass knocker shaped like an eagle gleamed in the afternoon sun, but Faith did not reach for it. She had never approached the house without Millicent's flinging the door wide before any sign was given that Faith stood waiting outside. So she stood. And stood a bit longer. This was odd. It wasn't Millicent's day to volunteer at the library or for the discreet trip she made every seven weeks to nearby Concord for a cut and perm—her Mamie Eisenhower bangs unvarying.

Finally Faith knocked. It sounded like a musket shot. After a few minutes, Millicent opened the door.

Faith stepped back in shock. She'd seen Millicent two weeks ago at a Historical Society meeting for which Have Faith supplied coffee and dessert. A noted speaker had come to talk about the "French Connection": Revere's French Huguenot father Apollos Rivoire and antecedents. Since this was Millicent's own research bailiwick, she was flushed with anticipation, eager to prove the Harvard professor wrong, which she did on a minuscule point—minuscule not to Millicent. Miss McKinley had certainly been the picture of health that day. Now she appeared to have lost at least ten pounds, and her face had gained several new lines.

"Yes?" Her tone was not welcoming.

"I thought you might like some anadama bread and other things." Faith held the basket out.

Millicent opened the door marginally wider and Faith noticed it was on the chain. Millicent's door was never chained—or even locked. Curiouser and curiouser.

Millicent unhooked the chain. "Well, I suppose you'd better come in then."

This did sound a bit more like the Miss McKinley she knew, but as Faith made her way to the parlor past the portraits of Millicent's forbears she noticed a fine layer of dust on the furniture. The smell of Old English, Millicent's preferred scent, was absent.

Faith perched on the slippery horsehair couch that had long been her appointed spot while Millicent commandeered the Windsor chair with a cushion near the window.

"Have you been all right? You look a bit—tired," Faith said. Beating around the bush never worked with Millicent.

She braced herself for the response, but when it came it was not what Faith expected.

"I *am* a little tired. I'm not as young as I once was. People don't realize that. They don't realize a lot of things about me." Millicent glanced over at her desk. Faith saw a thick business-size envelope on top.

"Do you want me to mail that for you?"

"Mail? No, I have nothing to mail," Millicent said, looking once more at the envelope on the desk and then quickly back to Faith. "I imagine you must want to get back to your husband and children." She stood up. This was more like it, Faith thought. The suggestion of Mrs. Fairchild's neglect of hearth and home. The snappish tone.

"I'll leave the basket here for you then," she said, setting it on a small piecrust table near Millicent's chair. The parlor abounded with small tables and made getting in and out tricky.

Millicent sat down. "And see yourself out, if you would."

That had never happened before. Another anomaly. Faith did as she was told, but Millicent must have changed her mind and followed her.

Miss McKinley closed the front door securely and Faith heard the chain click into place. And, she noticed with dismay, Millicent hadn't hung her usual holly wreath up. A yuletide sign that appeared the first Sunday of Advent as reliably as the sunrise that same morning.

Something was very, very wrong in the House of Rivoire/Revere.

I am so *thirsty!* Sophie sleepily reached for the glass of water she always kept next to her bed. Her silk sleeve brushed against her skin and she sat bolt upright, eyes wide open. *I don't have a silk nightgown!* She sank back, remembering the night before.

The shutters were drawn, but daylight was seeping in. Friday. It must be Friday morning. Or maybe not. It felt as if she had slept for eons. She looked around the room. It was as lovely as the rest of the house. Maybe she could stay here for a while. A few months, say. Someone had gone back to the other house, and her clothes were on a chair. She'd have to get dressed. But first she'd close her eyes again for a minute. . . .

She must be dreaming. The voice. The touch. Even the smell that was his alone, a kind of Ivory soap fresh-air aroma.

"Will," she murmured.

"I'm here. Do you want to sleep some more?"

"Oh, Will!" She opened her eyes. He was kneeling by the side of the bed and took her hand. She pulled him closer. "Oh, Will, I'm so glad you're here! It was horrible. That man! He was dead and then they said they couldn't find him and—"

"Not now. We'll talk later. You've had a very frightening experience. Are you hungry? Thirsty? What can I get you?"

"Water, but don't leave."

"There's some bottled water and a glass on the bureau. Don't worry, I'm not going anywhere. Randy's call scared me to death."

Sophie drank the whole bottle. "It must be the bourbon and then I think there was something in the cocoa to make me sleep."

Will smiled. "I'm sure there was. Carlene's medicine cabinet could be a branch of CVS. Now, do you want to get up or stay in bed?"

"What do you think?" Sophie said.

They spent the weekend back at Tybee and it was a second honeymoon. Sophie tried to apologize for duplicating Will's grandmother's dress and hoped that doing so would help Will talk about that difficult time in his life, but he closed her mouth with a kiss and said he had been the one at fault.

"Hard to explain, so let's agree to let it go. I was a total jerk. I should have known you wouldn't pull a stunt like that."

Sophie had decided not to mention Patty Sue's role in the "stunt." It wouldn't serve any purpose to drive a wedge between the two half sibs.

What was a problem was Will's steadfast refusal to believe that Sophie's story about Thursday night was all real and not a kind of half-awake nightmare. After several tries, she gave up, deciding not to spoil their precious time together.

Following an early breakfast at The Breakfast Club Monday morning, Will dropped Sophie off at the house before leaving for Atlanta. Randy and Carlene, as well as Anson and Gloria, had offered to have Sophie stay with them during the week while Will was away, but Sophie had refused. It was hard to be a guest and she told them she'd be fine. "How likely is it that another body will appear in the wardrobe?" They'd laughed at her joke. Except she wasn't joking.

She did change bedrooms, though.

"See you Friday," Will called as he went down the front steps. "As soon as I can get away. We'll go someplace nice for dinner."

"I'd love to go back to the rooftop spot," Sophie said. She'd told Will about having drinks overlooking the river with Randy and Carlene. She liked the idea of returning there, plus it was new. No ghostly Savannah lore.

"Whatever you want. Oh, I almost forgot. The real estate agent has lined up some listings for you to view. Tuesday afternoon okay? If not you can call and change it."

"No, that's fine," Sophie said. The sooner she got out of the current house the better.

No apparitions or unnatural noises disturbed her sleep Monday night, but when Ruth, Maxwell & Maxwell's recently hired office manager, buzzed her to say the agent was waiting, Sophie eagerly grabbed her purse. Gloria had said the agency was the best in Savannah and knew before owners themselves did that a house was going to go on the market! Gloria's favorite agent was a "crackerjack," she'd said. Maybe she'd find their house today, Sophie thought.

Or maybe not.

The agent rose to greet her, hand outstretched and lips curved in a smile. Sophie recalled seeing a similar grin on the gators in the lagoon at Tybee's Crab Shack.

The agent was Miss Laura.

Chapter 4

"We haven't been introduced, but I feel as if I know you from everything Will and the rest of the family have said. I'm Laura Belvedere."

And I'm furious, Sophie thought, nevertheless coolly taking the outstretched hand and returning the shake, which was the equivalent of an air kiss. There was no way she was going to let this woman know how she was really feeling.

Laura was in white again. It must be her signature color, and it certainly worked with her platinum blond hair. She'd paired a long white jacket with a short white skirt. Her strappy silver high-heeled sandals matched a silver silk tee. Today's necklace was a glitter of quartz gemstones. She reminded Sophie of Tilda Swinton playing the White Witch in *The Lion, the Witch and the Wardrobe.*

Wardrobe! Sophie was sure everyone in Savannah had heard about her call to the police and Laura's next words confirmed it.

"Are you feeling all right today? I understand you've been . . . ill." Laura placed an oh-so-comforting hand on Sophie's arm. It was all she could do to keep from pushing it off.

"Ill? You've been misinformed. I've never felt better in my life. Now, where are we going to start looking?"

"I thought we'd work our way in, starting with The Landings out on Skidaway. It's only twenty minutes from downtown. Why don't you tell me about the kind of houses you like? Old, new? What kind of houses did you grow up in? Will said something about one being on the water."

Sophie described the Victorian on Long Island Sound in Connecticut, telling Laura it had been and still was the family home.

"But I'm not married to any one style of architecture." *I am married to your old beau, though, and don't you forget it!* she was tempted to add.

"The Landings is a real pretty spot. You cross the Moon River Bridge and are in a place most people would think of as a vacation destination, not a residential community. It's right off the Intracoastal and Will could keep his boat in the marina there."

Will has a boat?

"I did see a house for sale on Habersham that I liked," Sophie said. "It's pale gray, stucco, I think, or painted brick, with a bright red door, and it's on the corner. There's an ivy-covered wall alongside with a gate that must lead to a patio, and it has a beautiful cast iron balcony across the second story. Is that one of the ones we're seeing?"

"Oh, honey! That shoe box! No room to swing a cat. I'm going to do much much better for you."

Should I want to swing a cat, Sophie thought sourly. Miss Laura wasn't doing anything for *her*. That was obvious.

It was beautiful at The Landings. Before they had driven too far, Sophie saw two graceful great blue heron fly overhead and commented how lovely they were.

"If you like birds, this is the place. The Audubon people even have a Bird Cam you can watch online. Cutest little baby owls last year."

The place did seem like a resort, complete with a number of golf courses, tennis courts, and pools, but after Laura pulled into the drive of the third house, roughly the size and style of Tara should the O'Haras have had a need for a four-car garage, Sophie said,

"I—I mean we—were thinking of something smaller. These are lovely and the views are spectacular," she added hastily, although why she felt the need to stay in this woman's good graces escaped her. The habit of a perennial good girl. She sighed.

"Now, don't be discouraged. We haven't even begun to look. Will gave *me* the impression that he wanted a good-size place. Why don't we head back toward town and I'll show you one in Ardsley Park that is my favorite of all the listings on the market right now. You said you liked stucco, right? Like that little bitty place on Habersham. Well, this one was built in 1911 and has recently been renovated from top to bottom. It's got a *few* more rooms than what you have your eye on." She gave a little laugh, like ice tinkling in an empty glass.

Sophie leaned back against the leather seat—Laura drove a Lexus SUV, white of course—and surrendered. Obviously she'd have to go online to look for what she, Sophie, wanted to view and not what this "crackerjack" Realtor was bent on showing her. Sophie recalled that the prizes in those boxes had been hit or miss. The one time she got something good—a ring with a "real" ruby—the stone had fallen out the next day.

The Ardsley Park house was on Victory Drive, a wide street lined with the palm trees she saw all over that Sophie could still not quite believe were real. Laura had been right. The listing was a special one—the front yard had a number of massive moss-draped oaks, and there was a carriage house as well. Inside, Minton tiles surrounded many of the fireplaces, and the woodwork everywhere was museum quality.

"I hear you are quite the little cook," Laura said, spreading her arms wide and twirling around in the state-of-the-art kitchen complete with stainless steel appliances, granite countertops, and an eight-burner stove.

Reduced in Laura's mind to a gingham apron–clad Betty Crocker clone, Sophie succeeded in keeping her voice even—if not warm. "It's lovely, but maybe we should look at the listings in town. So easy to walk to work. And I know you think it's small, but I would like to see that house on Habersham." Sophie felt it was time to dig her heels in, otherwise she would end up with an ill-fitting pair of shoes she couldn't afford.

"I'll have to get in touch with that agency." Laura made it sound like one specializing in trailers and tear-downs. "But we can look at a few others. Will really wants you to check out a steal on East Jones."

Sophie considered asking Laura—no, she would not call her Miss Laura, which sounded like a nursery school teacher or dance instructor—to drop her back at the office. Laura was making it very obvious that Will and she had discussed the housing market in detail—as well as a whole lot of other things? But Sophie was no quitter, and she'd see where Ms. Belvedere thought she—no, make that Will—should live.

After the next property—five bedrooms, three and a half baths, garden, garage, priced at close to two million dollars, Sophie had had it. She'd have to make a "steal" to buy the one on Jones, or any of the others.

"Will should have made it plainer to you that these homes, although wonderful, are way beyond our means. I'll go online and send you a few places I'd like to see if you don't mind. Starting with the Habersham one."

"Beyond your means? What on earth are you talking about?"

Laura must have heard about Babs, and, of course, Sophie had been wearing some significant jewelry at the party, which the Realtor would have assumed was Sophie's own.

"My stepfather is wealthy, but that has nothing to do with Will and me. The diamond necklace and bracelet I was wearing at the party belong to my mother."

"Oh, sugar, I know all that. I'm talking about Will. His grandmother left him everything, even the house Anson and Gloria live in. Will is richer than Croesus!"

The amused look Laura gave her said more than any words. *How well exactly do you know your husband?*

Sophie was so preoccupied she didn't realize Laura was pulling up to The Pirates' House, a restaurant catering to tourists on Broughton Street near the river.

"Now, Will said he hadn't taken you here yet, so it's the perfect place to have a drink and get an early dinner while we talk about the houses you saw today. Especially now that you know your budget!"

This is so not happening. "Thank you, Laura, but I need to get back to the office to finish something up. I'd planned on grabbing a salad later. I'm not really hungry now."

Her excuses fell on very deaf ears. Laura was already out of the car, key in hand.

"Now, I'm sure an educated lady like you read *Treasure Island* growing up. This is the place mentioned in the book. Captain Flint still makes an appearance on moonless nights, but y'all know about ghosts in Savannah." Sophie had no choice but to follow.

The hostess seated them in a small room that must have dated back even before *Treasure Island.* The blackened fireplace mantel was decorated with a line of skulls.

Their server appeared immediately. "What can I get you ladies to drink?" Sophie felt a sudden need for alcohol, the stronger the better.

"A vodka martini, please. Stoli if you have it. With two olives."

"She'll have a Skull Crusher," Laura said. "You *have* to have rum here. It's their most famous drink. Wait until you see the container!"

"I'll have a vodka martini, please. Stoli if you have it. With two olives," Sophie repeated firmly.

"Oh well. I guess I'll have a Cosmo then."

The server left and Laura assumed the role of tour guide. "You're sitting in part of the oldest house in Georgia, built in 1734. And the oldest bar in the state. General Oglethorpe banned rum—thought it was a bad influence—but it didn't last long. He had a lot of noble ideas that went out the window." Her tone clearly indicated what she thought of these "noble ideas."

Sophie had read up on James Oglethorpe. One of his other bans had been on slavery, which didn't last long, either.

"Now I'm going to go powder my nose. Y'all can read up on the history of The Pirates' House on the menu," Laura instructed. She really was very bossy. Was that why Will had broken up with her? It was clear that Laura hadn't dumped him.

When she returned she began to talk a mile a minute—houses, Savannah—and Sophie began to wonder whether she'd indulged in another kind of powdered substance in the ladies' room. She definitely was sounding high on something. Maybe it was just her love of the city.

The drinks arrived. "Are you ready to order?" the server asked. Once more Laura took charge.

"We'll start with a cup of okra gumbo—a bowl would fill us up—and then—"

"I'll have the grilled salmon salad, house dressing on the side." Sophie raised her voice slightly out of necessity.

"Pooh! You are a spoilsport—or don't you like Southern food?"

"I love it"—she'd even created her own recipe for cheese grits (see recipe, page 233)—"but I told you I wasn't hungry." Sophie knew she sounded truculent and didn't care. Her martini was doing the trick. She might have to have another. She was walking, after all.

"You can bring me the Fried Shrimp Savannah and I'm not going to share!"

There didn't seem to be much to say after that, and Sophie decided against another drink, even though Laura didn't. The alcohol seemed to restore her would-be hostess's genial mood.

"Now I just know I'm going to find you the perfect house. Which was your favorite today? I know! Ardsley Park! Oh, here comes our pirate. Y'all going to love this!"

Sophie listened politely as a man who did indeed look very much like an illustration from the Stevenson book related more Pirates' House history. By the time the gumbo arrived—she'd given in to the server's insistence, not Laura's—the mood of the place was starting to charm her. Yes, it was hosting at least two busloads of tourists in several of the seventeen rooms, but she thought it would be a fun spot to take her Yankee friends when they visited. She smiled to herself.

"That's better," Laura said, noting her expression. "Now isn't this the best okra gumbo you've ever had? Will's favorite."

Sophie's mood vanished as fast as the gumbo had—it *was* good, and she'd lied to Laura about not being hungry.

It was one of the longest dinners Sophie had ever endured. She listened to Laura's detailed description of her debut—Will was her escort—and more. The Belvederes were in shipping, the firm started by Laura's grandfather and now run by "Daddy and my brother—smart as a whip." Noting the brands Laura was sporting, Sophie figured someone was making money. And it could be Laura herself, selling houses. She realized she didn't know where Laura lived and asked her. At least it might move the woman from past to present.

" 'Course I moved out of Mama and Daddy's when I left Agnes Scott, but they keep my room just the way it's always been."

So much for present. Sophie envisioned a room fit for the Southern belle Laura embodied. An antique four-poster, shelves for the doll collection, an organdy skirted dressing table, and rose-colored walls, maybe even roses on the walls. Laura had revealed that she was the only girl and her family "just spoil the life out of me!"

Not knowing quite how to respond to that ("Lucky you"? "Poor me"?) Sophie asked her again where she was currently living.

"Since then I've been a flipper. You know. I've got the touch. Buy an apartment, fix it up while I live in it, sell it and double my money—or more. I'm in a condo near Gloria's new project now. That's a hot part of town, so close to the river and just starting to take off."

Filing away the information that Laura lived so nearby for further thought, Sophie stood up. "I really do have to be going, after I find the restroom."

Their server appeared to clear the table and pointed to the dessert menus. "I hope I can tempt you lovely ladies into one of the chef's sweets."

"Absolutely." Laura beamed, motioning for Sophie to sit down. "You can't leave without one of their desserts." She made it sound like a command. "I'll have the bourbon pecan pie with plenty of whipped cream. Why don't you have the peach cobbler? It's to die for and—"

Sophie remained standing but smiled her own gator grin as she finished Laura's sentence, "and Will loves it. But no thanks."

As she moved away from the table, she wondered how Laura stayed so thin. The old finger-down-the-throat trick or Ex-Lax?

Sophie did want the restroom, but she also wanted to give the server her credit card to pay for their meals. She didn't intend to owe Laura Belvedere a thing. After arranging the bill, she walked in the direction the server had indicated through the restaurant and stopped to read an out-of-the-way sign above what looked like the opening to an underground chamber. The drop was safely barricaded by an iron railing. She leaned over it to peer down and a voice next to her said, "First time here?"

Associating the phrase with pickup lines from Big Apple clubs, Sophie turned to move on but stopped when she saw the speaker was a handsome elderly gentleman with a thick crop of white hair leaning on a cane with a shiny brass pelican handle.

"That was where they kept the rum," he continued. "Workers uncovered the area sometime in the 1960s.

It leads to a tunnel that goes all the way to the river. Supposedly wide enough for a wagon. I'm Francis, by the way."

"I'm Sophie. And yes, I have never been here before. I just moved to Savannah in the fall, so all of it is pretty new to me. I've heard a little about tunnels under the city, though. I'm guessing this one was used to shanghai crew besides transport the barrels of rum?"

"That's what they say. Rope a poor unsuspecting young man in for a friendly drink—like the Skull Crusher they have now—and the next thing he'd know he was on a schooner headed for the Seven Seas. Other tunnels were used to move yellow fever victims, especially during the 1876 epidemic that took the lives of over one thousand people."

"That many!" Sophie exclaimed.

Francis nodded. "People say it's because Savannah is so swampy, and it's carried by mosquitoes, but it's also likely sailors brought the infection into the port. So, you're interested in our history?"

"Yes. Savannah is my home now and I'm finding out all sorts of interesting things about it." Including, she thought but didn't mention, a body.

"Well, you're talking to the right man. Here's my card. After I retired, I started working as a guide to some of the historic houses. I'm at the Mercer Williams

House right now and I'd be happy to give you a tour. No Mercer ever lived there and people come because of The Book—you know about that?—but there's much more to the house."

"I work nearby at Maxwell and Maxwell, so I'd be delighted," Sophie said. "And yes, I know all about The Book. Read it even before I knew I'd be living here."

"Maxwell and Maxwell, hmmm. You must be Will Maxwell's new bride. I was sorry to miss the party Anson and Gloria threw for you."

Sophie smiled mischievously. "The party to meet Will Maxwell's new *Yankee* bride."

Francis put out his hand and Sophie shook it. He had a firm grasp. "Welcome to Savannah, Mrs. Maxwell. Yankees are just fine with me. My grandmother was from Boston, and remember, even though he did a lot of damage other places, Sherman spared our fair city and gave it to President Lincoln as a Christmas present. We'll talk more. I have an endless supply of tales. Oh, and do be sure to take a look at the Herb House part of the restaurant when you are outside. That really is the oldest part and stands next to what was the Trustees Garden. Poor benighted Oglethorpe laid it out and planted mulberry trees plus other things that would never grow here. He thought he'd be feeding silkworms with the mulberry leaves, establishing a thriving silk industry. He had better luck with his peach trees. Now, I must go back to my friends. They'll be thinking I tumbled into the cellar here."

He gave a slight bow, and Sophie returned to her own table feeling happier than she had all day.

When she was finally able to get away from Laura, turning down her offer of a ride several times, Sophie's cheerful mood returned. It was dusk and she decided to walk down Bay Street and turn on Whitaker, which she knew led to Forsyth Park. And she'd come back by way of Habersham, past what she was fast thinking was *her* house, the tiny one with the red door.

It would be Christmas in a little over a week. Savannah didn't have Rockefeller Center–type decorations, but the city had plenty of lights, wreaths, and, unlike New York, blooming plants sporting big red bows in planters and window boxes. She was sure the large fountain at Forsyth would look seasonal. No worries about the recirculating water freezing.

As she walked she debated whether to ask Will if they could change agents. Laura wasn't going to show her the homes Sophie wanted to see—she was sure of it. She framed the argument in her mind. How would Will have felt if Ian, Sophie's former British swain, was their agent? Of course, Ian was a total snake, and although she didn't like her, Laura was a decent person. And the cattiness was explainable. Losing Will would make any woman resentful of her replacement. By the time Sophie reached the park, she was feeling sorry for Miss Laura—and if that's what her friends called her, so be it. It would be extremely petty for Sophie to insist on a new agent.

Yet, it was early days, a small voice way in the back of her head reminded her.

The fountain was lovely, and after sitting on a bench nearby for a while, Sophie walked on, intending to exit at Gwinnett to get over to Habersham. Dusk had given way to dark. There were not as many lights in this area, and she picked up her pace. Like any big city, Savannah had its share of crime—as she well knew. How could she convince Will that what she'd seen was real? And where had the corpse gone so rapidly?

It wasn't late, but she began to feel uneasy when she heard footsteps behind her. She sped up, and they did the same.

Until now she hadn't been the only person in the park.

The shadows were deeper here. The brightly lighted street ahead seemed far away, and Sophie began to feel truly afraid. She started to glance over her shoulder to see who it was but stumbled on the uneven pavement. Better to keep her eyes focused ahead.

It had been foolish to come to this part of the city, a city still so unfamiliar to her. She pulled her keys from her purse and clenched them in her fist, one pointing straight out between two fingers. When she'd moved to Manhattan, she'd taken a women's defense class at her mother's insistence. Bless Babs.

She was almost out of the park. Her heartbeats slowed. The person behind her must simply be eager to get home. But just as she was reassuring herself, a tall shape in a dark hooded coat rushed past her, pushing her roughly to one side. She let out a strangled cry as she struggled to keep her balance. The figure was taking off at a run.

Breathless, Sophie paused to collect herself. "Some people!" she muttered aloud.

The person had dropped an envelope in his or her haste to get wherever was so important. Sophie picked it up and was startled to see her name written on the outside.

The flap wasn't sealed and she tore it open. Six words were written on a single sheet of paper by the same hand as her name:

Go back where you came from

When Faith had picked up the phone Tuesday evening to hear Sophie Maxwell ask her if she had a minute, she hadn't expected they'd still be talking an hour later. After Sophie had related her encounter in the park, Faith had asked whether there had been any other frightening incidents. The floodgates opened. When Sophie got to the body in the wardrobe, Faith had exclaimed, "That happened to me, too!"

"You found a dead body in a wardrobe?"

"Not exactly a wardrobe, or it would have been an armoire. We were living in France at the time. What I meant was that I found a body behind the trash cans in the vestibule of our apartment building and fled upstairs. By the time the gendarmes arrived it was gone."

"So, you know how I feel. Nobody believed you, either, right?"

"Not at first."

"Even Tom?"

"Especially Tom. I was pregnant with Amy, and everyone put it down to hormones."

"Well, at least it makes sense that someone could have easily moved that body. How do you explain mine?" Sophie said.

"I can't. Especially without seeing where it was. Now, the business with the dress at the party was just pure spite on your sister-in-law's part. I remember her from the rehearsal dinner. I never trust those 'butter won't melt in my mouth' types. And, Sophie, could the person who jostled you tonight and left that sick note possibly have been her as well?"

"I suppose it could have. She probably got a report on today's house hunting from her BFF Laura, the woman Will *should* have married. I'll bet Laura called her right away. And I'd said I was going to take a walk to the park, as it was such a nice night. What's weird is that the figure most resembled the dead guy in the wardrobe—same size—but I think he can be crossed off the list of possibilities. Dead is dead."

"Definitely," Faith said. "Hold on to the paper and no more walks alone at night, okay?"

"Maybe this whole thing was a mistake! North, South. West Coast, East Coast. Maybe mixed marriages aren't meant to be. After all, we met in Maine. Neutral territory."

"Nonsense. I moved to Aleford from New York City. Much farther away if not in distance than in ways of life than Savannah is. It will take a while for the whole outsider thing to die down, but it will."

They ended the call, arranging to talk again the next day. Faith went back to the kitchen to run the dishwasher. The kids were doing homework, and Tom was at a meeting of the Vestry.

What she had been loath to tell Sophie was that it might take a very long time for the outsider label to blur—say, sixteen-plus years. . . .

Sophie wasn't hungry and she didn't feel like going over the papers she'd brought home from work. A cup of chamomile tea and early bed. She turned on the radio in the kitchen and started to boil some water. The station was playing holiday music. Randy had insisted that "Jingle Bells" had been written in Savannah. Sophie had laughed at what was obviously one of his tall tales. The idea of enough snow for a one-horse sleigh down here was ludicrous.

She'd ask her new friend Francis about it. "Francis Whelan III" his card read, all in an elegant font. She wanted to know more about Sherman's Christmas gift to Lincoln plus any special Savannah Christmas customs. If she asked Patty Sue, Sophie would surely end up committing another extreme faux pas. She could hear the woman now: "Oh yes, a new bride has to leave sprigs of gold-sprayed magnolia leaves on everyone's doorstep with her calling card."

The kettle whistled. Sophie poured it over the infuser and took her tea into the living room. Maybe she'd get a tree before Will came back and decorate it as a surprise. There was a perfect spot for it in front of the tall windows overlooking the square. She'd better check with Gloria to make sure it would be all right. It would be wonderful to be in their own house. Maybe Will would look at some listings with her this weekend. Some listings that were her choice.

She'd left the radio on. Dan Fogelberg's "Same Old Lang Syne" was playing and Sophie felt a lump in her throat. If the next tune was Judy Garland singing "Have Yourself a Merry Little Christmas," she'd be undone completely. She took a gulp of the tea, but it wasn't producing any comfort.

What would this Christmas be like? Last year she'd been in London with Ian and it was the before phase—before she'd found him in bed with another woman as he'd nastily planned. But that Merrie Olde English Christmas! She had never been happier—or so she thought. Now she was living an authentic happily-ever-after with Will. Wasn't she?

She sipped more tea and tried to think what was making her so blue. Yes, the encounter in the park and note had been upsetting—no, make that frightening—but the worst part of the day had been all Laura's references to Will. What he liked, their shared past, and especially his bank account. When Sophie had met Will last summer, he'd truly been a mystery man, but that had all been cleared up—or had it? How well did she know the man she had married? The man she loved?

They had not been able to spend that much time together since the wedding. He'd had to leave Maine before she did, and then she'd stayed in Connecticut to plan the wedding. Since the honeymoon, she could easily count the number of days they'd been together on both hands. And when they were together, other people, especially Will's family, so often surrounded them.

Her mug was empty. Sophie was feeling a little empty, too. Bing Crosby was crooning "I'll Be Home for Christmas." Damn it! Sophie thought. Why shouldn't she and Will go to Connecticut for Christmas? A White Christmas! A Christmas without grits.

It wasn't late. She'd call her mother and let her know. Babs went all out decorating the house for the holidays and threw a number of parties. It would be fun. Will had never seen New York City at Christmas. They could go skating, have hot toddies at The St. Regis's King Cole Bar, look in all the department store windows, catch the show at Radio City Music Hall. Surely he could get away for a few days. Her mood lifted as suddenly as an untethered hot air balloon.

Babs always let the phone ring at least four or five times to give the accurate indication that she was a busy lady and send a message that the caller better have a very good reason for getting in touch. At last she answered.

"Harrington residence."

"It's me, Mother, or rather 'I,' so you don't have to pretend to be the housekeeper."

"I'm not pretending. I've given Mrs. Bishop three weeks off to go see her son and his family who have moved to Canada. One of those places in the middle. Saskatchewan? Manitoba? They were living in Passaic, New Jersey, and apparently wanted a major change. I would have thought someplace closer would have sufficed. Ohio? Kansas?"

Mrs. Bishop had been with her mother for a few years, and Sophie wondered how Babs was going to manage the holiday season without the woman, who was known for her baking. Good thing Sophie would be on hand to help. Although Babs also used caterers. Which reminded her, she should ask Faith for some special holiday recipes.

"Good news—at least I assume it will be good news—"

Babs cut her off. "Well, I must say this is fast work. It's not that I don't want to be a grandmother—note to self, 'Get key ring with "World's Youngest Grand-mother" engraved on it'—but, Sophie, darling, I would have thought you'd have waited until you had a house and, more important, spent more time with Will. You haven't known each other long."

"I'm *not* pregnant! I called to tell you we're coming for Christmas!"

"Oh, darling, lovely, lovely thought; but sorry, no can do. Ed and I are leaving for Mustique in a few days. I'm just waiting for the final alterations to the clothes I ordered at Bendel's. Ed has rented a villa through New Year's. Just between the two of us, I wouldn't be surprised if that dear man ends up giving it to me in my stocking. He does love to play the course on the island and it's a hop to all those other island ones."

Probably Sir Paul will be their guest for dinner, Sophie thought bitterly. Rejected at the holidays by her own mother.

Babs was still talking. "It's not as if you haven't been here recently."

"That was my *wedding*, Mother!"

"I know, sweetheart, which is exactly my point. You are a married woman now and you should be spending this first Christmas with your new family. I'm surprised Will wants to leave them. Gloria and Anson are bound to have some fabulous soirees, and of course Savannah is known for celebrating the season."

Sophie mumbled something to the effect that she hadn't run the idea by Will yet, and Babs pounced.

"Don't tell me you two are still having that little tiff! Now, Sophie, I told you when I was there that whatever happened was best forgotten. So suck it up."

Such nurturance and such language, Sophie reflected. But her mother was right. She'd have to suck it up and deal with it.

"Have fun and send me a postcard," she said.

"You know I never send postcards. I'll bring you something nice for Christmas instead. Something from that fun shop, the Pink House. One of their silk sarongs for the beach?"

Tybee wasn't a silk sarong-type beach, but Sophie thanked her mother, sent love to Ed, and hung up.

The radio was playing Elvis's "Blue Christmas" and she was tempted to throw it straight through one of Gloria's very expensive glass-fronted kitchen cabinets.

When the phone rang, Faith grabbed it, thinking it might be Sophie calling back to talk some more. Sophie had sounded depressed. Very, very blue, and Faith wished she could take time off and meet Sophie for a long weekend in Manhattan. Retail therapy surrounded by the shiniest of ornaments. A poison pen letter was such a cowardly act and mean. Faith was beginning to equate Patty Sue—it had to be her—with the middle school girls making Amy's life hell.

But it wasn't Sophie, it was Ursula. "I'm worried about Millicent. She didn't show up for the Evergreens's sale today."

The Evergreens was Aleford's garden club and dated back if not to Eden then at least to the 1930s. Besides their meetings, their fund-raisers—plant sale in May and holiday greens in December—were events few ladies in town missed and definitely not a club member. Faith had stopped by when the sale started at eight thirty and scored a festive holly table decoration with peppermint-striped candles.

"Have you tried to reach her?"

"When she wasn't there by nine—and she was supposed to man the amaryllis table—I called. You know she won't have a machine, so I kept trying on and off all day until noon. We were supposed to stay open until one, but everything was gone."

Faith wasn't surprised. Many people waited for the sale to hang their wreaths, including First Parish's Altar Guild. Its members were always first in line for the few oversize ones that would adorn the church's facade.

"Would you like me or Tom to go check on her? She may be ill."

"Just as I've never known Millicent to miss an Evergreens event, and duty, I've never known her to be sick. I went over as soon as I could. She didn't answer the door, but I knew she was there."

"The curtain moved?" Faith guessed.

It was well known that Millicent's muslin curtains were sheer and a slight twitch gave her an even clearer view.

"Yes, so I just kept knocking. She hasn't hung the wreath she made for herself when we were making everything for the sale. I don't like this, Faith. I can tell you I am worried."

For a stalwart New Englander like Ursula Lyman Rowe, this was tantamount to admitting abject fear.

Ursula sighed audibly. "She came to the door eventually, opened it a crack, and instead of scolding me for making so much noise as I would have expected, she told me she was fine and had forgotten today was the sale. I didn't believe that for one minute. I hadn't mentioned the sale for one thing, so she certainly remembered it at some point. But what is concerning me is how she looked. I don't think she can be eating and her face was quite drawn."

Faith was assailed by guilt. Millicent hadn't looked well last week, and Faith being crazy busy was no excuse for not going back to check on the woman. "I'll go by first thing in the morning."

"I think it had better be Tom," Ursula said. "You and Millicent have, well, a complicated relationship. She's more apt to tell Tom what is going on. And something is definitely going on."

When Tom returned from his meeting, he was more than happy to stop by Millicent's and was reassuring about what might be wrong.

"You forget how old she is. Yes, forgetting the sale, or forgetting to tell someone she was missing it, is uncharacteristic. But she has probably picked up a bad cold and doesn't want to admit her distinguished gene pool could ever succumb. You've got chicken soup in the freezer, I assume. I'll bring that and whatever else you want to send."

Faith always had containers of that panacea—also known as Jewish penicillin—on hand, and before she went to bed she'd bake some pumpkin muffins, the closest Millicent came to sweets. She was preparing several more cookie varieties for the Uppity Women luncheon tomorrow—each would leave with a large plate of assorted treats—so whipping up the muffins would be easy.

But the deathwatch for Charles Frawley came to a peaceful end in the early hours of the morning, and

Tom's ministrations to the family took precedence. He made a note to see Millicent soon, but the living would have to wait for a while as he helped Godspeed the dead On Eagle's Wings.

Before Sophie went to work, she called Gloria about the tree—"Honey, you didn't have to ask me! You go ahead and do whatever you want to the house. Laura told me you'd had a good day looking at some listings, and if this one were a tad larger I'd adore for you and Will to have it!"

"A tad larger"? Less than twenty-four hours ago Sophie would have been completely mystified by the comment. When Gloria was finished, there would be four bedrooms, three and a half baths, an eat-in kitchen, living room, dining room, library, media room, garden room, and outdoor space. As it was she thanked her mother-in-law and before she hung up was told the best, and only, place to get a tree.

Sophie's mind was buzzing while she got dressed. If Gloria knew about her afternoon with the real estate agent, so did Patty Sue—or vice versa. Ridiculous to think that Gloria could have been her assailant in the park. She had been nothing but welcoming to Sophie, but she *was* close to Laura. Laura the person Gloria had hoped would be her daughter-in-law? Besides, she was a petite woman. But she might have written the note. She quelled her impulse to call back and ask if it would be all right to drape the Connecticut State flag from an upstairs window with its singularly appropriate state motto, "Qui Transtulit Sustinet"—"He Who Transplanted Still Sustains"—or in this case, "She."

Tree ordered and delivery scheduled, Sophie stepped out into the kind of Savannah morning that never failed to enchant her. The air was warm but crisp, and everywhere she looked she saw things to delight the eye. The houses, the landscape, but also the people off to work or just off walking. There was something to be said for living in this sort of warm climate. People looked happier, and were friendlier. She knew the summer would be an endurance test, but for now she was enjoying the weather and not missing the cold at all.

She planned on decorating the tree very simply with tiny white lights, maybe some sort of garlands and a few special ornaments. Will and she would be collecting ornaments for years to come. The Christmas Shop on Bull looked enticing and she'd already decided to look for Will's present at the Savannah College of Art and Design's shop. And then there were the historic house gift shops as well. She'd missed the big Christmas Made in the South craft fair at the International Trade & Convention Center on Hutchinson

Island just across from downtown. She hoped to get to something else there just for the experience of taking the Savannah Belles Ferry instead of the Talmadge Bridge. She'd taken Will on the Staten Island Ferry. Maybe they should do a round-trip this weekend for the fun of it.

One of the other resolutions she'd made when she woke up—the main one being to snap out of it and, yes, suck it up—was to invite Ruth, the office manager at the firm, to lunch this week. She knew Ruth had already been welcomed by everyone else. Sophie liked the competent young woman, and she should have invited her earlier. With that in mind, she went directly to Ruth's desk when she got to the office.

"Could you spare some time to grab lunch today or tomorrow? You probably know places better than I do, but someone told me that the Jepson Center has a good café. Maybe squeeze in some Christmas shopping?"

Ruth beamed. "I'd love to, and I haven't been to the café but have heard it's excellent."

It occurred to Sophie that Ruth was the New Kid on the Block, too.

"I know the former assistant was here for many years. I hope it wasn't too hard to step into her shoes."

Will had told Sophie about the legendary Sophronia Webster, "Miss S." to all. She'd been like family.

"From what everyone has said, she was a lovely person and I'm sure a big help," Sophie added.

Ruth shook her head, and her smile vanished. "I never met her, although I've heard about her, too, from so many people. It was tragic. She was killed instantly by a hit-and-run driver right in front of her own home."

Chapter 5

"A vaporizer, two years in a row! Granted, the second year he included some Vicks VapoPads. CVS on Christmas Eve is his go-to solution for what to put under the tree." The women gathered around Sandra Katz's dining room table erupted in peals of laughter.

It was the Uppity Women's holiday luncheon. They had long ago added both Faith and Niki to the group, insisting the kitchen door be left open so they could both hear and contribute. The question Pamela, a tall slender Wharton grad with her own financial planning firm, had thrown out was: "What was your worst Christmas, Hanukkah, Kwanza gift ever?"

They had started in the living room with flutes of prosecco and a simple hors d'oeuvre of bite-size melon wrapped in prosciutto. Faith knew the group would be counting their calories and was giving them a delectable dessert—her own eggnog ice cream with Niki's take on mince tarts. Hers had a rich butter crust that tasted like shortbread, and she added clementines to the traditional spiced currant/apple filling, spiking it with brandy.

Niki wasn't able to do the luncheon today. It had especially become her gig when her husband, Phil, had lost his job and the group's amazing networking capability landed him a plum new one in less than a week. But little Sofia had picked up a bug, and Niki needed to be home. The women had expressed regret but also delight at seeing Faith after "too long," they all told her.

Sandra's dining room looked beautiful, with a shiny brass menorah that she told them had been her grandparents' on the sideboard. Blue-and-white porcelain cachepots filled with white amaryllis and cyclamen were placed throughout the room. Margaret, a dean at a local college, had brought favors she'd made—pomanders studded with cloves and cured in cinnamon, orris, nutmeg, and allspice. They were heaped in a Simon Pearce glass bowl in the center of the table, their spicy orange fragrance perfuming the air just enough not to overwhelm the food.

While Faith plated the first course—endive spears with fresh chèvre and pomegranate seeds in a light vinaigrette—she thought about what a great mix the group was. Married, divorced, never married, and stay-at-home moms—present and past—working full- or part-time—pretty much a cross section of forty-something women. What they all had in common was a well-developed sense of humor and interest in a wide range of topics from politics to how to get ink stains off a silk blouse. And books. They were omnivorous readers. At the moment they were still on the worst gifts.

"Mine was a *Love Actually* moment," Nora, a petite woman with short dark curls, said. "You remember when Emma Thompson opens the gift she believes is the necklace she saw her husband buy—"

"Alan Rickman," Sandra called out. "He was practicing to play Snape in the Harry Potters obviously!"

Nora nodded. "So it's Christmas Eve and Emma and the kids are each opening one gift. It's not the necklace, but a CD."

"Joni Mitchell, however," Margaret added. It was no surprise to Faith that the group seemed to have the film memorized. It was one of her favorites, too. "So, Nora, don't keep us in suspense, what happened?"

"It was pretty damn similar. Just after Thanksgiving I found a receipt from Tiffany's in one of his jackets that had to go to the dry cleaner—"

She was interrupted again by somewhat raucous laughter and a comment, "Men are sooo stupid!"

"It was for the Elsa Peretti diamond open heart that I had admired when we were picking out gifts for his partners and some other business contacts. Sure enough, on Christmas morning there was a little blue box in my stocking—gift wrapping is not his thing— and I gave him a big kiss before I opened it."

There was a hushed moment before she continued, "It was a sterling key ring with my initials and the 'big' gift under the tree was a Natori peignoir and gown set I'm sure his secretary picked out. The Peretti neck- lace appeared around the neck of our recently divorced next-door neighbor whom I'd invited to our annual New Year's Eve party because I felt sorry for her!"

"It could have been a coincidence," Pamela said.

"True. But the fact that they were sucking face even before midnight when I went out to the fridge in the garage for more champagne was not."

Faith knew Nora was divorced, but had never heard the backstory.

They continued around the table and were moving on to best gifts when Cheryl said, "How materialistic are we? Shouldn't we be discussing the election?" Faith did not remember seeing her at an Uppies before. She must be a new addition.

A chorus of nos and one boo greeted her.

"Nothing serious today, ladies," Sandra said. "It's my house and I'm making the rules! Now, we definitely need more wine."

That was Faith's cue, and she moved into the room quickly to pour a Geyser Peak sauvignon blanc and an Arboreto Montepulciano. "Montepulciano," she whispered to herself. So much fun to say and a place where she and Tom had celebrated a significant anniversary. As she cleared the plates, she was struck by how much she would miss jobs like this—and other longtime clients. Niki could certainly keep working at the Uppity luncheons, but would she be able to do it from whatever location Faith found on the South Shore? Niki was constantly offered jobs from Faith's competitors and she could also set up her own firm. Was that what would happen if Faith had to move?

"Why is change so hard?" Faith thought she had spoken her thoughts aloud and almost dropped the plates she was carrying, but it was a recent member of the group speaking, Jessica. "When I was younger it was all I wanted. New jobs, new places to live, new men. New experiences across the board. Now I want to stay put! Have a great guy. Great place to live. Great job."

"So what's the problem?" Margaret asked.

"He wants to move into town. Says we're in a rut. So if I want to be with him—and I do—I have to move."

The discussion took them through the next course, with suggestions and questions flying: "Does he know how you feel?" "Is he worth it?"

It was the second night of Hanukkah. In honor of the hostess and a few of the other women, Faith had prepared latkes—silver-dollar-size crisp potato pancakes. They accompanied lightly smoked grilled salmon with mustard dill sauce and roasted root vegetables. By the time the last latke had disappeared, the conversation had moved on to aging parents and growing kids—topics that came up at every one of the luncheons Faith had attended. Today her ears were wide open.

She brought in the dessert with one for herself. She, or Niki when it was her turn, always joined the women for the final course. Sandra had selected a Moscato that was not overly sweet as the final wine, and Faith poured herself a glass, too.

Laura, who looked like a teenager herself, was speaking. "We haven't even gotten near a tuition bill yet and we're already feeling pinched by the application fees. We've tried to get him to narrow his choices, but he's afraid he won't get in anywhere. And I guess we are, too. He hasn't built an orphanage in a poverty-stricken country or happened upon a cure for something in the chem lab, so he's going to have to rely on a decent GPA and varsity soccer. I kept telling him to join the drama club or model UN, broaden his scope, but would he listen?"

Margaret reassured her, "There's a lid for every pot and he's a great kid. The whole application process has gotten insane. It's something we're all talking about in higher ed."

"Any change will be too late for us. Billy's our one and only," Laura said ruefully.

Sandra changed the topic—and mood. "Faith, this meal was the best ever—and that's saying a great deal. You've been so busy serving us that we haven't heard from you. What's new? And how's Niki?"

Quelling her desire to talk about Tom's recent decision, Faith gave them an update on Niki, including the Sofia-meets-a-paper-clip incident, and then decided to talk about Amy. Maybe she'd get some suggestions. "My daughter Amy has started middle school."

Several groans greeted the news, and Sandra said, "Would not go through that again for anything. Is she still speaking to you?"

"Pretty much. The big problem is school. She's at Hancock, not Adams, where everyone from her elementary school went. It turns out we were in a different district all along and she should have been in another elementary school, too."

"And the powers that be wouldn't budge. Been there and not done that," Sandra said.

Faith nodded. "It's been really tough. There are a—"

Just as she was about to launch into the whole Mean Girls problem, Laetitia, also one of the group's newer members, broke in. "My daughter Cassandra is in the seventh grade at Hancock, too! She has tons of friends and I know they'll all be happy to welcome your daughter. Your Amy probably knows my Cassie already!" She beamed.

Cassie. Oh yes, Faith thought. There couldn't be two. Cassie, short for Cassandra, the Greek princess with the gift of prophecy and the curse never to be believed. A seer and a liar. Cassie, Amy's nemesis.

The next day was Charles Frawley's funeral and Faith was sitting in her accustomed spot in church. Her first Sunday as a new bride she had slipped into one of the pews farthermost to the rear, her mother's longstanding choice, and was politely but firmly escorted by one of the ushers to the front pew, right-hand side just below the pulpit. "The minister's wife has *always* sat here."

The spot had its advantages. She could look inattentive—her mind tended to wander during a service—and only her husband would know. However, it also had disadvantages: she couldn't count the house and see how many parishioners had shown up, and who had not bothered.

As she waited for the service to begin, her mind was on several things at once. The thought that she'd be occupying a different designated spot in a new church and Amy, always Amy. After Laetitia's announcement about her daughter—and what was with these oh-so-classical names?—Faith had jumped up to serve coffee and holiday cookies for those Uppity Women secure enough with the way they looked to nibble on them—a surprising number indulged. At the end of the luncheon, she'd been tempted to pull Laetitia to one side and confide—what? "Your daughter is making my daughter's life a living hell"? Instead she'd thanked her for the offer of Cassie's friendship and said she was sure the two girls' paths would cross. She'd also crossed her fingers.

The church was beginning to fill up. Charles had been a treasured member of the congregation and the whole town. He'd been widowed ten years ago and his children lived at a distance, so Aleford had filled in as family. He'd been a frequent guest for Sunday dinner and other meals at the parsonage. Ben and Amy were very fond of him. He was a great storyteller, a self-described amateur historian, who had more knowledge about Aleford and New England than most professionals. Faith was starting to feel sad. He'd had a good long life, but she was filled with mixed emotions. Happy that his suffering was over, but depressed by the increasingly rapid passing of his generation. As for her own death, it was something she hoped was many years in the future and would occur at the exact moment of Tom's passing. As for an afterlife, she planned on being pleasantly surprised.

Her end-of-life thoughts strayed to Sophie's discovery of the corpse in the wardrobe. Faith had no doubts about what the young woman saw. When she herself had discovered a body that then vanished, everyone's disbelief was the worst part of all. She still got angry when she remembered the gesture one of the gendarmes had made when he thought she wasn't looking— his hand to his mouth as if tipping a bottle. She'd call Sophie soon and find out if there was any more news.

"She's not here," a voice hissed.

Faith was startled from her reverie. Ursula had slid next to her. The act was such a departure—the Rowes' spot was third row left-hand side since before Revere's midnight ride—that for an instant she was frozen in place, then quickly responded. "Who's not here?"

"Millicent."

Faith darted a look over her shoulder. When Millicent did come to a service she occupied the last pew, always seated next to the aisle. The spot Faith longed for. It was indeed empty.

"There's still time. She might just be late."

"Millicent late?" Ursula said. "Aside from the fact that she's never late, she lives only a few steps away. Did Tom go talk to her?"

Faith shook her head. "Not yet. He's been busy planning the service with Charles's family."

"Please tell him I am very concerned about Millicent and hope he can go see her as soon as possible. She *must* be ill to miss Charles's funeral."

Charles Frawley had been a past president of the Aleford Historical Society, as was Millicent. Both were board members emeriti, although Millicent chose to ignore that part and attended all the board meetings as if she were still an active member. The fact that she would miss her old friend's funeral—a person who shared her passion for the past—was more than troublesome.

The first hymn was beginning, and Ursula slipped back across to her pew. Faith stood as her husband came down the aisle, watching as she always did with pride and a slight lump in her throat today.

It was a beautiful service. Charles himself had chosen one of the readings—Longfellow's "A Psalm of Life"—and asked that his son-in-law, who was an actor, read it. It was a good choice, especially as one of the children might have choked up. The son-in-law did not, and "Act,—act in the living Present!" rang out just as Charles must have wished.

A final hymn—"Abide with Me"—and everyone moved into the parish hall for the collation. At Charles's request, interment would be private. Faith headed for the restroom, slipping through the throng intent on getting a deviled egg and one of the chicken salad triangles. The anchovy paste sandwiches and cream cheese pinwheels always sat on the platters as last resorts. Yesterday she'd dropped off a white lasagna—béchamel sauce instead of tomato—along with salad makings, and an apple cake for the Frawleys to have for dinner tonight when the day drew to a close. Whatever they were eating now, if they were, wouldn't provide much sustenance.

She ducked into a stall to check her phone—it wouldn't do to have one of the parishioners see her scrolling through her cell at such a time. Niki and Tricia were handling a holiday luncheon at one of the Historic New England properties. Faith was sure all was well, but it always made her feel better to check. They would also have to get everything loaded into the van later for an exhibit opening at Aleford's Ganley Museum this evening. She'd added more staff than they needed for the event in case she wasn't able to get away.

Nothing from work, but there were ten missed calls from Hancock and a text from Amy that said, "*Where r u? Call school!*"

Students were strictly forbidden the use of their phones during school and had to leave them in their lockers. Amy's elementary school principal had told Faith she'd ban them outright, but the parental backlash would not be pretty. They needed to know where their kids were 24/7.

Faith began to panic. She'd told the kids at breakfast where she would be. It had to be serious if Amy was trying to get ahold of her.

She quickly texted back. "*R u sick?*"

The reply was immediate. "*No. In trouble.*"

Faith flushed the toilet for authenticity and went out the church's side door to make the call. It was freezing. She was wearing her funeral dress, a black Lauren with three-quarter sleeves that she'd bought years ago. After it had served for occasions like this too many times, she could never wear it anyplace else. While she waited for the school to answer, she gazed at the old cemetery that divided the parsonage from the church and tried not to feel her fingers getting numb.

"Hancock Middle School."

"Hello, this is Mrs. Fairchild. You've been trying to reach me?"

"Yes, would you hold for Principal Frazer, please?"

Worse and worse.

"Mrs. Fairchild?" Anthony Frazer had the kind of voice perfectly suited for his job—authoritative, stern, with a hint of empathy. Thinking this, Faith thought her description could fit a good Merlot as well and wished she had a warming glass.

"Is Amy all right? What's happened?"

"I'm afraid we're going to have to suspend her for the rest of the day and possibly longer. She left school without permission using an emergency exit that set off a fire alarm. One of the aides was outside and was able to bring her back into the building. However, as the alarm had been triggered, we of course had to clear the building and valuable classroom time was wasted."

Faith tried to match her own voice to his and remain calm.

"Why was she trying to leave?"

"I'm afraid"—Faith was already tired of hearing the words and doubted very much that he *was* afraid—"we have not been able to learn that from Amy." The hint of empathy was totally absent, replaced by a dash of irritation.

Her poor little girl. Whatever happened, it had to be big to make her rush off, ignoring the emergency exit sign. Faith pictured the flight and then what? Tackled by the aide? She was sure of one thing, though. The incident must have been triggered by some kind of bullying.

"Unfortunately," she said, "I am at the funeral of a dear friend and parishioner at my husband's church. I can't get Amy for some time yet, but I will ask Mrs. Miller, who is listed as our emergency contact, if she can do so."

"I think that would be best and perhaps you could give me a call when you are free?"

"Yes. I'd like to talk to my daughter now, please."

"Fine. Good-bye, Mrs. Fairchild, and tell Mrs. Miller that Amy will be waiting in the front office."

"Hi, Mom." Amy's voice was barely a whisper. Faith knew it was her "I'm trying not to cry" voice.

"Don't worry, darling. Pix will come get you. I'm at Mr. Frawley's funeral. Everything will be okay."

"I don't think so."

"Well, we'll work on it. I love you."

"You too."

Faith went back inside, took a moment to allow her circulation to resume, and then went in search of Pix. Maybe Amy would tell her what had happened. Having raised Samantha, Pix might have some advice, advice the Fairchild family desperately needed. She closed her eyes and pictured Amy in graduation robes. Many years hence.

"You'd think it would be easy to find time for lunch, what with us working in the same place." Ruth Stafford laughed. Sophie had made the suggestion a week ago and it had taken this long to find a time when they were both free.

They had ordered at the counter of the Jepson Center's attractive café and were told a server would bring the food to their table. They'd chosen one overlooking the museum's atrium. When Sophie had walked in she was stunned by the architect Moshe Safdie's soaring space—all white marble and a wall of glass. The staircase was the showpiece, leading up to each floor in an unbroken progression, as if it also were a piece of sculpture the museum was displaying.

"I know I'm in Savannah, because I can see out to Telfair Square, but this is pretty different from what's usually on the city's menus, except for the deviled eggs, and even those have curry today," Ruth commented.

"There are lots of places with eclectic and ethnic menus, but so far everyone seems to want me to enjoy all the local specialties," Sophie said. "I've loved them, but this is a fun change. That's why I ordered the *banh mi*. I used to eat them in New York. There was a great little Vietnamese place near my office." Although, Sophie reflected, she had been inside it only once, sending her secretary out for the sandwich so as not to waste a second of those billable hours.

The food arrived. Ruth's was the Jepson's take on a BLT: sliced prosciutto, tomato-bacon jam, herbed goat cheese, and greens on a ciabatta roll. It looked delicious. Sophie resolved to order it next time, although her sandwich was almost as good as the ones she remembered.

"Everyone has been so nice," Ruth said after a mouthful. "I really didn't know what to expect. I've never been out of Illinois. No, I take that back. We went to Disney World when I was a kid. I plan to take mine—hope to have a bunch—way more than once!"

Sophie was intrigued. "What brought you to Savannah?" She'd realized after she invited Ruth that she didn't know much about her other than assuming she wasn't from the South. There wasn't even a hint of a "y'all" in her accent.

"A lot of things. I'm the youngest. My brother and sister went to college, got married to people my parents approve of, have produced grandchildren—done everything right. Kind of the opposite of me. I just couldn't seem to find someone—or rather an acceptable one—or something, either. I'm not real academic, but I turned out to be good at word processing, IT, so always had a job. All the happy family stuff and the freezing cold were getting to me. You can't imagine what it's like in Chicago in the winter."

"I've seen the TV footage. Brrrr! So you decided to get away and get warm?"

Ruth nodded. "There was a show about Savannah on the Travel Channel and I decided what the heck, I'd give it a try." She took a swig of her iced tea. "So far, so good. Would I be having a cold drink now back home? No way."

"Everyone keeps saying wait until summer, but I'm with you. This is my first warm winter as well."

"I know. Your husband's family has been great. Inviting me to lunch and helping me find an apartment. I saw the ad for an office manager online and came down for an interview with Randy, I mean Mr. Watson, except he keeps saying to call him Randy, and Carlene says to do the same with her."

"It's an informal firm, and I hope you'll call me 'Sophie.'"

"Big change from up north. And I guess my family, too. Nobody was begging me to stay. It's going to be a little weird without snow for Christmas, but not weird enough for me to go home. Besides, I might get stranded."

Ruth was pretty, tall with a runner's body. She'd told Sophie she'd joined a running club, the Savannah Striders, and got up to run before work. She'd had a decent finish in November at the city's 5K Rock 'n' Roll Marathon. Her light brown hair was sun streaked whether by nature or art, and her brown eyes, large and luminous, were her best feature.

"When I told Randy where we were going for lunch he said to be sure to finish the meal with some of their homemade truffles," Ruth said.

"That sounds like excellent advice." The problem, Sophie soon found, was selecting. She picked dark chocolate honeycomb, and it was so rich she had them pack up her other choice—salted caramel—to savor later.

Outside, Ruth asked if they had time to walk back by way of the Cathedral of St. John the Baptist. "Everyone keeps telling me the Christmas decorations are the best in the city and I've never been inside."

"Why not?" Sophie said. The lunch had been fun. She hadn't had this sort of "girls" outing in years—it had a "Let's go shoe shopping" feel —but looking inside the church, which Sophie also had yet to do, was a better idea. She'd been feeling more and more Christmassy as each day passed.

As they walked, Sophie thought back to the weekend. The tree was up in time for Will's arrival home

Friday, and it looked beautiful. He'd arrived with a heavy cold and offered no resistance to being packed off to bed. By Sunday he was better and told his wife the whole nurse thing had been a total turn-on. She'd been plying him with hot toddies and teased him that must be what was creating all their heat.

While she was sorry he'd been sick, once he felt well enough to sit with her before the fire, the tree shining next to them, she'd been happy for the time alone together. Savannah had swung into full holiday party mode and they'd had more invitations than they could accept. Calling to let people know they couldn't make it, she heard genuine regret in the hosts' voices and thought once more how nice people were down here. Not that Northerners weren't, but there would be undercurrents about the numbers not being balanced in the case of a dinner, having to square things with the caterer, and so forth. Savannahians were simply way looser.

Sophie had also thought that once word got around about her wardrobe/corpse encounter, she might be someone to avoid—"that crazy Yankee." But word reached her through Carlene that it was just the opposite. Having seen a ghost she was flavor of the month and everyone wanted her on the guest list. They always wanted Will, even though he wasn't single anymore.

He was a universal favorite for his easygoing sense of humor, like his stepbrother's. And Will's occupation as a PI added a soupçon of glamour—although according to Will it was mostly tedious fact-checking and legwork.

The only fly—or gnat, this being Savannah—in the ointment was a visit from Patty Sue on Saturday morning. When Sophie answered the door, her sister-in-law was standing outside holding a large shopping bag. "I just came by with a care package for Will. I hear he's feeling poorly."

Sophie took her into the living room where Will was stretched out on the couch, covered in a blanket. He'd been dozing until the bell woke him up. At the sound of Patty Sue's voice, he'd roused himself and urged her to take a seat.

Patty Sue put the bag on the floor next to him. "I stopped at Back in the Day—best bakery in the universe, Sophie, and right here—for cinnamon rolls, since it's Saturday, and I couldn't resist the red velvet cupcakes. Some of their bourbon bread pudding, too."

It might not cure Will's cold, Sophie had thought, but the sugar rush would pep him up. She'd offered Patty Sue something to drink, assuming coffee or tea, but the young woman had said, "Could go for a glass of wine. White if you have it."

Will had chided her, "Hair of the dog?" and she'd laughed.

The wine had disappeared fast and when Sophie walked her out, Patty Sue had turned to her and whispered, "He really *is* sick!"

"Well, yes. Running a temperature and a very sore throat on top of his stuffy nose," Sophie said, a bit shocked. Did Patty Sue and the rest of the family, as well as friends, think they were making it up? An excuse to miss the festivities scheduled for the weekend? "He didn't want to give it to anyone. I'm hoping he'll wait until Tuesday to go back to Atlanta. Please let everyone know how sorry we are to miss seeing them. He says he'll definitely be better by next weekend."

Patty Sue had managed to leave Sophie with a parting shot. "I'll tell Laura. She's been *very* worried."

All thoughts of Miss Laura, Patty Sue, and even her beloved Will promptly disappeared as Sophie walked with Ruth into the cathedral. St. John's two tall spires were a familiar landmark and had been helping her find her way for weeks, but she'd had no idea of the splendor within. She recognized the late 1800s Gothic Revival style that drew the eye toward heaven up the slender columns to the fan vaulting and deep blue starry ceiling. The sun was streaming in the richly colored stained glass windows, creating new patterns on the decorative flooring. The church was indeed bedecked for Christmas—wreaths down the nave, a tall poinsettia tree and more bright poinsettias and cyclamen at the altar. Everywhere Sophie looked her eyes took in red and gold.

"Let's go see the crèche," Ruth whispered. She appeared as awestruck as Sophie.

It was magnificent and Sophie was swept back into childhood memories—going with Babs to see the carved Neapolitan crèche figures and angel tree at the Metropolitan Museum of Art. These were every bit as lovely. She sat down in a nearby pew to gaze on them, turning to see the organ and spectacular rose window. She must come to a service, she thought, recalling, too, that this had been Flannery O'Connor's church. Savannah was turning out to be a good fit, she realized, and said a quick prayer of thanks.

Ruth joined her and after a while they both left quietly. Outside Sophie said, "Thank you so much for thinking of this. It was the perfect thing to do."

"I'll start going to Mass again now. Sitting there reminded me why it was important to me. My faith, that is." She darted a look filled with compassion at Sophie. "I said a little prayer for you. I know you had that awful nightmare or whatever it was. I prayed for it not to come back."

Amen, Sophie said to herself, adding—it was a nightmare, but it wasn't a dream. She gave Ruth's arm a quick squeeze, and they headed back to pick up the threads of their workaday world.

When Faith got back from the cemetery, she called the Millers to tell Pix she was back. A few minutes later Amy's woebegone face appeared at the kitchen door. Faith opened it quickly and took her daughter in her arms. That was apparently all Amy needed to unleash the day's emotions, and she started sobbing.

Faith steered her to the window seat by the big round kitchen table and let her cry. After a while the tempest began to pass. Faith detached herself to get Amy a glass of juice and a box of Kleenex.

"Honey, what happened?"

Amy gulped some juice and then sat for a while without saying anything. Faith was beginning to think being so direct was the wrong tack when Amy took a deep breath and started speaking.

"It was stupid. *I* was stupid. Nobody did anything. I wasn't late, but I was the last one to history class. The doors have glass on top and I looked in at all of them and it felt like they were looking back at me with these faces like 'what is *she* doing here?' And I began to feel really bad." Amy's words began to accelerate, crashing into one another, the wreck ahead just waiting to happen. "I couldn't move. I couldn't go in and couldn't not go in, and then I stopped breathing and thought I was going to pass out. I don't remember running, but I must have because I was at one of the outside doors. I just had to get some air. Mom, I never saw that it was an emergency exit! You believe me, right? The principal kept saying I must have seen the sign on the door, but I didn't."

"Of course I believe you!" Faith hugged Amy harder and began to angrily rehearse in her mind what she'd say to Anthony Frazer later. "What you had is something called a panic attack. You wouldn't have noticed a brass band, let alone something posted on a door. Everybody has them, hopefully once in a blue moon when things in life start to pile up on you. And your body does feel as if it's going to pass out. You *did* need fresh air, but it wasn't oxygen so much as carbon dioxide. Maybe you learned about this in science. That's why when this happens people breathe into a paper bag."

"Better stock up," Amy said wryly. Faith took the remark as a good sign.

"It's not going to happen again soon, if ever," she said. "You mustn't worry about it. Instead we have to try to figure out what to do about school."

Amy appeared skeptical. "They all hate me, Mom. I honestly don't know why. I never did anything to them except be new at their precious school."

Faith said, "I know that this girl Cassie has a lot of influence, but I'm sure there are kids who don't care what she and her friends think. Kids who go their own way?"

"If there are, I haven't found them." Amy sounded resigned. "Mom, the principal said I could be arrested for setting off the alarm and that there is a big fine." Her eyes widened.

Good job, Tony, scare the poor child to death after what was a horrible incident.

"He's wrong, honey. If you are okay to sit here for a bit, I need to make a call or two and we can clear this part up."

She went to use the phone in Tom's study, having settled Amy with more juice, a plate of oatmeal chocolate chip "comfort" cookies, and the not-for-school book Amy was currently reading, James Klise's *The Art of Secrets.*

As she dialed, she thought that this was a time when she was particularly happy to live in Aleford, a small community. The retired chief of police was a close friend, and the current one as well. Faith was known to the force—in a good way. She was put through immediately.

"Hi, Brian, it's Faith Fairchild. I imagine you already know, but my daughter accidentally set off the fire alarm at Hancock earlier today. She was feeling sick and pushed the door to get outside for some air without seeing the sign."

"Thought it must be something like that. I'll let the fire department know. Hancock hasn't had a fire drill for a while, so that's what we'll call it. I'll tell Frazer, too." Faith wished Amy could hear the chief's calm voice. It was no biggie to him. "Hope Amy feels better. There's a nasty stomach bug going around and it would be a shame if she was sick for Christmas. Can't believe it's just a week away. Have to come up with something for the wife instead of hitting CVS Christmas Eve as usual."

Apparently this was the favorite shopping venue for gift-challenged husbands. So that was why there was always a big display of cosmetic gift sets near the shaving cream aisle.

"I'll tell her and many thanks," Faith said. Although she had thought this is what Brian would say, she was extremely relieved.

"No problem. Come by after the holidays and I'll show you the jazzy new fingerprint machine we have."

"Will do. Bye."

Amy looked up from her book as Faith returned. She'd been crying again and her cheeks were streaked with tears. "I have a lot of babysitting money saved up if I do have to pay a fine. It was for the rest of my Christmas presents, but I was going to make some anyway—"

Faith cut in. "There's no fine, no arrest. Chief Mooney understood completely and hopes you feel better soon." She put her hand on her daughter's forehead. "I think it could be that you *are* coming down with something. Let's go upstairs and take your temperature."

Amy brightened. "So it maybe wasn't one of those attack things and I have the flu?"

"Exactly," Faith said firmly, and it was what she planned to tell the principal, too, as soon as she tucked Amy into bed.

Ben burst in the back door after school. "My little sister pulled a fire alarm and the whole department showed up! What the f— I mean, heck!"

"She was sick and didn't see the sign, just had to get outside." The principal had listened patiently to Faith's explanation, which she had delivered in as even a tone as she could muster.

"Oh," Ben said. He looked slightly disappointed. "Well, it's gross when kids throw up in the hallway so I guess she did the right thing."

"Absolutely—and please spread the word tomorrow."

"Where is she now? In bed? I don't want to catch it."

"Nice show of sympathy, sweetie. Yes, she's in bed, and I don't think you'll catch it. I'm keeping her home tomorrow, though." Faith did not reveal that the principal had nevertheless extended Amy's suspension by a day. Before hanging up, she'd countered that she had planned to keep her daughter, who was running a temperature and showing flu-like symptoms, home in any case. Amy *did* have a temp, 99.6, probably from all the crying.

Ben went off to do homework after opening the fridge and grabbing some food, pretty much a reflex. Faith made a mental note to get more milk—keeping a cow might keep them more reliably stocked.

Tom got home at five. He looked so tired that Faith hated to tell him about Amy. She poured him a Sam Adams in a chilled beer glass.

He smiled. "Thank you, but I already know my daughter set off a fire alarm at school."

The Aleford grapevine, faster than a speeding bullet. Faith should have known.

"Bumped into Brian Mooney on my way to see Millicent. She wasn't at the funeral and that's not like her. Besides, Ursula ambushed me as I was leaving for the cemetery, wanting to know when I was going to drop by on 'our Millicent.'"

Faith had never thought of Millicent as this sort of collective, but it was true—she was theirs, through thick or thin. She filled Tom in on what had happened at school and he went upstairs to see Amy, coming down almost immediately. "She's asleep. I don't like to say this is your department, but never having been a teenage girl, I am pretty much at a loss here."

"I *was* one and I'm at a loss. If she could make just one friend that would do it."

Tom sighed. "Wouldn't that have happened by now? The sad fact is that everybody sides with the bully so the bully won't target them."

Faith hadn't told Tom she'd met the bully's mother and did so now. "It would only make things worse if I said something to her, but it's time to talk to one of the teachers or the guidance counselor. Obviously not the principal. I'll call Amy's teacher from last year. Maybe she knows someone at Hancock who would be approachable. Now, tell me about your visit to Millicent."

Tom put his beer down. "She asked me what I would do if someone I respected had been lying to me for many years."

Faith was stunned. Whoever it was who'd been lying to Millicent Revere McKinley was definitely going to what the lady herself called "H-E-double-hockey-sticks."

Chapter 6

♠

Faith had had a very trying morning. Ben had texted his mother a link to Cassie's Facebook page, adding a sad face emoticon. The girl had posted the fire alarm story. She didn't use Amy's name, but Faith was sure everyone knew who it was. Adopting the role of citizen cop, Cassie said the perpetrator had committed a felony and should be punished to the full extent of the law for putting people at risk. She opined, "What will happen when there's a real emergency? It will be like 'Crying Wolf.'" Future politician here? Faith wondered.

After texting thanks to Ben and taking a moment to feel good about whatever parenting skills Tom and she had employed to create a son who was this concerned about his sister, Faith poured herself a cup of coffee and went over the pros and cons of calling Cassie's mother. There was never really any question. This was not a time when she could keep her mouth shut.

It hadn't gone well.

There was silence for a moment after Faith explained why she was calling, asking Laetitia to please let Cassie know that no felony, or any other crime, had been committed. That the police were treating it as a fire drill. That Amy had been feeling extremely ill and was in fact home today.

The silence broke. "Now, Faith, I believe your daughter is home because she was suspended, and I'm sure the whole sorry business *has* made her sick. It was a very irresponsible thing to do." Laetitia's voice was gently scolding.

So much for sisterhood, or rather motherhood. "Technically, yes, she was suspended, but she *does* have the flu." Amy had thrown up twice in the night.

"I will correct Cassandra," Laetitia said, restoring Faith's belief in humanity. "Amy committed a misdemeanor, not a felony."

And then destroyed it. Faith gave one more try. "Facebook can be so hurtful."

"I am shocked that you would imply that my daughter would do anything to hurt a fellow student—or anyone else. You do know she received the Outstanding

Citizenship Award at school last year for her volunteer work."

Faith had planned to suggest Cassie take the post down. It wasn't going to happen. Laetitia barreled on, her tone escalating from a scold to an indictment. "I do not police *my* daughters' online activities. I have never needed to, as they have demonstrated nothing but responsible behavior. Now, I am sorry but I am running late and must say good-bye. Happy holidays."

And she hung up. "Running late" for what? Her nail appointment? It certainly wasn't a stint as the Welcome Wagon lady.

Sophie had taken the Friday off to do more Christmas shopping and pick up ingredients for dinner. Will had said he might be quite late. Whenever he did arrive, though, he'd be hungry. She decided to do New England clam chowder, but give it a Southern twist by substituting shrimp for clams and diced country ham for salt pork. With plenty of Old Bay, of course. She had an industrial-size tin of it now. The chowder would get better the longer it sat in the fridge.

Will had no need to count calories—the opposite, in fact—and recalling how delicious the baked goods Patty Sue had brought were, Sophie decided to head for the Back in the Day bakery, too. When her cell rang and she saw it was Faith, she answered quickly. It had been awhile since they had talked.

"Is this a good time? You said you were working half days Friday, but I don't know which half."

"This is perfect. I'm not going in at all today. No more Workaholic Sophie."

"How is everything? Any corpses, poison pen letters, dirty tricks in general?"

"Nothing, but I can tell from your voice that something is going on there. What's happening?"

"Is it that obvious?" Faith replied with a sigh and told her about Amy's most recent adventure in the labyrinthine corridors of middle school complete with Minotaur.

"Have you thought about private school? I wish I could tell you this will all blow over, but I doubt it. A girl in my third grade class wet her pants when the substitute wouldn't let her go to the bathroom because she was saying 'can I' instead of 'may I.' Kids were asking her if she needed more Depends until we graduated from high school."

"Private school has crossed my mind, especially because Aleford kids go to the regional high school, since we're such a small town. She could go to someplace like Concord Academy for these two years and then be in an entirely different milieu. It would be a very expensive solution, but we may have to consider it seriously if this keeps up."

"I've heard Facebook has a strict policy about bullying," Sophie said. "She can report the post as such and have it removed."

"Ben mentioned that, too, but we both agreed it would make Cassie turn to other, possibly even worse, ways to attack."

" 'Attack'! I can't imagine that anyone would pick on Amy like this. It makes me want to take the next plane and smack that queen bee up the side of her head!"

Faith laughed. "What a great image! Cassie in a bee costume with a tiara toppled from her throne, but sadly life doesn't imitate imagination. I suggested Amy close her Facebook account and take a break from it when someone, probably Cassie, posted about Amy saluting the flag—that was really evil, just when I'd thought I'd succeeded in making her proud of her newly developed boobies! She did, and I'm happy she hasn't seen the latest, but I'm not naive enough to believe that news of it won't reach her. Now, tell me about Savannah. It's supposed to be wonderful at Christmastime."

"Beyond wonderful, although the best time so far has been staying in by the tree and in front of the fire last weekend when Will came home with a bad cold. He's better now and back in Atlanta."

Sophie proceeded to tell Faith about Christmas on the River—a weekend-long craft fair on River Street culminating in fireworks, her visit to St. John's with Ruth, and how gorgeous the houses in the historic district looked, especially as so much was blooming. Nothing needed to be artificial to add color. And, she added, unlike Manhattan, everywhere she looked people were smiling, filled with the holiday spirit, and maybe other kinds of spirits as well.

"Have you had a chance to find out more about Will's grandmother?" Faith asked.

"Not yet, but we're going out to Bells Mills for Sunday dinner and I may get some time alone with my father-in-law. There are always so many people around, though."

"And how about with Will himself during your cozy weekend together?"

"I tried. I tried to bring up the dead man, too—sitting on the couch, the wardrobe was pretty much directly over our heads in the front bedroom. I moved us to another bedroom in the back of the house right away, but if Will noticed he didn't say anything. When I started to talk about it this time he just said 'Now, shug, don't worry about it.' Same when I brought up family history—tried your idea of starting back in the nineteenth century and working up to more recent relatives, but that went nowhere, as well. I think we have a problem communicating, Faith."

"No you don't, darlin'—I can do Southern, too, their endearments always sound so much more affectionate. Anyway, a good friend, my business partner Niki, set me straight years ago when Tom and I were avoiding an elephant in the room. I was complaining that he wouldn't talk and she came right back at me with 'If you wanted someone for meaningful chats, it's not going to be a guy. Not in their DNA. That's why women have women friends. You'll get more and more frustrated if you expect otherwise.' And she was right."

"Ian was chatty."

"I rest my case," Faith said. "It's not that men never communicate—they just do it differently. Think body language.

"But back to the body that went bump in the night. No police reports or anything about a missing person?" During the conversation following Sophie's gruesome discovery, Faith had advised her to read the police reports in the *Savannah Morning News,* online sites, and anywhere else information that might identify the victim was posted.

"Nothing. I'm still not convinced that the body wasn't stashed somewhere in the house with the killers. The police would have had to use a ladder to get into the attic. Gloria hadn't installed a pull-down one until recently. They'd have to have been quick, but could have used a ladder from the yard—they're still all over the place—and hoisted him up, pulling the ladder up, too."

"And then while you were at Randy and Carlene's, they could have taken him out and gotten rid of the body—where?"

Sophie had thought this through as well. "We're very close to the river, easy to dump him in. But surely the corpse would have been found by now, washed up someplace?" Faith had more experience with this sort of thing, so Sophie put it as a question.

"Yes, unless they weighted him down."

"The proverbial cement overshoes?"

They both laughed, and then Faith asked, "Have you seen Patty Sue lately?"

Sophie told her about her sister-in-law's visit to check up on whether Will was really sick. "She is so transparent. And someone with too much time and too little to do."

"I thought she had a job—and doesn't she live in one big social whirl?"

"Her job at the art gallery seems to be an at-will one—Patty Sue's will that is. I've never caught sight of her there unless there's a back office you can't see from the street. And she must spend a lot of time shopping.

I haven't seen her in the same thing twice. She doesn't mention work except when they're having a party for an opening. She's definitely a party girl." Sophie remembered the way Patty Sue had gulped down her wine at what seemed like a very early hour of the day. "I think she may drink too much, but it's hard to say."

"She's young and it *is* Savannah," Faith said.

"I guess. Will is very fond of her. Maybe I should invite her to do something, just the two of us, and try to forget what happened."

"But keep your guard up," Faith warned. "Will is such a nice person, he may not be tuned in to some of his stepsister's little tricks."

"He *is* nice," Sophie said. She was missing him terribly.

"It's a shame he has to be in Atlanta so much."

"I know. He did warn me that his job would sometimes take him away for extended periods of time, but he'd try to stay local as much as possible. And Atlanta isn't that far." Although, Sophie thought to herself, as far as she was concerned it might as well be Alaska.

"Sophie." Faith sounded a bit hesitant. "You don't think any of what's happening to you could have something to do with whatever case Will is working on?"

"I thought of that when I found the body, but Will isn't a Sherlock or whatever type of PI. The bad guys he goes after rub out entries, as in cooking the books, not people. I suppose if the stakes are high enough, it could lead to murder. But I have no idea what this case is about. He's told me from the start that he wouldn't be able to discuss his work except in the most general terms."

"Sounds like *my* marriage, and Tom's employer is very strict. Well, it was a thought. Now, go have fun shopping—and buy something for yourself!"

"Will do. I have my eye on a pair of shoes at this old-fashioned store on Broughton, the Globe Shoe Company. It's been there forever and the shoes are displayed in lighted wood cabinetry like gems. But forget Enna Jetticks. They have Cole Haan plus all the latest European manufacturers. The ones I'm lusting after are a pair of Stuart Weitzmans—a red satin ridiculously high-heeled pump with red crystals on the toe. Think: I caught Mommy kissing Santa Claus, but naughtier."

Laughing some more, they said good-bye and hung up.

Armed with a list—Sophie was a great list maker—she stepped out into the Savannah morning sunshine, making sure to lock the house up tight. The contractor had been working on the backyard this week, telling her he didn't want to get in the way of her holiday preparations inside the house. Sophie had been touched by his thoughtfulness, and glad not to have the commotion, and dust. The gazebo was partly done, and enough shrubs and trees to set up a mini Longwood Gardens spilled out into the front of the house, waiting to be planted. You couldn't get even the sharpest shovel into the frozen ground back home, Sophie realized. Then corrected herself. *This* was home now.

The older woman who had had the presence of mind, and the information, to call Randy the night of The Body, the Switch, and the Wardrobe, as Sophie was calling it to herself, was in the square, walking her little dog, and Sophie went over to her.

"I wanted to thank you for calling my brother-in-law the other night." She put out her hand. "I'm Sophie Maxwell."

The woman took it. "And I'm Lydia Scriven. Pleased to meet you on a better occasion."

She had a warm smile, and age had not diminished her beauty—her dark hair was only slightly streaked with gray and pulled tight off her face into a low cluster of braids, emphasizing her cheekbones and deep brown eyes flecked with gold. She looked like a sculpted head by Elizabeth Catlett that Sophie had seen in an exhibit of twentieth-century female African American artists.

"Yes, a much better one! I'm taking the whole day off. I had never been to Savannah before my marriage, so it's all wonderfully new—especially the weather. I'm from New England. A Yankee."

Lydia gave her an appraising look. "I'm not much for labels. Let's just call you a happy new bride—I've seen you walking with your husband from my window and I can tell. Where are you off to now?"

"Finishing my Christmas shopping and picking up some things to cook for dinner."

"Not one of those busy ladies relying on takeout and the microwave, I see." Her smiled broadened. "I like to cook myself. If you want, I can share some of my Lowcountry recipes—surprise your new family."

"I'd love that," Sophie said and told her what she planned for tonight, noting Lydia's approval.

The dog started to pull on his lead. "Now, Charlie, you be good," Lydia said, then turned to Sophie. "He thinks he rules the roost and maybe he does. He's my only company since my husband passed ten years ago." She paused for a moment before adding, "I'm on my way over to my church, First African Baptist. I volunteer as a guide and in our small shop. If you have the time, would you like to come with me?"

"It's at the top of my list of places I want to visit and haven't yet," Sophie said. "I know it's the oldest

African American congregation in North America and that it was a stop on the Underground Railroad, but not many details."

"Oh, there's so much more. I hope I won't bore you. For example, it's the place where Dr. King first gave his 'I Have a Dream' speech—a moment I have never forgotten. I'm getting sidetracked already! I just have to put Charlie in the yard and get my purse. Meet you out front in ten minutes?" She pointed to a narrow brick house painted the color of churned butter with a wisteria vine covering the two stories that must have magnificent blossoms come spring. It was just the kind of house she was looking for—something about it said a happy family lives, or lived, here.

Sophie nodded. "This is so kind of you. Is photography permitted? If so, I'll get my camera."

It was, and Sophie hurried back home.

An hour later, she was reluctantly leaving the church. She had taken up too much of Lydia's time as it was. In a quiet voice Mrs. Scriven—her surname that of the name of the Savannah owners of her deceased husband's ancestors—had related the history of the church, starting in December 1777 with the purchase of land by free and enslaved African Americans. The slaves used money they'd saved to buy their freedom for the freedom to worship instead, and the first church was built at night after long, torturous days in the indigo and rice fields. Lydia described it all so vividly that Sophie knew she would hold these images in her mind forever—the many miles walked from the plantations to attend services by an astonishing number of African Americans. The congregation numbered 1,400 by 1841. As Lydia pointed out, of the first pastors pictured in the stained-glass windows, the first six names were all prefaced by "Born a slave."

But it was the twenty-six sets of apparently random holes drilled into the pine floor of what was now the lower auditorium of the church that moved Sophie the most for what lay below—a cramped space where men, women, and children had huddled awaiting safe passage on the Underground Railroad. The holes were the only ventilation, and the pattern wasn't random at all to those who knew. It was a Kongolese Cosmogram symbolizing the four movements of the sun and the journey of the body from the physical to the spiritual world. A symbol of hope.

There were other tunnels beneath present-day Savannah; one in Crawford Square, Lydia said, and no doubt many more undiscovered—or still kept secret.

With a promise to come to a service soon—judging from the drum set to the left of the altar, some of them would prove very lively—Sophie bought a book of photos and pictures on the history of slavery in Savannah that focused on First African Baptist to send to the Fairchilds. She also bought a small square wooden box with a quilt square carved on the lid from the shop. She hadn't known the stories of what each quilt, draped over a fence or gate, symbolized, sending messages in the calico of safety, danger, food, and more for those following "The Drinking Gourd."

Lydia had hugged her and, keeping her hands on Sophie's shoulders, looked squarely into her face and said, "I don't know what you saw or didn't see the other night, but be careful. We may all smile at you and greet you as a friend, but just like any place on this earth, Savannah has a dark side. You know you can come knock on my door any time, day or night. I don't sleep much these days—don't want to waste precious time before I meet my Maker. Besides, Charlie's snore is a loud one."

Heading now for Parker's Market and last-minute gifts at the Savannah Bee Company—she had already sent gift baskets of honey and honey-related items to many on her list—Sophie turned the woman's words over in her mind. And was warned.

Tom came home for lunch—easy to do, since it was a mere hop, skip, and a jump over the tombstones in the old cemetery that divided the church from the parsonage. His face did not indicate this sort of merry behavior and Faith's heart sank. *What now?*

"Did you know Amy is not going to read 'The Queens Came Late' in the pageant?"

"Oh no! She's done it since she stopped being a sheep. And she was so excited when Roberta asked her that first year." Roberta Ballou, the church school director, had added poetry and song to the pageant to provide more parts. Parents had been delighted—and that did seem to be what the whole thing was about, keeping the parents happy. The kids were happy with whatever part they were assigned.

"The Queens Came Late" was a wonderful Christmas poem by Norma Farber that described their arrival—"The Queens came late, but the Queens were there . . ." and the gifts they brought. Much more sensible than the frankincense and myrrh from the Kings, Faith had always thought—" . . . a homespun gown of blue, chicken soup—with noodles, too—and a lingering, lasting cradle-song."

"Did Roberta say why Amy doesn't want to do it?"

"Because the pageant is the *children's* service and I'm not a child anymore," came a firm voice from the door. Amy stepped into the room. "And you can't make me."

"Of course we can't and don't want to." Tom was by his daughter's side instantly. "Come have lunch with us." He put his arm around her shoulders and led her to the chair next to his. "Mom made egg salad."

It was Amy's favorite, and the choice was no accident.

"A half, okay? I'm not really very hungry."

Faith put the food in front of her daughter with a tall glass of milk. "We thought you liked reading the poem and you have such a fine voice." This was true. No stumbling, partly because the Fairchilds had always recited it together Christmas morning and all of them had it memorized.

"I'll still say it with you and Ben here," Amy said, taking a bite of her sandwich. "Good egg salad, Mom. I'll finish this later. I've been thinking." Amy swallowed hard. "There's only Monday and Tuesday, plus Wednesday's a half day, so I really should stay home to help you. I can come to work and do stuff. You know I'm good at baking."

This was true, but Faith said to herself when you fall off the horse, etc. Tom stepped in before she could think of the best way to phrase the no. "That's extremely thoughtful of you, honey, but school is your job just now, like Mom's and mine. We'll be at work and you'll be at your work."

What was implied was you go whether you particularly like your job or not. Amy didn't argue, but her sad face made Faith angry all over again. She was itching to tell Tom about the phone conversation with Laetitia when he jumped up.

"Damn, I'm late for a meeting!"

Amy giggled. "Quarter in the jar, Dad, and good thing only we heard you. And . . ." She pointed upward.

Ben, in his never-ending ways to raise money for his trip, had instituted the practice. So far only Tom and Faith were contributors, and Faith vowed the moment Ben's plane left the ground for La Belle France she was sticking the Mason jar back with the canning goods never to be used again except for natural purposes.

Tom gave his wife and daughter quick kisses and rushed out the door, leaving his coat behind. At least his socks matched today, Faith thought, and was glad he had spare outerwear at church. It was supposed to snow later. She regularly replenished the supply with all the coats he left at home in a kind of revolving door. Occasionally she was even able to spirit away some of the tattered items he held on to in his belief that they were still good enough to wear. Maybe so when he was in high school. . . .

"So you're not mad at me?" Amy said.

"Of course not. I'll miss hearing you do the reading, but I know you're growing up and you *should* be deciding what you want to do."

Amy nodded, sighed, and covered her sandwich, putting it in the fridge before she left the room. Who was all this growing-up stuff harder on, Faith wondered—her daughter or her? Maybe a toss-up.

She would have to bring Amy to work this afternoon, though—and yes, she could mix some of the cookie doughs. It was a very busy weekend for Have Faith, the last before Christmas. Since he'd made the call to the search committee head and arranged to preach in January, there had been a spring in Tom's step that Faith hadn't seen in a while. She knew what she had to do. Tom came first—always. But that wasn't going to make it any easier, or her happier as she contemplated the holidays. Their last Christmas in Aleford?

"So I hear you've become a churchgoer, Sophie," Randy said. "Glad someone in the family is paving the way for the rest of us."

"Randall Lee Watson! You know I go to church every Sunday, and I've been a member of the Altar Guild and the Flower Committee since I married your father right in that same church." Gloria turned to Sophie. "I know we may not make it every Sunday, to be truthful, since we spend so much time out here, but I am there in spirit. Have you been going to services? It is your denomination, right?"

The whole family was having a Sunday dinner at Bells Mills that was so festive and sumptuous it made Sophie wonder what would be weighing the table down here, or in town, at Christmas. There was an enormous baked country ham with a brown-sugar glaze, pickled peaches that had been put up last summer, corn pudding, baked Vidalia onions, collard greens, cream biscuits, heavy cream that is, and oyster stew to start. All of it was the work of Blanche Harper, longtime housekeeper and cook at Bells Mills, with help from her granddaughter Tiffany. There was also the ever present cruet of hot sauce that made Sophie's eyes water just to look at, but that Will put on everything from scrambled eggs and grits to fried chicken. A Southern thing, especially Southern males.

"Randy must have heard that Ruth Stafford and I went to Saint John's to look at the decorations—and the church itself. Neither of us had been inside. It was stunning." She added hastily, "I'm sure Christ Episcopal will be beautiful, too." She certainly didn't want to slight a member of the Altar Guild *and* Flower Committee who also happened to be her stepmother-in-law.

"It is, and if you don't have a chance to get there before, we always go to the candlelight service on Christmas Eve after a small family dinner at the house. We like to dress up for it. Black tie for the men and I get some of my jewelry from the bank to go with a new Christmas gown each year!" She sounded as giddy as a schoolgirl contemplating what to wear for the prom.

"It sounds wonderful," Sophie said.

Anson was beaming from the head of the table. "You be sure to wear some of the sparklers Will gave you, my mother's and his mother's. I had thought you might wear a piece at your welcome party—Grandmother Aurora's pearl choker is famous in Savannah, better than any of Queen Mary's, my father said when he gave it to her for their tenth anniversary."

Will was sitting directly across from his wife and seemed about to say something, but Sophie beat him to it.

"They are all exquisite, especially the pearls, but my mother had brought a necklace and bracelet that she particularly wanted me to wear, and I didn't want to disappoint her."

"Of course," Anson said. "But you go all out this holiday, you hear, darlin'. You'd shine without them at the parties, but it would give me pleasure to see Will's bride wearing our family treasures."

Family treasures that Sophie had never heard about, let alone seen. She looked over at her husband. There was no mistaking the relief on his face, and he gave her what she read as an apologetic smile.

"It was nice of you to do something with Ruth," Randy said, picking up the previous topic. "I worry about the girl so far away from her family at this time of year. I caught her weeping the other day."

Sophie was puzzled. She had thought Ruth was happy not to have to spend the holidays with her family in Chicago. Was there something else going on? Her love life or lack thereof? She resolved to ask the young woman for lunch, or a drink after work. Christmas was speeding toward them. Only a few more days. It would have to be Monday or Tuesday. She'd also have to do some serious shopping for a formal dress. As she savored a mouthful of ham, she felt her spirits rise. After all, she had the shoes. Killer ones.

Conversation rose and fell around the table as the main course gave way to a chocolate layer cake, lemon buttermilk chess pie, and a compote of winter fruits—plump prunes, dried apricots, sliced apples and pears in a slightly spicy sweet syrup. Besides Anson, Gloria, Randy, Carlene, Patty Sue, Will, and Sophie, two elderly female cousins—Maxwells or Watsons, Sophie wasn't sure—were in attendance. They seemed to be permanent fixtures at family gatherings, and though they weren't sisters, they looked like twins, especially because they both wore 1950s shirtwaist dresses—original?—in identical shades of lilac. For old ladies, they seemed to have the appetites of a teenage boy and kept up a steady litany of appreciation throughout the meal—"Uh-huh, I do love a good cream biscuit" and "Nobody does a pickled peach like Gloria's Blanche." The other guest today was the ubiquitous Miss Laura, who was seated between Will and Patty Sue. Before dinner, Sophie had taken the Realtor aside and told her that the house hunting would have to wait until after the holidays, especially since Will would be able to join them then.

"Of course, Sophie," she'd said. "I am simply run off my feet what with everything going on and it won't slow down until New Year's Day. Last night I believe I was at seven soirees, although with all the champagne and punch I can't be sure. You were at the Beauregards', I saw."

Will and Sophie had limited themselves to two of the many gatherings they'd had invitations for and the Beauregards' was one. Will had wanted Sophie to see the rooftop garden atop a beautifully restored nineteenth-century house in the Victorian part of the historic district. It had been lovely, but even lovelier to get home for some rare quality time alone.

Sophie was about to say something to the effect that it had been a great party, but Miss Laura in typical fashion continued to talk. "Of course Will won't be any freer after New Year's than now. The case won't be wrapped up, so it will just be you and me, sugar." She'd linked her arm through Sophie's and they'd entered the dining room as BFFs to all appearances.

Sophie shook off the jealousy that was threatening to creep over her like poison ivy. It was unlikely that Laura knew anything more about Will's work than Sophie. She was just being, well, Miss Laura.

Randy leaned back in his chair, the picture of a man who had consumed a very satisfactory meal. "Wasn't just taking in the poinsettias at Saint John's I heard, Sophie. Next day was First African Baptist, I believe. You need to hit Temple Israel, too. Oldest in Georgia and one of the oldest in the country, period. Don't skip the Unitarians, the Jingle Bell church, since you're on a religious kick."

How did Randy know she had gone to First Baptist with Lydia? Ruth had probably mentioned St. John's. Savannah was feeling smaller and smaller. Sophie kept her tone light. "I do mean to see everything in town, including the places of worship, but a Jingle Bell church is a new name. I'll add it to my list."

Patty Sue, flushed from preprandial cocktails served in front of the largest Christmas tree Sophie had seen in a private home, and the excellent burgundy that had liberally accompanied dinner, spoke up. "I'll bet you've always thought 'Jingle Bells' was written up north, but it was written right here! Just before the war. James Pierpont might have been born a Yankee but he was the music director of the church; his brother was the minister. James even served in the Confederate army!"

Sophie assumed when Patty Sue said "the war," she meant the Civil War, although in Patty Sue's mind it was the "War of Northern Aggression."

"That's fascinating. There wouldn't have been much snow to dash through, though!"

"It's a pretty church," Will said. "We'll go there soon. Pierpont composed the carol when the church was on its original site at Oglethorpe Square. The church fell on hard times with a dwindling congregation—abolitionists not being real popular. It was sold and moved to Troup Square. The Unitarians, merged now with the Universalists, were able to buy it back in the late 1990s."

Sophie smiled proudly at him. "If the PI thing doesn't work out, you could certainly be a tour guide."

"That pretty much applies to any real Savannahian," Will said. "But I'll give it some thought. I'd like to drive one of those horse-drawn victorias."

They moved out to the back veranda for coffee. The weather was so mild Sophie didn't need the jacket she'd brought. She leaned back against the soft cushion on the wicker armchair and felt herself relax. It was hard to believe that a short while ago she'd been almost desperate to spend Christmas in Connecticut. Now she was looking forward to her first one here surrounded by her new family.

She hadn't been able to get time alone with her father-in-law to talk about family history, but it didn't seem so important anymore. Her eyelids felt heavy and she heard Will say, "Y'all have put my bride to sleep! Time to go home."

"For some shut-eye, bro?" Randy teased and everyone laughed, including Sophie. Maybe shut-eye later, but that was not what was on her mind now.

As they were leaving, Gloria said, "You'll need to squeeze Laura in. She came with Randy and Carlene, but they're staying on to pick me some more holly and mistletoe for our Christmas Day open house."

Will had told Sophie that Christmas Day would mean a pleasant round of open houses at all the family's friends.

"No problem," Will said, and the three headed for the sports car. The sports car that was built for two.

"I'll get in the back," Sophie offered nobly.

"I wouldn't dream of it," Laura objected. "I'm so much smaller than you are!"

It was true that Sophie was taller—a good match for her over-six-foot husband—but the remark made her feel like a giantess, a freak.

"No," she said firmly. "You sit in front." And proceeded to squinch into the tiny space.

Conversation was impossible, as Laura had insisted Will put the top down. "I just love to feel the wind in my hair!"

As they drove into town Sophie realized that Laura must have moved while Will was in Atlanta, moved quite close to them. She expected Laura to give him directions. Not necessary. Will drove up to her door and helped her out like the gentleman he was.

He knew exactly where Laura Belvedere lived.

It was the last Sunday in Advent. Since they would have Christmas dinner in Norwell with Tom's parents as always, Faith had prepared an early version.

Today's service had been lovely. The choir outdid themselves, and humming "Once in Royal David's City," she put the finishing touches on the plum pudding she had been aging for weeks and carried it into the dining room. Amy followed with the hard sauce. The pears and Stilton were already on the festive table. The main course had been goose with all the trimmings. The Millers and Ursula had joined them. Faith had invited

Millicent as well, but had been rather abruptly turned down, as Millicent was "too busy."

Tom had given Faith a full report of his visit after revealing Millicent's odd query. They'd discussed its meaning. What person Millicent respected could possibly have been lying to her for years? Tom had been struck by how ill Millicent looked, as Faith had been. "As if she'd suddenly aged ten years overnight and lost twenty pounds." He'd also noticed the dust and disorder, which, given the state of his study with its piles of books and papers, was something out of the ordinary as well. Faith was afraid Millicent would be offended if she took a full Christmas dinner over later—"not a charity case"—but she would pack up a large portion of the pudding sans the hard sauce. Millicent was an ardent member of the W.C.T.U., and Carrie Nation was one of her heroes.

Amy and Ben cleared the table while the adults moved into the living room, where Tom lit the fire he'd laid in the fireplace and Faith served coffee. She started to turn on some lights, but Ursula stopped her. "It's so lovely with just the tree and the fire. We can imagine ourselves back when the parsonage was new."

"Would there have been a tree then?" Sam Miller asked. "I thought the custom started later. Wasn't it introduced by the minister at the Follen church in Lexington who originally came from Germany?"

"Yes—some thirty years before the Civil War. The church sells trees every year, and some people refer to it as the Christmas Tree Church," Tom said, poking the fire. "Think I'll add another log."

Pix and Faith exchanged a look. They had had many discussions about the male love of all things pyrotechnic, as well as an innate penchant for chain saws. Oh, Faith thought with a stab of regret that was becoming all too familiar, how can I leave my best friend? She quickly quelled the feeling and concentrated on the happiness in the room.

Tom sat down next to his wife. "Christmas Eve: the pageant, the early family service, and then the late one, plus Christmas morning. We're getting close to the finish line!"

Everyone laughed, and Ursula commented dryly, "One would think you didn't enjoy your job, Reverend."

"Oh, I do, I do. But it's like what Faith always says when we're the ones giving a party. Lovely when it's over and can be contemplated instead of planned."

There was more laughter and Tom got out some Rémy Martin along with the bottle of Cockburn's port that he kept stocked for Ursula. He had just filled his own snifter when the phone rang.

"I'll get it," Faith said. "And it better be someone with a good reason." She kissed the top of her husband's head as she went past. She knew how tired he was.

"Hello?" She was surprised to hear Millicent abruptly ask for Ben after a hasty "Hello, Faith."

"Of course, I'll get him." Millicent was never one for chitchat, so Faith didn't extend their conversation and called, "Ben, it's for you. Miss McKinley."

"I'll take it in the kitchen," he answered, and she put the receiver down when she heard his voice.

She returned to her place next to the fire and picked up her glass. "It was Millicent. And she very specifically asked for Ben."

"Maybe she wants to contribute to the French class travel fund," Pix offered.

Millicent was not known for this sort of largesse. The group as a whole looked skeptical.

"I'm sure Ben will let us know," Ursula said. A worried look had appeared on her face.

The conversation was a short one and Ben came bursting through the door. "Miss McKinley wants me to go over and help her. It's not too late. I said yes. Okay?"

"Help her do what?" Faith asked.

"She wants me to bring my laptop and teach her how to Google."

Chapter 7

There was a moment of silence, then a wave of conversation swept over the room. "A laptop? How would Millicent know about one, except possibly as a type of colonial desk?" Pix wondered aloud. She was drowned out by several other voices, all saying "Google?" in various tones.

"Are you sure she said 'Google,' Ben?" Tom asked and was quickly followed by Ursula. "She may have meant 'gaggle,' a 'gaggle of geese,' although why she would need you to come over for that I can't imagine."

Ben was standing patiently by the front door. "She said 'laptop' and 'Google.' So, can I go?"

Permission given, Ben left, and after some further discussion of what certainly was the most curious bit of news to strike Aleford in many a moon, the guests left as well. Tom went to pay a call on a parishioner he sensed was feeling more than the usual holiday blues, and Faith decided to get a start on wrapping gifts. This activity usually took place in the early hours of Christmas morning when the rest of the family was dreaming of sugarplums. It was the first leisure time ever available in the hectic week before, and she had come to like it, pouring herself a glass of wine while listening to the carols she'd loaded on her iPod. The only drawback was how early Christmas morning dawned, although the kids slept later now.

Even though the dinner had been hearty enough to satisfy most hunger pangs until the next day, Faith knew both Tom and Ben would be asking what was for supper, and in fact those were the first words out of Ben's mouth when he came through the door after his time with Millicent. Faith was prepared, but first went over to Amy, who was curled up in front of the fire reading a book for English class, Lois Lowry's *The Giver*. It was one of Amy's favorites, and Faith had been pleased that the teacher had assigned it. One person at the school who was on Amy's wavelength.

"Are you hungry? Would you like a cup of soup? It's split pea."

"No thanks, Mom, I'm good."

Faith didn't correct her grammar—the description was too apt and tugged at Faith's heartstrings as she went back into the kitchen.

After putting a large bowl of soup on the table in front of Ben and a pastrami sandwich similar in size to those at New York's Carnegie Deli, Faith pulled a chair close to her son's. "So, what was all that with the laptop and Google at Millicent's about?"

Ben put his spoon back in the bowl. "Mom, I promised Miss McKinley that I wouldn't discuss her affairs with anyone, not even my parents."

Faith was pretty sure this was a direct quote and was annoyed.

"I'm sure it can't be anything much, sweetie. And I am not going to tell anyone else. Parents are exempt from the secret rule. You remember this from when you were much younger, right?"

Now Ben looked annoyed. "It's not that kind of secret, and there's nothing involved that you or Dad should worry about. She's paying me for my time and this constitutes Computer Guy/Client Privilege. Good soup."

Faith pushed the chair back, stood up, and went to check on Amy. Now that she thought of it, Amy hadn't eaten all that much at dinner. She'd helped Faith make most of it and that may have been why. Faith often found that after preparing all the food, she wasn't hungry.

"Computer Guy/Client Privilege!" she said over her shoulder to her son as she left the room. "What is she paying you? Fifty cents an hour?"

"No. She offered five bucks, and I got her up to seven."

Truly something very weird was going on behind the McKinley white picket fence. And Faith intended to find out what it was. This was definitely beginning to feel very Nancy Drew. Not *The Secret of the Old Clock*, Faith laughed to herself, but *The Secret of the Old Crock*.

The next morning Amy didn't get out of bed. Unlike her brother, who had his alarm set at ten-minute intervals before he managed to get up, Amy was always up as soon as the clock buzzed, often before it did, to be first in the bathroom they shared.

"I don't feel well, Mom. I think I have a temperature." She coughed very convincingly, sounding like a five-pack-a-day smoker.

"I'll get the thermometer," Faith said. She was afraid this would happen. If Amy didn't go today, they would have an even bigger problem—school phobia.

She tucked the thermometer under her daughter's tongue and, noticing that the light on Amy's bedside table was on, sat down on the rocker that was still in the room, the rocker that Faith had used to lull both babies to sleep.

"Faith," Tom called, "I can't find a clean collar!"

"I'm sure there's one in the top left-hand drawer of your bureau."

"I looked and there aren't any. I guess I can take yesterday's from the hamper."

Faith dashed out of the room. It would look clean— she didn't recall that Tom had spilled gravy or hard sauce on himself—but it would give off a vibe, and all those handmaidens of the Lord, aka female parishioners convinced their beloved reverend was ill served by his flighty wife, would get some sort of inkling. They had uncanny powers.

The collars had been pushed to the back of the drawer and Faith was back soon, but not soon enough. Amy had obviously held the thermometer to the light. Faith shook it down and said cheerfully, "Absolutely normal, darling. Now hurry up or you'll miss the bus."

Waving from the door as her daughter trudged down the front walk, Faith felt as if she were seeing Marie Antoinette off in the tumbrel. Two and a half days to get through and then the nice long vacation. She poured some coffee into a travel mug and headed for the catering kitchen. They had a big luncheon today, the D.A.R.'s annual holiday party, "Back to the Past." The Masons kindly let the group use the Masonic Hall, a larger space than the meeting room at the library—appropriate, as fourteen presidents had been Freemasons, most especially Washington. Today's D.A.R. was not the one that barred Marian Anderson from performing in 1939, and Faith was looking forward to the event. Many of the women would be sporting period dress from different eras in American history.

The menu represented a similar nod to the past and was an homage always to Fannie Merritt Farmer's 1896 classic, *The Boston Cooking-School Cook Book*. Each year's committee gave Faith a menu drawn from the book, which she followed with a few tweaks here and there. Faith had the 1915 edition, which she treasured for the photographs, especially those in color that created a rainbow of hues never seen in nature. They were starting with Poinsettia Salad—a whole tomato cut into eighths, seeds removed, and spread out to resemble petals. Faith mixed fresh chèvre with the mashed cream cheese called for, adding the specified French dressing sparingly and more of the finely chopped parsley and green pepper that transformed plain French dressing into "Martinique" Dressing. This was followed by soup—the ladies liked a soup course, and today's was Cream Chestnut. Faith roasted the chestnuts before cooking and sieving them. The main course was Chicken à la King (Faith always wondered which one—a Louis?) in puff pastry—vol-au-vents. Not cafeteria Chicken à la King—no hint of library paste and plenty of mushrooms. And yes, the pimento strips as well.

Fannie Farmer was dubbed in her own time and since as "The Mother of Level Measurements." Not a bad way to be remembered with its reassurance for the ages that if you followed her recipes all would be edible. Faith had always hoped that one of the committee would request the cookbook's Canapés à la Rector for the social hour that started the festivities with Mock-tails, especially Virgin Marys and Shirley Temples. The ecclesiastical canapé recipe called for strips of stale bread covered with caviar on the toasted side and three sections—the middle with finely chopped cucumber pickles, one end with finely chopped red peppers, and the other with a piece of anchovy fillet. The women always opted for toasted almonds and cheese straws, however, as they didn't want to get too full.

And they were surely saving room for dessert. The first year Niki didn't get the dessert memo, or ignored whatever it was, and made a chocolate Bûche de Noël with hazelnut cream filling, the individual slices crowned with tiny marzipan Golden Eagles holding a sprig of holly. Forever after, that was the desired dessert.

They'd arrived at this point in the job now, and Faith could begin to relax. The ship had been launched, stayed afloat, and was now steaming off into the sunset. The ladies were still having a very jolly time as the servers poured coffee. Faith heard one of the older members say, "What the heck. Make it regular! I've had enough decaf to last the rest of my life." It seemed hair was about to be let down and there hadn't been a drop of alcohol except for the rum truffles also being served now.

She felt her phone, which she'd tucked into the pocket of her checked chef trousers, vibrate. A surreptitious glance sent her scurrying into the kitchen. It was Amy's school.

"Hello, Mrs. Fairchild?"

"Yes. Is everything all right?" She didn't recognize the voice. It was a woman, not good old Tony the principal.

"I'm Eleanor Woodward, the school nurse, and I'm afraid you have a very sick girl here. She's running quite a high temperature and I'd advise you to get her to your doctor immediately. She has been crying, apparently someone said something to upset her, but that wouldn't account for this spike, and she seems to have a very bad cough."

"I'll be there right away."

Faith went to tell Niki and the others. Grabbing her coat and purse, she said, "Please make my apologies to the chapter president and the committee who organized this. They're having a carol sing soon, but you should be able to clear everything except the coffee and cookie plates."

"Go, don't worry." Niki gave her a little shove toward the door and then a quick hug. "And you shouldn't be too hasty at kissing Mother of the Year good-bye. Everybody does stuff like this."

Maybe, Faith thought. But it didn't help. She'd sent her seriously ill daughter to school and hadn't believed her. Amy might be coughing, but Faith was choking on guilt.

Will is like one of those puzzle balls she used to get as a favor at childhood birthday parties, Sophie thought. When she'd get it home, she'd carefully unwind the thin strips of crepe paper, revealing tiny charms or other surprises before reaching the solid small ball at the center, which was good for playing jacks. Maybe all married, or other, couples went through this getting-to-know-you process—the unwinding—but it seemed a bit more complicated in her case.

Last night he had tried to explain about the jewelry even though Sophie had said it was fine and not to worry about it. She didn't need expensive pearls and diamond brooches or whatever else was in the safety-deposit box. That kind of jewelry would cause her to worry about losing it if she did wear a piece, she insisted.

Will had listened and said, "I *want* you to wear them. I don't really know what I was thinking, or not thinking. I just forgot about them. Really. Until Dad said something, it hadn't occurred to me that I should have given them to you when we got engaged. I'm sorry, Sophie."

She'd repeated what she had said, and it had all ended most satisfactorily in bed where he'd murmured, "You don't need anything to add to the gem I have right here."

Smiling, she'd started to slip into a deep sleep when he'd added, " 'Fraid Atlanta is going to take longer than I thought, honey. After New Year's I won't be back for a while."

Laura had been right.

This morning Will was up early but delayed his departure to go to the bank with Sophie. "I want to make sure you can access the box. I'm assuming you can, since we added you to my account. Maybe you can find something to wear Christmas Eve. It would please Dad—and me, too. I won't be back until late on Wednesday, so we can't do it then."

There had been no problem at the bank, and Will gave her a hasty kiss, telling her to have fun. Sophie had an appointment with a new client scheduled and she had a call she needed to make, but she sat down with what seemed like an extremely large box just to hold some jewelry and unlocked it, carefully removing some documents on top. One appeared to be a will. Sophie wished she had more time to go over everything. She was curious about where the money Laura said Will had inherited was. Sophie had been keeping track of their monthly statements, and they had a healthy balance in both checking and savings, but nothing like the kind of money the Realtor had hinted at.

The box was filled with velvet-covered and leather cases. Some looked quite old. Sophie pulled out several that were large enough to hold the pearl necklace. She had already decided that she would wear it Christmas Eve. The first box did not hold the pearls but a beautiful diamond and sapphire Art Deco necklace. It must have been Will's great-grandmother's. Aurora and Paul's mother? Another box contained a tiara, surely the one Will's mother was wearing in her wedding photo. Sophie picked it up. The delicate diamond leaves and rosebuds sparkled in the light. There was a separate chain of small diamonds, and Sophie realized the tiara could also be worn as a necklace. Would it bring up too many sad memories for Will and his father?

She put it back. The pearls were in the next case and they were extraordinary, perfectly matched, and Sophie thought they must be natural, not cultured. A bit looser than a choker, the three strands met in front, held together by an exquisite ruby clasp surrounded by diamonds. She put the necklace on, and it fit as though it had been made for her, the clasp at her collarbone. Yes, she would wear the pearls—and after quickly searching through some of the other boxes, she found a Tiffany Jean Schlumberger ruby-enameled gold and diamond bracelet that she was sure had been worn with the pearls. The reds were an exact match.

Sophie didn't know how dressed up she should be for the Christmas Day open houses, but she tucked a lovely wide flat gold collar and diamond earrings shaped like half moons into her bag as well. A bag that would not be leaving her side until she could get back to the house and think of a secure hiding place. Definitely not under her lingerie or in the toes of her shoes. Or even the freezer. Faith had told her she hid her good jewelry in Ben's Legos—a pack rat, he still had a container of them. The one time the Fairchilds were robbed, the thieves hadn't even gone into the kids' rooms.

Sophie closed up the box, promising herself to return with Will and ask him about the pieces. Treasures selected with care and love—she could almost feel it—for his grandmother and mother, perhaps great-grandmother. Jewelry of such value had obviously been birthday, anniversary, or other occasion gifts for these very special women.

Ruth was at the desk when Sophie walked into the office, and she was reminded that she wanted to get together with the woman before Christmas. Randy could be right about Ruth's depression. She would most likely be alone for most of the holiday. But lunch today was out. If all went well, Sophie would be taking the new client somewhere to eat. And tomorrow could be just as busy, then it was Christmas Eve, and the practice was closing at noon.

"Do you have time for a drink after work?" she asked Ruth. "I was thinking we should go someplace traditional like the Pink House bar for our first Savannah Christmases."

Ruth brightened. "That would be great. I'm pretty much done with my shopping. Most of it had to be mailed. There's a running club party tomorrow after work, so today is perfect."

"Great. This gives me an incentive to clear my desk after I meet with Mr. Smith."

"He won't find any better representation," Ruth said loyally, and Sophie went up to her office on the second floor.

Anson and Randy both had larger offices on the ground floor of what had been a cotton factor's—cotton broker's—home, but Sophie liked her small office better with its view overlooking the square. There was an enormous magnolia growing to one side of the window that Will had told her he used to climb as a kid. He'd looked longingly at it when he told her and she'd almost expected him to dart out the window onto the nearest branch.

Before Sophie could get to work she had an important phone call to make first. Babs had had the same personal shopper at Bergdorf's for so long and relied on her so much that Pru Wolcott seemed like a relative. And Sophie needed to rely on her now.

"Sophie! How delightful to hear from you! A married woman! Where did the time go? It seems like just the other day you would sit in your little smocked dresses and Mary Janes while your mother tried things on."

Since Pru sported the same dark brunette chin-length pageboy and bangs she'd had since Sophie's earliest memories, kept a trim figure, and didn't show even the hint of crow's-feet, time did not seem to have gone anywhere for her. Not so for Sophie and her wardrobe call. Mary Janes, unless they were Manolos, wouldn't do.

"I need your help desperately! Could you overnight me two outfits? I didn't know I'd need a formal gown to wear Christmas Eve for the family dinner. Stupid of me. I should have asked my mother-in-law ages ago. Or tried to get an instruction booklet after I said 'I do.' They do things differently in—"

"Savannah, the South in general—much dressier," Pru finished for her. "We have your measurements from the wedding dress, and unless you've either lost or gained weight they'll be recent enough. Tell me what you have in mind."

"Well, I have the shoes." Sophie texted a photo and then spent a fun half hour viewing the possibilities Pru shot back to her before choosing two outfits. Her Christmas Eve dress was cocktail length, not long, and strapless to show off the pearls. What made it formal was the fabric—ivory satin—and the style, a fitted bodice with a wide, almost vintage Dior New Look skirt. There was a stole in the same material lined in ruby red. For the open houses Pru found a sleeveless gold silk sheath paired with a long-sleeved tunic jacket that could have come straight from a Renaissance painting—deep burgundy with black and gold embroidery.

A girl could get used to this, Sophie said to herself after thanking Pru profusely and hanging up.

"I'm thinking *Wall Street* meets *Midnight in the Garden of Good and Evil* in a pub."

Sophie laughed. She'd liked Patrick Smith immediately—warm handshake and smile, but not too much so, plus he'd immediately gotten to the point. A literary agent had sold his thriller for a very nice figure, but Patrick wanted someone specializing in intellectual property to represent him for the film rights, which he'd kept out. He'd already had several offers.

"It's a classic story of greed—young lad of Irish ancestry's head is turned by the amount of money he sees dangled in front of him if he will only agree to cut a few corners and keep his mouth shut."

"And why the Savannah locale?" Sophie asked.

"To start with, I'm Savannah Irish myself. You do know that our St. Patrick's Day parade is second only to New York's—three hours long last year? The fountain in Forsyth Park flows green. Hard workers that we be, we built much of Georgia back in the day, especially the railroads. There's even a Dublin, Georgia. And as for politics, well we're a part of the city's history there, too. Have you not noticed all the Irish pubs?"

She laughed again and not just because of the accent he'd suddenly adopted. "There are so many places to imbibe that I'm afraid the names haven't jumped out at me, only that there is no shortage of them."

Patrick was a young lad himself, late twenties, and an investigative reporter for the NBC Atlanta affiliate, as well as a contributor to several print outlets. He'd brought an advanced reader's copy of the book for her, and as he talked, listing his plot elements—everything from money laundering to smuggling—Sophie heard echoes of what Randy had mentioned. How the port of Savannah was becoming an ever-increasing major hub. If Patrick wrote as well as he spoke, the book would be a page-turner. She definitely wanted to represent him and only hoped he wanted Maxwell & Maxwell in turn.

"May I take you to lunch and we can continue the conversation? Clary's? Or anywhere you like," Sophie said.

"Have you been to Kevin Barry's? The pub on River Street?"

"No, but it sounds as if I should have."

Patrick nodded. "You've obviously been to Clary's, since you suggested it, and I do love their grilled pimento cheese, but we need some Guinness and the banana bread pudding with Jameson whipped cream for dessert to celebrate."

"So this means . . ."

"Yes, Sophie. I'm assuming I may call you that, since you're going to be representing me and making bushels of money for us both."

Lunch was delightful—and long, as they considered places in Savannah as possible locations for the film. "Pretty much anywhere," Patrick said at one point. "And easy to find extras on every corner. We love it when Hollywood comes to town."

Leaving the restaurant Patrick said, "Maxwell is a pretty common name, but I've been running into a nice guy from Savannah named Will Maxwell, a PI, in Atlanta this fall. He read a story I'd written on illegal arms trading and called to ask me some questions, which led to a drink. He's a local boy, too. Any relation?"

Sophie stopped short. Illegal arms? That didn't sound very white collar!

"Will's my husband. We got married in November."

"Congratulations. And this explains the lack of an accent." He grinned. "I kinda like the idea of a Yankee lady lawyer."

"So do we Yankee lady lawyers," she shot back.

They returned to the office to finalize the details and Sophie promised to have everything ready for him to sign before he left for Atlanta the following day. Randy and Anson would be pleased by the deal, and who knew? Hard to imagine another book and film putting the city on the map the way *Midnight* had, but fiction *could* sometimes be stranger than fact.

She sent all the information to Ruth and settled in to clear her desk of other work so she could relax over the holiday. Relax with Will. Had they just been together that morning? It seemed a week ago.

Early in November she had looked for a piece of artwork for his Christmas gift at the Savannah College of Art and Design store, one of the best gift shops she'd ever visited. She'd liked the notion of giving Will something for the home they would be sharing together, something new that neither of them had ever had on their walls. There were several possibilities, but she'd decided not to decide in a hurry, although she found great earrings for Faith, and gifts for others on her list. And then she'd walked past a large pine on her way back to the office that instantly reminded her of some prints, mezzotints, they'd seen in a gallery on Sanpere last summer by an artist named James Groleau. She quickly found him through the magic of Google and ordered *Fog over Eggemog-gin* and *Morning at Water's Edge,* both evoking the time and place where they'd met. She was sure Will would love them—a suggestion of the Arts and Crafts movement, but the colors and technique very much today's.

At last she decided she'd done enough catching up—and she was coming into the office tomorrow, she reminded herself—so she logged out, setting her protective password. The time at the top of her screen jumped out. Ruth! It was almost five thirty. She grabbed her things and rushed downstairs into the reception area. "I'm so sorry! I didn't realize it was getting so late! You should have let me know."

"No worries. I wanted to finish these, and some other things," Ruth said. "I'm not in a hurry. Do you have to be someplace? We could postpone until after the holidays."

"I'm completely free, unless *you'd* rather wait."

"Nope. Free as a bird, too," Ruth said. The woman didn't look depressed at all, Sophie noted. In fact she looked extremely happy. "Glowing" was the appropriate adjective.

The bar at the Olde Pink House was the perfect choice. It was decked out for the season and a pianist was playing "Greensleeves" as they walked in.

"This place is supposed to be loaded with ghosts," Ruth said as they sat down near the fire.

"Will told me all about it," Sophie said. "I think the one down here in the bar is the original owner, who welcomes guests on occasion!"

"I'm happy to be greeted by a friendly ghost. Like Casper. Just no pink elephants." Ruth giggled.

Ms. Stafford, Sophie thought, was in a very cheerful mood and hadn't had the other sort of spirits yet.

"We're not driving anywhere, so how about a bottle of champagne to mark our first Southern Christmas?" Sophie suggested. Patrick Smith had had his Guinness at lunch, but she'd stuck to iced tea—unsweetened. The whole sweet tea thing had to be genetic. Or an acquired taste she hadn't developed yet.

"Oh that sounds lovely! I haven't had champagne since last New Year's."

"And oysters to start?" Sophie said.

Ruth sighed. "This is going to be the best Christmas ever." And then she blushed.

By the time the champagne bottle was half empty, the pianist had moved on to a medley of more recent carols and a few people had clustered round, singing along. Sophie and Ruth had ordered another dish, Southern Sushi. As Ruth said, "How can we not? When in Rome, or I should say Tokyo."

"I think you should say 'Savannah,'" Sophie said. They were both getting what her mother called "tiddly," and it felt great.

"Southern Sushi" turned out to be smoked shrimp and grits rolled in coconut-crusted nori. It was so good they ordered another portion.

The food, and drink, emboldened Sophie. "So, have you met anyone special here? I don't mean to pry. . . ."

"Yes, you do," Ruth teased her, "and it's fine. There *is* someone special, and he makes me feel special." She blushed again. It caused her to look even younger, even prettier. "That's all I can say for now."

Sophie reached across the table and patted Ruth's hand. "I'm happy for you." She almost added that she wanted Ruth to have what she had and then thought, but Will is taken, and thought further, *whoever invented champagne should have been given a Nobel Prize if they had them then, and wasn't it a monk? The inventor that is.* The server refilled their glasses and a few minutes later Sophie pulled Ruth over to the crowd around the piano, lustily joining the chorus of "Jingle Bells." She tried to tell her the story of the Jingle Bell church but gave up and just sang.

"Hey, Ruth," a woman called as she came into the bar with some others. "You didn't run this morning! Starting the holiday early?"

Ruth waved them over. "I went into work early. Come sing with us!" She turned to Sophie. "These are a few of my running buddies." She made introductions, but the only name that Sophie knew she would remember was Esmeralda Higgins—"Someone gave Mama a copy of *The Hunchback of Notre Dame* when she was pregnant. Most people just call me Emmie."

"Good thing you weren't a boy," Sophie said before she could stop herself. "Quasimodo?"

"I get that a lot, too, and thank the Lord every night. I do have a little sister named Cosette. Mama's Victor Hugo was a two-volume set, and she'd kept going with *Les Misérables!*"

Ruth's friends were breaking training for the night and proved to be great fun. The runners ordered platters of assorted appetizers and Sophie decided mac 'n' cheese poppers were possibly the best thing she'd ever eaten. They went perfectly with the next bottle of champagne she'd decided they all needed, and the next. Forget the oysters? And weren't carbs supposed to be good for marathoners?

That night she slept more soundly than any night since discovering the body in the wardrobe. There were no ghostly noises or visitations of any kind. Just sweet Christmas dreams.

Faith called their family doctor, Dr. Michael Kane, before starting the car. Amy had graduated from a pediatrician a year ago. Faith was put right through when she explained the emergency, and after Dr. Kane listened to the symptoms he told Faith to bring Amy to the hospital immediately. He was on his way there now to check on a patient.

"My office is a petri dish of germs. At the hospital, you can bring her straight into an examining room. It sounds like she'll need a chest X-ray. I don't want to diagnose without seeing her first, but it sounds like pneumonia."

"Pneumonia!" Faith hung up quickly and tried Tom's cell. It was his day as chaplain at the VA hospital in Bedford, and she left a voice message when, as she'd expected, he didn't answer.

Amy was lying down in the nurse's office, tears rolling into her ears. Her face was puffy and bright red. When she saw her mother she started to cry harder. Faith pulled her into her arms. "Hush, it's all right. Dr. Kane is waiting for us at the hospital, and he'll make you feel better in no time."

"Hospital! No!"

The nurse came over. "Amy, don't worry. Your doctor needs to take a picture of those lungs of yours to help you get over this cough." She mouthed the word "pneumonia" over Amy's head. Faith didn't think she could feel any worse, but she did. She helped Amy get her parka on, wishing she could carry her, but those days were long gone.

By the time they reached the hospital, Amy had stopped protesting. Her eyes were glassy with fever and she was too sick to say anything even when the nurse inserted the IV Dr. Kane ordered for dehydration She was taken to have an X-ray, then back to the curtained cubicle in the ER. Faith sat by her daughter's side, holding her hand.

It wasn't long before the blood tests and X-ray revealed the culprit. It *was* pneumonia. Viral pneumonia, which Dr. Kane said they usually saw in older adults or younger children. The virus—RSV, or respiratory syncytial virus—did not respond to antibiotics, as bacterial pneumonia did, but he was prescribing an antiviral medication to keep it at bay along with ibuprofen to reduce Amy's fever and deal with the pain.

"It's caused by flu initially, and the schools are filled with kids whose parents send them to school sick."

Like me, Faith thought glumly.

"Have you noticed that she has seemed tired lately, run-down? Maybe too much homework."

"A little, but I thought it was because she's in a new school and it's been very stressful for her."

Dr. Kane frowned. "Stress is not our bodies' friend. She'll be fine in time, with plenty of rest and fluids. Use the humidifier. Still, I want to keep her overnight."

"I can stay with her, can't I?"

He smiled. "I wouldn't have it any other way. Miss Amy will need to be kept quiet and as relaxed as possible. She's always been in good health and the X-ray did not show any permanent lung damage, just fluid. I'll keep checking on her while she's here and you have my pager number."

"Thank you. Tom's at the VA today, but I left a message, so he should be here soon."

Dr. Kane left, giving Faith a hug and reassuring her once more that Amy would be fine. "And, Faith, these things come on suddenly. Don't beat yourself up."

He knew her well. After he left, she pulled a chair up next to Amy. It wasn't a private room, but the other bed was unoccupied at the moment. She ought to call Pix and text Ben, the most reliable way to reach him, but right now Faith just wanted to sit with her precious daughter and watch her.

After a while, she heard Amy's soft, "Mom?" and instantly bent closer.

"Darling, how do you feel? There's juice, and Dr. Kane said you could have something to eat if you're hungry. I can ring for the nurse."

"Thirsty," Amy said.

Faith gave her the juice and after correctly interpreting Amy's startled look at the IV explained what it was and that she had pneumonia but would be better soon.

"In time for Christmas?"

"Maybe not that fast, but by Thursday you'll definitely feel better than today."

"So no school tomorrow?"

"No school."

Amy sank back into the pillows. The hospital made her look smaller than she was. Over the summer she had shot up and was as tall as Faith now. Her expression was fearful and the tears were starting again. Faith reached for the buzzer to summon the nurse.

"What's wrong? Are you in pain?" Faith brought her face near her child's, wiping away the tears with a tissue. "Amy, what is it!"

"Ben can't go to France! You mustn't let him! Cassie said he'll be targeted by terrorists as an American and that her parents wouldn't let her brother go on the trip. She said his plane will probably blow up before he even gets there!"

Faith was torn between violent rage and the need to stay calm for her daughter.

"Honey, yes, the world has seen some horrible things over this year, but aside from what Dad and I would allow, do you think the school and Ben's teacher would put students at risk? If there were any question at all that the trip would be dangerous, it would have been canceled. Ben and the others will all be staying with families. Families like ours. Cassie was just saying this to hurt you. I'm not sure she even has an older brother."

"But why, Mom?" Amy moaned. "Why does she hate me so much?"

Faith paused. Why indeed? "I don't know, sweetheart. You may not believe me, but she's probably jealous of you. Afraid her friends will like you better. You certainly are nicer, prettier, smarter."

This drew a wan smile. "You think so because you're my mom."

Faith smiled back, although it *was* true. Faith had never seen Cassie, but she doubted she had Amy's beautiful big blue eyes and shining straight blond hair, and there was no question about who was nicer. As for smarts, both her children were distinctly above average, as Garrison Keillor would have said.

"Besides," she said, "there are things we don't know that cause people to act the way Cassie has. She could have family troubles or be unhappy, and is taking her hurt out on you." Faith paused. "Or she could just be evil."

"Mom!"

The nurse came in and looked at the two of them. "I'd say someone, or both, may be feeling better. Let me check Amy's temp and a few other things while you get a snack. I'll be bringing Amy something soon if she feels as though she could eat."

Faith left reluctantly but was immediately cheered by the sight of Pix and Tom coming off the elevator. She rushed over.

"The nurse is with her. She's going to be fine. I mean Amy, not the nurse. It's viral pneumonia, and that Cassie made her sick!"

Sophie rang Lydia Scriven's bell early Wednesday afternoon. She'd seen the woman walking Charlie a half hour ago so was hoping she'd still be at home and not off somewhere for Christmas Eve. She was.

"Sophie Maxwell! Merry Christmas! Come in, come in. I was just about to have a cup of tea, but we can have something more celebratory if you like."

"Thank you," Sophie said, stepping into the hall, which was painted deep peach. The banister on the stairs to the second floor ended in a mahogany carved acanthus newel post. A large oval mirror made the narrow space seem larger and the walls were covered with botanical prints. The color continued in the parlor, but these walls were covered with folk art paintings like those Sophie had seen by Jacob Lawrence and Horace Pippin.

"My husband and I used to pick these up at tag sales, and sometimes from the trash! When he retired he decided to try his hand. The ones on this wall are his."

Sophie recognized the house and square—brightly colored, sunny pictures—and a warm, deep-hued portrait of Lydia herself.

"Now, what will you have? Some scuppernong wine? My cousin in North Carolina keeps me supplied."

"Knowing my husband's family, I think I'd better have tea. There will be plenty to drink at dinner tonight, and I should start with a clear head, tempting as the wine sounds. I know it's a sweet one, but I've never had it."

"Tea it is and a slice of Scripture Cake. A recipe that's come down in my family from about the time Eve was having to come up with a pie recipe."

"Scripture Cake?"

"Now, don't tell me you haven't heard of it. You must have it up north, too."

Sophie shook her head.

"I'll make a copy of the recipe for you. But to give you an idea, each ingredient refers to a passage from scripture, twelve in all, just like the twelve apostles. For example First Kings, chapter four, verse twenty-two says, 'And Solomon's provision for one day was thirty measures of fine flour.' Over the years, ladies have worked out the amounts. There are figs mentioned in Nahum and 'sweet cane' in Jeremiah. My favorite is Second Chronicles, chapter nine, verse nine, 'And she gave the king spices in great abundance.' Or as we say now, 'Season to taste'!"

"I love it! I'm sure my friend Faith Fairchild has heard of the cake, but I'll send her a copy, too, if I may. She's a pastor's wife and a caterer."

"She will most likely know of it, but *our* recipe tastes good, too. It's not just a gimmick!"

Sophie followed her hostess into the kitchen. It had not been touched, except for updated appliances, since the 1950s, and happily so. Sophie wondered if her new friend knew how much the cabinets, counter-tops, canisters, and dinette set would bring in a mid-century-modern shop in Manhattan. After Sophie's appreciative remarks, they talked about the way new kitchens lacked character—"all that stainless steel and granite, so cold," Lydia said. It turned out she was an HGTV devotee nonetheless. Sophie agreed about the soullessness and told her how much she was looking forward to doing up her own kitchen, adding to herself, as soon as possible.

"Your mother-in-law must be chewing nails at how slow the work is going on her place here on the square.

They started almost a year and a half, no make that two years, ago. Word is that she switched contractors, so that may be the problem."

Sophie was surprised. From what Will had said, Gloria was a quick flipper. Maybe she had other plans for this particular house. She hoped she wouldn't offer it to them. Sophie wanted a place all their own at this point, no matter how lovely Gloria's finished product would be.

"We always end up in the kitchen, now let's be proper ladies and sit in the parlor. Will you take the tray?" Lydia said.

Over what was truly a heavenly slice of cake, Lydia told Sophie she would be going out to her sister's south of Savannah near Jekyll Island for the holidays. "You must be so happy to have your husband home. Your first married Christmas!"

"I am, but he won't be getting here until late this afternoon, I'm afraid."

"But I saw . . . no these old eyes of mine do play tricks on me. Now, I have a little something for you two to enjoy over the holidays. Divinity. Do you know what that is?"

"I have a notion, but I'm pretty sure it's not the one you're giving us unless you have even greater powers than I already think you have," Sophie said. While

Lydia was out of the room, Sophie wondered about the woman's "eyes playing tricks" comment. Was that what it had been or had she seen Will today? Will, who was still supposed to be in Atlanta.

Lydia returned with a tin filled with what looked like small snow-white meringues, each morsel topped with a pecan. "Try one. It's basically sugar, corn syrup, and egg white. Southern nougat."

"I'll have to put these on a high shelf out of temptation's way or there won't be any left for Will! Thank you so much, and here's a little something for you."

Sophie had ordered one of L.L.Bean's Christmas gift bags—a small version of their famous canvas boat bags decorated with an embroidered Christmas tree and filled with Maine treats: a jar of wild blueberry jam, a jug of maple syrup, and barley sugar lobster lollipops.

"I will be the envy of my book club when the bag is empty! It's the perfect size for my reading material and my reading glasses."

Lydia's last word reminded Sophie of the earlier comment—about the older woman's eyes playing tricks on her—and hoped that's what had happened.

They were expected for drinks at six and Sophie was ready by five thirty, excitedly waiting for her husband. The pleasure of putting on the new dress and the heirloom jewelry had chased any other thoughts far away. She pulled her hair back into a sleek French twist to show off the pearls. When she heard Will's key in the door she ran to greet him.

"Merry Christmas, darling!"

He stopped still for a moment, stepped in, and closed the door behind him.

"Sophie!" He sounded choked up as he reached for her. "You look like you just stepped down from the top of a tree, a Christmas angel! Oh, shug, I love you so much!" He pulled her close.

It was all she could do to keep tears of joy from falling, wrecking the makeup that had taken her so long to put on. She usually just went for mascara, blush and lip gloss, but tonight she had gone all out. It was obviously working.

"I don't want to muss you up," Will murmured. "Think we have time . . . ?"

Just as Sophie was about to say they would always have time, the doorbell sounded.

"Damn! Who could that be? It's Christmas Eve! Can't a man have a moment with his wife?"

"You go change." Sophie sighed. "And I'll see who it is. Probably a late delivery." Babs had sent a large package of gifts, and others had also arrived, including one from the Fairchilds. Surely Uncle Paul wasn't near a post office in the remote part of Asia where they were spending the holiday? But he was very resourceful, Sophie thought, opening the door.

"Merry Christmas, y'all. Where's Will? We always exchange gifts Christmas Eve and I have his right here."

Miss Laura. Sophie bet the ice queen—all in white velvet tonight—had a very special one in mind. She stepped over the threshold.

"I'm so sorry, Laura, but Will is changing for our family dinner." Sophie emphasized "our" and "family." "We're running late. Give me the gift and I'll put it under our tree." Again with the "our."

Just then Will came downstairs, his hands at his neck, his jacket draped over an arm. "I can never tie these things, but if I try to get away with a ready-made one, I'll never hear the end of it. Oh, hi, Laura. Merry Christmas."

Will must have changed at warp speed, Sophie thought sourly.

"Merry Christmas, Will. I brought your gift." Laura kissed him on the cheek. Very close to his mouth.

"Well, best be heading out. Merry Christmas to you, too, Laura," Sophie said, grabbing the stole and an evening purse she'd left on the hall table. The hall was getting rather crowded at this point and it was time to leave. More than time.

But when she turned around, Laura was tying Will's formal bow tie and neither of them seemed to have heard Sophie.

She tried again. "I'm sure we'll see you at the open houses tomorrow, Laura. Good-bye for now."

"Ice cold. Just the way you like it." Laura pulled a bottle of Veuve Clicquot champagne from the bag she was carrying. "And here's something to tuck into your stocking."

Sophie recognized the familiar robin's egg blue of a Tiffany's box. Cuff links? Key to Laura Belvedere's heart?

"Aren't you the sweetest thing?" Will said. "Sophie, get some glasses and we'll toast old Saint Nick."

"Honey, I don't think we have time—"

"Y'all obviously don't know this family, Sophie." Laura laughed. "Time is not something they pay much attention to, unless it's like now and we're pouring drinks." Her laugh was one of those tinkling, glass-shattering ones. Sophie wanted to smack her. Instead she took the bottle and went into the kitchen to pour three glasses.

They were sitting in the front room when she came back with the tray. Three glasses, the bottle left in the kitchen. No cheese straws, sugared pecans, or any other nibbles.

"Here's to us," Laura said, raising her glass and draining it. Sophie had no choice but to return to the kitchen for the rest.

When they arrived at her in-laws over an hour late, Randy started to tease them the moment they walked in. "Hey, sister-in-law! That a little love bite I see peeking out from under the pearls?"

Sophie took the joshing good-naturedly, only wishing it had been the truth.

"Hush now, Randall," Anson said. "These two have some catching up to do. I don't know what y'all put in your eggnog in Connecticut, but here we like it with a lot of heavy cream and a healthy amount of bourbon."

Sophie took a sip. It was so thick you could almost stand a spoon in it, and she'd finished the cup before she knew it.

"Sinfully delicious," she said. Anson promptly topped up her cup from the enormous Waterford punch bowl and looped his arm through hers, pulling her aside.

"Now, you come tell me all about this new client of ours. I didn't get to be in the other movie and I'd like to have a cameo—isn't that what they call it?—in this one."

"It is, and I'll make sure that's part of the final agreement," Sophie said. She filled him in quickly, looking back into the front parlor and thinking they could be on a movie set now. The crystal chandeliers, gleaming period furniture, lavish holiday decorations, and above all the cast. The women were in elegant gowns— richly colored satins and silks. Sophie had obviously not been the only one to go to the bank, and jewels gleamed at throats and wrists. Carlene was wearing a diamond and emerald necklace that would not have been out of place in Cartier's window. And the men in black tie—handsome without it, but elevated to George Clooney status with the change in dress. And they were all wearing socks. No flip-flops or loafers tonight, although Sophie wouldn't put it past Randy.

As soon as she had given Anson the highlights of the deal, he said, "I just want you to know how happy I am to have you as part of our family, Sophie. This is the happiest Christmas I can remember in years." They were standing in front of the portrait of his mother. Of Aurora. "Her pearls look lovely on you, darlin', and she would have loved you."

Impulsively Sophie gave him a kiss. "I know I would have loved her, too, and Will's mother. I wish I could have known them both."

Anson's eyes filled with tears. "I wish you could have, too. They surely didn't deserve the ending dealt them. . . ."

Gloria bustled over. "Now what's with the long faces on Christmas Eve? Santa's not going to be happy! Y'all sit down. The rest of us are starving."

But not for long. Sophie had thought the dinners at Bells Mills had been generous, but this Yuletide table was groaning loudly. A ham *and* roast beef, shrimp in many forms, greens, cheese grits, beaten biscuits, and Savannah red rice. This was Sophie's first taste of the city favorite, and once more she thought of Faith, resolving to get this version of the recipe for her— smoked sausage, tomatoes, hence the name, and all sorts of other yummy things. (See recipe, page 232.)

The meal was as merry as it was delicious. Sophie hadn't had much to drink after the eggnog, having had Laura's champagne to start, but she now realized she was drunk on the food and there was still dessert to come, served in the double parlor, where it had been laid out on the pair of Duncan Phyfe sideboards that had belonged to Will's great-grandparents.

She slipped away to freshen up and, finding the powder room on the main floor occupied, ducked into a small room off to one side, not wanting to embarrass whoever was using it by waiting just outside. She left the door ajar and when she heard footsteps going past, she started out only to find herself pushed back by the firmly closing door. Odd.

But what was even more odd was the woman's voice that reached her. "She must have felt overserved and gone home to lie down."

"Overserved," a euphemism for "drunk." Who'd gone home? And who was speaking? It sounded like Patty Sue or Gloria, even Carlene. Sophie realized their voices all had the same pitch. As did Laura's. Well, she'd find out in a moment, she thought, reaching for the doorknob.

A doorknob that wasn't there.

Chapter 8

The whole thing was absurd. Sophie banged on the door, calling, "Hey, I'm stuck in here!" She heard footsteps and gave a sigh of relief, but the steps went right past the door and kept going. She hit the door harder, rapping with her knuckles until they stung. The oak was thick, and only someone right outside would be able to hear her. She tried again anyway with her other hand.

Nothing.

She felt around the door and located a light switch. An overhead fixture revealed where she was. Larger than a closet, it was a storage space that must have been created when the powder room was added. There was a vacuum cleaner and various boxes plus an ample coatrack that would probably be put to use during tomorrow's open house. She'd surely be discovered then, she thought ruefully, well aware that someone—someone female—had deliberately shut her in and lied about Sophie's leaving.

There had been a knob on the outside of the door, which meant a shank to open it. She knelt down and peered into the opening. The metal piece was close and she tried to grab it, but even her slender fingers were too thick. What she needed was something like needle-nose pliers.

Sophie stood up and started opening the boxes. They were filled with china and glassware—the kind caterers used for large gatherings. Her hopes rose. There would be cutlery. She could try using two knives to turn the shank.

One box did contain layers of knives, forks, and spoons. The knife blades were too broad, but she continued to search until she reached the bottom of the box and was rewarded by a layer of thin-bladed steak knives.

Again, she couldn't get purchase to twist the knob open, but she realized she could try sliding one blade between the door and the jamb, pushing the latch in. She'd never leave home without a Swiss Army knife in the future.

The trick worked with credit cards in mystery novels and the movies. She took a deep breath and slid the knife into the crack. It didn't budge. She tried again, coming from the top and giving the blade a sharp twist when she felt it reach the metal lock.

Bingo!

Sophie switched off the light—leaving the door wide open—and went to the powder room to put on some lipstick, then calmly entered the parlor where the family had gathered for after-dinner liqueurs and coffee.

"Sophie!" Will came over to her side and put his arm around her waist. "We thought you'd gone back to the house. You should have told me. I was just about to leave to check on you."

No one else said anything, but all eyes were on her. Was one pair more surprised than the rest? Wondering how she had escaped? Sophie couldn't tell.

"No. I feel fine. Fine now, that is. I've been locked in that little room next to the powder room. Someone—"

Gloria quickly interrupted. "Anson, I keep telling you we have to get that wonky doorknob fixed! I'm surprised this hasn't happened before! But whatever were you doing in the box room, darlin'?" She laughed. "Never mind. You're here now and that's what counts."

Carlene came over with a snifter of brandy. "Get this down. You do seem to have had bad luck since coming here! Did you happen to see anything in the dark? I've never heard this house has ghosts, but you may have coaxed one out!"

"Sorry. I turned the light on right away and if there was one, it disappeared." Sophie smiled at Carlene, who seemed genuinely disappointed, and patted her arm. "Maybe another time." The brandy did the trick and she felt much less shaky.

Her appearance—or reappearance—seemed to signal the end of the party. And it was time to head out for the Christmas Eve service. Sophie and Will found themselves leaving before the others. Sophie managed a "thanks for a lovely evening" when she actually wanted to say "a strange" one. There were Merry Christmas hugs all around, and so far as she could determine, none was less effusive—or more—than the others.

As they walked toward Christ Church and Johnson Square through the streets of Savannah, Sophie debated telling Will about the way she'd been shoved in the box room—and the words she'd overheard, even through the thick door. Back in the parlor, she'd tried to separate out each woman's voice, even the two cousins who were, as usual, dressed in twin outfits—long plum-colored taffeta gowns with lace fichus. None of the voices stood out for certain.

No, she wouldn't tell Will. It was their first Christmas Eve. Later in the week before he went back to

Atlanta she would, however, ask him who'd said Sophie had left, that she was "overserved." She didn't need to know now and a part of her was afraid it might not be Patty Sue, her prime suspect. She liked Carlene and Gloria. And the cousins were straight from the pages of a Gothic Southern novel. Maybe slightly "porch light on, but nobody home," but Sophie ruled the two ladies out.

Approaching the church from across the square, Will stopped in the shadows of a live oak festooned with moss and took his wife in his arms. "I want a picture of you in this dress. Not that I'll need one to remember the way you looked tonight. Oh, Sophie, how did I get so lucky?"

His kiss was filled with longing, one she knew she'd satisfy soon. For now it was enough to hold each other under the magical Christmas sky with all its promise. When reluctantly, she sensed, he moved his lips away from hers, Sophie whispered, "And how did I get so lucky?" before they slowly walked the rest of the way to join the others.

It was only when Sophie walked through the church door that she remembered one more thing from the evening.

No one had asked her how she'd gotten out of the room.

Faith was anything but thankful for the reason, but she was appreciating this quiet Christmas Eve. Truly all was calm and all was bright. Amy had been improving steadily since she'd been discharged from the hospital yesterday morning. Since Monday Niki, Tricia, and the rest of the staff had taken over for Faith. Today was the last big job until New Year's—a staff luncheon at one of the IT firms in Burlington, and Niki reported it had all gone so well the president had booked them for next year already.

Instead of her usual late night/early morning gift wrapping, she had been doing it this evening in her bedroom, checking on Amy in between tying bows and writing tags. To welcome her home from the hospital Pix had brought over a beautifully trimmed tabletop tree for Amy's room, and Faith had left the tiny lights on. With both bedroom doors open, she could see the soft glow in the hallway. Dr. Kane had told them not to worry if Amy slept most of the time, which she was. "Keep an eye on her temperature and wake her to keep her hydrated with whatever she feels like drinking, preferably something with protein and calories— smoothies would be great, but she may just want fruit juice for now." That had been the case until this evening, when Amy asked for ice cream and Faith made a strawberry-banana shake with a large scoop of soy powder.

Yet what had proved the best medicine so far was the get-well card Amy's English teacher had delivered signed by the whole class. Some of the students had added messages, and Faith made a list of those names. Once Amy was better and back at school, Faith hoped to help her make some new friends. Maybe a small party at the catering kitchen for some of the girls. Cupcakes were the in food these days, and they could make some fun ones.

Over the next week Faith knew she and Tom would have to work hard to convince Amy that things would be better at school, avoiding the start of what could become a deep-seated phobia. She only hoped Amy would be well enough to go back. Also, they had to keep assuring her that Ben's upcoming trip would be safe. Ben had already told his sister this, showing her the letters he'd received from the family in France. The son was his age and the daughter was the same as Amy. "Just like us except the dad is a lawyer and the mom teaches school." He'd promised to bring her back a few special Tintin books, a favorite, and large bars of Côte d'Or chocolate in flavors not available here.

Tom and Ben would be at church late, but Faith knew they'd both be ravenous despite the early dinner she'd given them. She'd left a stack of roast beef, sharp cheddar, and horseradish mayo sandwiches—their favorite—on the kitchen table next to the plate of cookies for Santa and a carrot for Rudolph. Last year when she'd suggested they skip it, both kids were appalled. "Mom, it's a custom!" Amy had declared. There was ginger beer for Ben and Sam Adams Old Fezziwig Ale for Tom in the fridge.

She wasn't listening to her usual carols; she wanted to be able to hear Amy, and without the music Faith's mind drifted. Sophie had called yesterday to chat and again this morning, wanting to check on Amy. The fancy family dinner must be about over and they would be headed to their Christmas Eve service. Yesterday's conversation was all about Amy, but today Sophie had told Faith about the dresses she'd ordered from Bergdorf's and the jewelry she would be wearing. From the sound of it, the Maxwells' safe-deposit box was not that far removed from Aladdin's cave. Tomorrow there would be more revelry in Savannah. The Maxwells and their circle of friends had Christmas Day open houses, not the traditional Southern New Year's ones, although Faith was sure there would be plenty of those.

Sophie wanted Faith and the kids to come for the February school vacation, and the notion of leaving a

New England winter was extremely appealing. Sophie hoped to be in her own house by then, but even if she wasn't, there was plenty of room where she was now. Faith wanted to take a good look at the famous wardrobe—and the anonymous threatening note. At least, she thought with relief, nothing had happened since, and soon Will would be finished with the job in Atlanta.

The Maxwells were very different from the Fairchilds, but Faith kept being reminded of her own first year of marriage when she thought about the young couple. Like Sophie, she had come to a place that was unlike the place where she had grown up. And now it was where her children called home, like Sophie's would. Her children. Faith felt a small lump in her throat. Growing up fast. Too fast.

Throughout the holidays, she had tried not to suppose that it would be the last Thanksgiving, the last Christmas in Aleford. Tom had been open with the church on the South Shore, telling them he was interested but that he needed to get to know them better and they him. When he preached in January it would not be as a candidate.

As the weeks had passed, he was torn about whether to tell First Parish's Vestry about the possibility. Faith wasn't sure if he was concerned they would hand him his hat in a hurry or the opposite. From long experience she knew it was difficult to predict what a church's governing body would do at any given time. She had remained supportive, listening to Tom and trying to match his enthusiasm. Change was healthy, she told herself. New chapters. Tom mustn't feel stuck. But why didn't she? In earlier years she would have jumped at the chance to leave the small town. But Tom's sabbatical year in Cambridge made her realize how embedded she—and her children—were in Aleford. No Pix, all the Millers, Ursula, the Averys, other friends, the business. She needed to stop thinking about it now. Whatever Tom decided would be fine. The whole "whither thou goest" thing. She shelved the prospect of leaving once again—it was getting to be a reflex.

The last gift was wrapped. She peeked in on Amy and took the packages downstairs. She still had the stockings to fill. Tomorrow Tom and Ben would head down to Norwell for the Fairchild Christmas dinner. Faith would bring a book and sit with Amy in her room or maybe move her downstairs to the sofa in front of the fire if the patient felt up to it.

It would be a good day, this Christmas Day, and rare for the lack of work—all obligations—save tending to Amy. A day Faith wished away with all her heart. Wished Amy would be opening gifts under the tree and finding the most special gift—an open ticket to go see Daisy in California—in her stocking. Wished this last week, Amy's entire difficult fall, had never happened.

She went to make a cup of tea. She would sit by her daughter's side all night, as she had these last two, and be there when she woke up in the morning.

"Merry Christmas, my love," Will said. Sophie, half awake, had moved closer, her head nestling into the crook of his arm. Now fully awake, she was torn between wanting to stay exactly where she was—possibly for the entire day—and giving Will the presents she'd put under the tree last night when they'd come back. He solved the problem for her.

"Come on! Let's see what Mr. Claus left—and I need coffee."

Sophie jumped out of bed and reached for the dressing gown at the foot of it, putting it on.

"Sure you need that?" Will teased. "You're not in the frozen north anymore and I kind of like the idea of seeing my wife in the buff with maybe a little bit of tinsel around her neck."

"Will! What if someone drops by or peeks in the window!"

"Have it your way, but I still think it's a fine idea."

He pulled on some sweats and they went downstairs into the kitchen.

As the coffee was brewing, Sophie heated up some muffins she'd picked up. Despite the amount of food she expected they'd be consuming the night before, she knew her husband's appetite. In addition to the muffins she had a Savannah Rum Runners cake from the bakery of the same name, which she kept hearing was delicious at any time of year but a special holiday treat. She'd sent one to the Fairchilds along with River Street pralines and an assortment of honeys from the Savannah Bee Company.

"How about some eggs?" she asked. "I can do an omelet or just scrambled? There's bacon, too."

"Presents first. Let's have this under the tree for now, but I might could eat eggs and bacon later. Maybe even much later."

Sophie gave him a kiss. No question. Best Christmas ever and it was only eight o'clock.

"You first," Will said, handing her a large box wrapped in shiny gold paper, tied with scarlet ribbons.

"No, you!" She couldn't wait to see whether he loved the prints she had had framed as much as she did.

He did and there was a time out for more of what Uncle Paul called "canoodling" before Will said, "Come on, Sophie. Your turn."

She smiled broadly as she opened the box. It appeared to be filled with shredded paper. "I hope I don't have to paste all this together to find out what it is!"

"Would I do that to you? Keep digging."

She did, expecting a small box buried at the bottom. Earrings or something else that Will had picked out. Much as she was pleased by the jewelry that had belonged to his mother and grandmother—who wouldn't be?—Sophie knew she would treasure more modest pieces selected by Will just for her.

But there was no box. Just an envelope with a lump at one end.

"Open it!" Her husband was clearly tickled with himself.

Sophie tore the flap and pulled out a sheet of paper. A key dropped out. She took one look and threw her arms around him, giving a little shriek of joy. The paper was the listing for the house on Habersham.

"Will Tarkington Maxwell! You didn't! You didn't just go and buy the very house I wanted in all of Savannah?" She had suddenly developed a Southern accent, she noticed.

"I guess maybe I did, although it's going to be in your name, too. Haven't closed on it yet. But they did accept my offer."

She pulled him to his feet. "Can we go see it now? Oh, of course we can't." She frowned. "They haven't moved out yet, right?"

Will shook his head. "But they *are* away for the holidays and they did say I could bring you by."

Sophie was already at the bottom of the stairs. "Let's get going! We don't have to be at your parents' open house or any of the others until this afternoon, right? Oh, Will, I can't believe you did this!" She had a sudden anxious thought, remembering Laura's words. "You don't think it's too small, do you? I mean we're both tall and there are only two bedrooms and two baths. But there's a garden and a garage."

Will was following close behind and kissed the back of her neck. "Maybe we'll have to move after child number five, but for now it should do just fine."

"Five!"

"Maybe six."

On the way over Will told her that the only drawback was the move-in date. The current owners couldn't get into their new place until March, so that was a condition of sale.

"That's not far away at all," Sophie enthused. "And it will give me plenty of time to pick out paint colors. Oh! Our very own house. Pinch me!" She had told him about the listing and how much she liked it, but that had been a while ago and he hadn't seemed to take it in.

There was a large magnolia wreath with a silver bow on the bright red front door. Two cast iron urns were filled with more greens. Sophie paused to admire the wrought iron balcony that stretched across the front of the house. It was all even more beautiful than she had remembered.

They stepped inside into the hall and faced an elegant curving staircase to the left just beyond a curved arch marked by two columns.

"You've probably noticed this kind of foyer in other houses. My family house has a large one. The design is intended to create the illusion of a tiny 'yard' separating the rest of the house from the street. From the other side, looking out the open door, the columns frame the view. I should be carrying you over the threshold. We'll do that once it's totally ours."

The house didn't feel small at all with its high ceilings. "I won't have to do anything," Sophie said, almost disappointed. "These are exactly the colors I'd choose!" Celadon in the hall and butter cream frosting in the parlor, which also had a beautiful fireplace. The house was decorated sparsely for the holidays—no doubt because the owners were away—but there was a row of red amaryllis in bloom marching across the ornate mantel, reflected in the bull's-eye mirror above.

"Right away the house reminded me of the house I grew up in," Will said. "I had the feeling I'd been in it before. It just felt like home. Come on—check out the kitchen. They redid it last year, but it's not all stainless steel and concrete counters."

In fact it looked like an updated version of Lydia Scriven's. Sophie hadn't had a chance to tell Will much about her new friend and did so as they toured the rest of the house.

"I've seen her walking her little dog. Let's have her to dinner here. Have lots of dinners. Maybe get a dog, too."

Will was in very high spirits.

The master bedroom was at the rear and there was a door to a screened-in veranda overlooking the small garden.

"Gloria can give y'all advice about these plantings. They seem to be in good shape. But there isn't anything she doesn't know about gardens and any plant you can name. Dirt under her fingernails is why she never gets a manicure, she'll tell you. A waste of money when she's just going to be digging again."

Sophie had assumed Gloria hired garden designers and others to do the actual work. She looked forward to showing off her own little plot and asking for help. She wanted lots of old-fashioned perennials.

The master bath had the original big claw-foot tub, but a modern rain forest shower. "Glad they didn't change this out," Will said, pointing to the tub. "Think we can both squeeze in. Want to give it a dry run?"

She took his hand and then kissed him hard. They were going to be very happy here.

There was another veranda off the kitchen across the back of the house leading to the garden, and the garage was on one side.

"I don't have the key, but there's storage space above. It's large enough for another room. They had planned to put in a mother-in-law apartment. We could do that for guests and my mother-in-law. I'm very fond of Babs, and Ed can get plenty of golf in."

"I can't wait to tell her about the house. Let's try calling before we have to go out." Sophie gave a little sigh. Much as she enjoyed Savannah social life, and her in-laws, she wished they could have spent the day alone together—if not here in the new house, then in the borrowed one.

Will was looking at her, and it seemed he was thinking the same thing. "We'll have lots and lots of time for just the two of us. Now, let's go find us some of that mistletoe from Bells Mills Gloria has hanging all over the town house."

Faith waved good-bye to Tom and Ben. They'd opened stockings in Amy's room early, enjoying eggs, bacon, and biscuits dripping with some of the honey Sophie had sent. The other presents waited until after church, and now her two men were off to the South Shore for the Fairchild Christmas dinner. Faith didn't dare give them even a crumb that might spoil their appetites. Marian had been cooking all the family favorites for days, starting with the blue cheese and scallion spread on Melba toast and pigs in a blanket that had appeared as hors d'oeuvres probably since the first Fairchild set foot upon some sort of rock. There would be turkey with all the trimmings and, late in the day, pies, fruitcake—a palatable one—and that New England staple: Indian pudding. Faith was not sure which tribe had passed the recipe along and suspected it might have been one associated with a recipe on the back of a corn-meal box, but no Fairchild holiday was complete without the warm golden brown pudding chock-full of molasses, brown sugar, ginger, nutmeg, cinnamon, and topped with vanilla ice cream. It had taken her awhile, but she had come to enjoy it—or maybe it was just eating it with the whole family amid their chorus of "yums."

There was a knock on the kitchen door, and she darted to the back of the house. Amy hadn't wanted to move downstairs and was asleep now, biding time until she could Skype with Daisy on the West Coast to tell her about the best Christmas present ever that she'd found in her stocking.

Pix was at the door, carrying a tray covered with plates wrapped in aluminum foil. "Since you can't come to Christmas, Christmas is coming to you. I was pretty sure you would just make a sandwich or eat cornflakes!"

Pix knew Faith didn't eat packaged cereal, but the thought behind the comment was dear. She hadn't planned on cooking anything. "You are a love! And Merry Christmas! This smells delicious. Do you have time to sit down and have a glass of wine or are you about to have dinner?"

"We're still waiting for Samantha and her new boyfriend. They had to go to his parents first. Poor babies. They'll be stuffed by the end of the day—two Christmas dinners!"

Faith took a bottle of prosecco from the fridge. "Cassis or au naturel?"

"A drop of cassis sounds very celebratory."

They talked for a bit, and as Faith was pouring refills—the flutes were small—she stopped suddenly.

"Pix! I just remembered something! These last days have been so eventful that it went completely out of my mind. Millicent wasn't at the D.A.R. luncheon Monday." She filled the glasses to the brim and sat down.

Pix looked stunned. "And she wasn't in church last night or this morning. But then she often goes to her own church at the holidays, even though she considers herself an unofficial member of First Parish."

"Has your mother said anything about her? Now Ben has been meeting Millicent at the library for whatever she's doing on the computer, but not since last weekend. He's leaving for France in a few days and busy getting packed, although from what I can tell it's all fitting into a small knapsack. He may not realize he has to pack clothes in addition to his iPad, phone, and power converters."

"Ursula hasn't said anything. I'll ask her as soon as I go back. But, Faith, this is serious. Millicent would never miss a D.A.R. event, especially not the holiday luncheon!"

"I can't leave Amy. Maybe when Tom gets back he can go over, but it could be late."

Millicent kept New England hours, rising with the birds and going to sleep with them. Faith still hadn't gotten used to the fact that any call after eight o'clock at night meant an emergency in Aleford.

"I'll go now," Pix said. "She may not be home. I think she usually goes to some cousin in Weston for Christmas Day. I can make up a plate of desserts as an excuse."

"Add some of these. I know she doesn't like sweets, but these pralines that Sophie sent have a little kick." Faith transferred some of the confection from the large box to a Ziploc bag. "And call me."

After Pix left, Faith sat down to eat. The smells were tantalizing, and while Pix tended toward meals from cartons that had HELPER written on them, she could cook a turkey, stuffing, mashed potatoes, creamed onions, and gravy with the best of them. The cranberry sauce with orange peel was Faith's own from the jar that she'd given Pix on Sunday.

She slowly sipped the rest of her wine. What on earth could be going on with Miss McKinley?

They'd decided to start with the open house at Will's parents, and from the sounds that greeted them as they walked in, so had most of Savannah. Carlene, resplendent in Christmas, or more likely University of Georgia, red velvet, was the first to greet them. "Merry Christmas y'all!! I swear, Sophie, where do you get such gorgeous dresses?"

Now that she was here, Sophie was glad. She wanted to celebrate—being in such a wonderful family, wonderful marriage, and now wonderful new home. She told Carlene, who squealed appropriately, grabbing a spoon to tap her glass for quiet. "Hey! Will and Sophie have bought a house! Best of all it's right around the corner from Randy and me!"

This brought congratulations and hugs from people Sophie knew and many she didn't yet. Standing next to Will, she was bursting with joy. Then Laura appeared. She moved in close to Sophie and hissed, "So you got your way. I told Will the place was too small, but he was dead set on making you happy."

Like that's a bad thing? Sophie thought to herself, realizing that Laura knew of the purchase before Sophie herself because Will would have used Laura as the Realtor. Even if she hadn't actually shown the house, it was multilisted, and for better or worse, Miss Belvedere was their agent.

It was Christmas, and in that spirit, Sophie said, "You'll have to come for dinner once we've moved in."

"Sure"—the acceptance sounded somewhat halfhearted—"now I have to go home or my family will about kill for not helping with our do. Y'all be sure to come to us next. You've never seen the house. It's the big old Savannah gray brick on the corner by Telfair."

There was a definite emphasis on "big." Sophie just smiled. Nothing could bother her today. Not even Laura.

She moved into the back parlor—the pocket doors were open to make one large space. A flash of bright green caught her eye: Ruth Stafford, in a brilliant emerald dress that left no doubt about how toned the body beneath was. She was talking to Randy, and the blinking holiday-tree-light earrings she wore were sending tiny bits of color across her animated face.

"Hey, Sophie," Randy called out. "Or I should say 'neighbor'?"

She went over, and after giving her a hug, Randy said, "Something is very wrong here. There is no glass in your hand. Don't move an inch; I'll be right back to fix this terrible calamity." He moved off into the crowd.

"I am surely not in Illinois," Ruth said, looking after him fondly. "It was lovely of your family to invite me today."

"Maxwell and Maxwell is like family," Sophie said, happy that someone had remembered to include Ruth and chastising herself for not thinking of it. The firm's associates and significant others were all here. But then it wasn't her house. Or was it? According to Laura, it was Will's. And what was his was theirs. She shook her head to clear her thoughts. She didn't want any house except the very one she now had.

She turned her attention to Ruth. "Did you do the Christmas run this morning?" Sophie asked.

"Yes, it was wonderful! Afterward we all crowded into the Sentient Bean for breakfast. It's a great coffee shop near Forsyth Park."

"I'm surprised it was open," Sophie said.

"I was too, but someone had checked and it's where we go a lot, so a perfect start to the day. And being here is the cherry on top!"

Will came over and greeted Ruth. "These folks"—he gestured to his wife and Randy, who was back with a cup of punch for Sophie—"think they're the ones keeping the firm in business. But I know who is really keeping things on track. They'd be lost without you. Merry Christmas!"

Ruth blushed, which made her even prettier.

A server approached with a tray of assorted hot hors d'oeuvres. Sophie recognized a version of the Southern Sushi they'd had at the Olde Pink House, as well as small crab cakes, skewers of shrimp, and hush puppies. She'd have to pace herself, as they'd planned to go to three other houses after this one. Still, all she'd had for breakfast was a muffin.

"The hush puppies are great—they have a little cayenne," Randy said. "And be sure you get some oysters. Mama fusses about this party every year—that there won't be enough food, but I always tell her—"

"Tell her what?" Gloria gave her son a playful tap on the arm. "What could you possibly tell me that I don't already know?"

"Nothing, Mama," Randy said in mock obedience. "Was only adding that folks come for the drink, too, and your famous fancy to-go cups." He pointed toward the front door, where rows of sturdy silver and gold plastic cups stood waiting.

"You girls go mingle. Don't let this naughty boy of mine monopolize you," Gloria instructed. "And, Randy, I want you to go tell the caterer to have the servers top up everyone. Will, you'd better go with him. Make sure he doesn't get sidetracked talking to everybody on the way. It's a thirsty crowd!"

Sophie gave Ruth a hug. "Merry Christmas. I guess we'd better do as we're told. New Year's lunch?"

"Absolutely," Ruth agreed and went off toward the front of the house.

Sophie stayed put for a moment, taking in the scene. As usual Savannahians had come determined to have fun. Even the elderly cousins had abandoned their muted colors and were sporting bright silk shirts, one red and one green, with circle skirts to match.

But where was Patty Sue? Sophie thought it was all hands on deck for the start of the family open house. Maybe she was late? Overserved last night? Sophie was almost sure it had been her sister-in-law who had locked Sophie in the box room. No one else made sense. The question was why? Could it all be because Will hadn't married the right woman? Surely it couldn't be a grudge against Sophie's Northern roots. She'd been hoping to catch a telltale look of guilt on the young woman's face when she saw Sophie today.

"You look very serious for such a festive gathering."

It was Francis Whelan—Sophie remembered to add "the third" mentally as well—the elderly gentleman she had met while peering into the tunnel at The Pirates' House. Today he was wearing what she had heard referred to as "an ice cream suit"—ivory linen—over a red-and-white-striped shirt, the pelican cane over one arm.

"Merry Christmas," she said. "I don't feel serious, just the opposite! Will and I have a new house."

He nodded. "So I hear. That little jewel on Haber-sham."

Sophie was not surprised. Word traveled fast here. "I'm sorry I haven't had time to come to the Mercer Williams House for a tour," she apologized.

"We'll both be there for a while. No rush."

They were standing in front of the portrait of Aurora Maxwell. Francis gestured toward it. "We were all more than a little in love with her. You can see from this how beautiful she was, but it doesn't show other qualities she had. You felt as if you were the most important person in the world when she talked to you. That what you had to say was exactly what she had been pining to hear. Cherished. That's it. She made people feel cherished."

For the second time in twenty-four hours, Sophie said, "I wish I had known her. And Will's mother, Amanda, as well. Paul McAllister married my great-aunt Priscilla, and I'm looking forward to learning more from him about his sister and his niece."

"I know Paul well. And knew Priscilla. I'm sorry for your loss, and then these two women as well. Tragic. Just tragic beyond the imagining, especially Aurora. I still find it hard to believe."

This wasn't the time nor place to ask him more, but here was her best source, Sophie realized. Before she could frame a way to ask him something that might lead to a future conversation, Francis said, "I often go out to Bonaventure to visit them—and plenty of others, too. It's a beautiful place, isn't it?"

Sophie had to admit she hadn't been to the cemetery yet. He seemed surprised. "You don't have a disinclination for such places, I hope?"

"No," she said—in fact she found most cemeteries places of peace and beauty—and certain ones, like Highgate in London and Mount Auburn in Massachusetts, fascinating. "Somehow I haven't gotten out to Bonaventure." It was a partial truth. After the incident with Aurora's wedding gown the night of the party here in the same house, Sophie had avoided thinking about the famous burial ground.

Francis was studying her face. "I'll take you. After New Year's. You'll be fine." He kissed her hand, smiled, and Sophie felt rather cherished herself.

She remembered he had promised to tell her about Sherman's gift to Lincoln. "Do you have time to tell me more about that Christmas present you mentioned when we last talked?"

"I always have time to relate events of the past. The future is a tad murkier." He straightened up. "You know about Sherman's infamous March to the Sea, how all Savannah was prepared to suffer the same fate as the rest of Georgia? On December twenty-first at four o'clock in the morning Dr. Richard Arnold surrendered the city, waving a white flag, and Sherman took possession, making the very handsome Green-Meldrim house on Chippewa Square his headquarters—a pleasant change, I should imagine, from a tent. Green was a British cotton factor, so self-interest definitely played a part. The general sent Lincoln a telegram on the twenty-second, and I quote: 'To His Excellency President Lincoln, Washington, D.C.: I beg to present you as a Christmas gift the city of Savannah, with one hundred and fifty heavy guns and plenty of ammunition, also about twenty-five thousand bales of cotton.' "

"Why did he spare Savannah after having destroyed so much else?" Sophie asked.

"There are a number of theories, some much more plausible than others—the least being that he had a lady friend in the city. You've seen photos of him, no doubt. To say he was plain is being kind, and besides, he was a devoted family man despite what we may think of him otherwise."

"Maybe because of the city's beauty—the way Paris was saved during the Second World War?"

"I'd like to think so, but I believe it was the valuable cotton—piled up because of the blockade—and the fact that the port was essential to the Union cause to ferry supplies and reinforcements for the next phase of the war Sherman had planned. The port, and all

Savannah as a base, would have been rendered useless if destroyed. A discussion to be continued, my dear. Now, I must go on to several other houses before I lose what energy I have."

Sophie kissed him on the cheek and said, "Merry Christmas, and thank you for telling me the story." And much, much more, she thought.

Patty Sue was at the Belvederes' house and greeted Sophie with apparent warmth. She cooed about the "precious little house Will put in your stocking" and then headed for her real pals, who were clustered around Laura and the punch bowl. Laura's family home was indeed wonderful, as were the two others the Maxwells stopped in at before Will called it quits.

"We've done our duty, pleasant as it has been, but what would you say to some just-you-and-me time? Starting as soon as you pack a small bag. I'm thinking Tybee for two nights."

Their honeymoon house was available. Will had arranged it the week before, and someone had even come in on Christmas Day to turn the heat up. Sophie loved beaches in winter, but winter walks along the ocean until now had always involved many layers of outerwear. She needed her down jacket, but it was a light one she'd picked up at Uniqlo last fall. She'd heard about the

New Year's Day Tybee Polar Plunge, when thousands of people gathered to rush into the frigid—by their standards—ocean and thought what the Bostonians who did the same thing, in lesser numbers and *much* lower temperatures, would say about their Southern counterparts.

They stayed out until dusk began to fall and then returned for the supper Sophie had packed from the provisions she was glad she'd picked up for the Savannah house, not knowing about Tybee. After all the heavy food of the last two days, the version of Salade Lyonnaise she put together—frisée lettuce, crisp bacon, and poached eggs—with a ripe camembert and crusty baguette was more than enough. Friday they slept in, went out for a late breakfast, and returned to the cottage. The beach beckoned, but the wind had picked up and Sophie decided that Will beckoned more.

Saturday morning Will said, "I've got some stuff to do in town and we have to leave this afternoon, I'm afraid. Gloria's brother and his family are arriving, and it does belong to them. But you can stay a few hours more. I'll come back and get you."

Sophie knew that they had to vacate the house but had hoped to have one last lazy morning. "No, that doesn't make sense. I'll come with you," she said, hoping to pick up on what sort of "stuff" Will might have to do.

After making sure the house was in even better shape than when they arrived, and leaving a bottle of champagne in the fridge, they went back to Savannah. Will hadn't responded to any of her gentle queries about what "stuff" he had to do. He didn't change out of his jeans and tee shirt, long sleeved as a nod to the season, but otherwise like all the ones Sophie had seen him in last summer, his gimme hat on his head. Today's was red with Uga the bulldog embroidered in white. Whatever it was, it didn't require dressier garb.

She watched him get back into the Triumph Stag— they'd put the top up today—and made a sudden decision. She'd do some "stuff" of her own—pick up some groceries, buy about a hundred home decorating magazines, and start out in the same direction her husband might be going. She had finally agreed with Will several weeks ago that she needed her own car and bought a small Subaru.

It was easy to keep the vintage sports car in sight. She wasn't following him, she told herself, just taking the same route. He was headed out of town and south. She kept back, feeling a little like she should be wearing a trench coat and fedora. Soon they were outside downtown and before long she recognized the route as the one she'd taken to look at houses at The Landings on Skidaway Island across the Moon River Bridge. Was Will going to see someone out there? Maybe get in a couple of rounds of golf? But he would have said. Golf was in his blood just as much as almost every other person she'd met since moving to Savannah. She'd have to take it up one of these days, if only to keep the stunned expression from faces when she revealed her unfamiliarity with the sport.

No, he wasn't going across the bridge, but turning right onto another road. There was a sign for the Pin Point Heritage Museum, surely closed for the holidays. She let him get far ahead. According to the map on her GPS there weren't too many streets nearby. There were a lot of Subarus—not as many as in Maine, where the brand was the state car—but she didn't want to chance Will spotting her.

And so she lost him. She went down the winding streets, but her husband's car had completely disappeared. At last she turned around and headed for the Piggly Wiggly.

Will still wasn't back when she got home, and after seeing an e-mail from Patrick Smith asking for a small change in wording before he signed the contract, she decided to go to the office and do it herself. Maxwell & Maxwell was closed until January 2. It was a simple change, and she could do it without bothering Ruth. She left a note for Will inside the front door and went out.

Letting herself into the firm, Sophie was surprised to hear a voice from Randy's office. The door was open, and as she passed by she saw it was Randy himself on the phone. Hearing him say, "I'll have to get back to you on that," she lingered to tease him about being a workaholic.

"Hey, sis," he said. "What are you doing here?"

"I was about to ask you the same thing. I've been abandoned by my spouse, who had some 'stuff' to do."

"Ah, how quickly the honeymoon ends." His grin took the sting from the words. "But seriously, Sophie, what is so gawd almighty important to bring you into work?"

She told him and he congratulated her again on the new client. "Always wanted to go to the Oscars. Well, Carlene is waiting on me. You be sweet now." And he was gone, locking his office door behind him.

Sophie sent off the revised contract and was rewarded by an almost immediate response. Patrick was working today, too. He planned to be back in Savannah soon and invited her to dinner, "with your husband if he's back." Sophie certainly hoped Will would be. She was tired of being a lonely bride.

But when Will returned late that afternoon she learned to her dismay that he would have to go to Atlanta Monday and Tuesday, driving back "as soon as the Triumph will get me here" on Wednesday for New Year's Eve and New Year's Day. They would be going out to Bells Mills for Hoppin' John, the traditional black-eyed peas and ham dish that guaranteed good luck for the following year.

New Year's Day, it felt as if Sophie had just gotten to sleep when the phone started ringing. Will had gotten home in plenty of time to celebrate their first New Year's Eve together, and they had gone to dinner at Elizabeth on 37th with a small group of Will's college friends who were in town. When they left the restaurant, Sophie realized the whole city was one very big party. They headed to the City Market, which was offering music of every sort imaginable. Later the fireworks over the river had been spectacular. They'd watched from the rooftop bar she had been to with Randy and Carlene. It had been perfect, but they'd finally called it a night, or early morning.

And now her phone was ringing. Mother? But they had just spoken Tuesday. Babs and Ed were leaving Mustique early to visit "dear, dear friends" with a "sweet little place with twelve bedrooms" on Virgin

Gorda. Reassured that Sophie had indeed received the sarongs for Christmas, Babs had been in a rush. They'd agreed to talk once next week.

"Hello?"

"Sophie, it's Randy. I'm afraid I have some very bad news. Ruth Stafford is dead. She killed herself last night."

Chapter 9

"And then he started crying. Oh, Faith, it broke my heart even more. Randy is a happy-go-lucky guy. I never thought he would be the type to break down like this—he couldn't talk. Carlene took the phone and told me what had happened." Sophie's words were coming fast. Faith murmured, "I'm so sorry!" and Sophie barely paused.

"They'd come in around four this morning and were on their way to bed when they saw the answering machine was beeping. Carlene said they were about to ignore it, but she knew she wouldn't sleep—she suffers from an 'overabundance of curiosity,' her words. The message was from Ruth and had been left at midnight. Her voice was slurred and she told them to have a happy New Year and she'd see them in heaven. They thought she might just be drunk, but when she didn't answer her phone, Randy decided he'd better go over and check on her. Carlene went with him. The door to the building was wide open, people were still partying, and her apartment door was unlocked. She was on the couch, an empty bottle of vodka and an empty pill container on the floor next to her. They called nine-one-one and Randy started CPR. They couldn't get a pulse. Carlene said it seemed like only seconds before the ambulance was there and the EMTs. At the hospital the ER doctor said she had probably been dead for some hours. That if she had gotten help right away there was a slim chance she would have made it, but the amount of alcohol she'd drunk swiftly acted to increase the effect of the Ambien—that's what she took. Sleeping pills!"

Faith said how sorry she was once more, but Sophie's words continued to spill out. "I just can't believe it! I saw her Christmas Day. She was so happy! So alive." She started to sob. Until now she hadn't been able to cry, but relating what had happened unleashed her emotions.

Will had gone to the hospital to be with Randy. They were trying to reach Ruth's family in Illinois. Carlene had gone home.

"I wish I could be with you," Faith said. "Suicide, especially when it's someone so young, is the death with no answers. We can't know what was going through Ruth's mind. Sadly, too, the gaiety you saw at Christmas is often a signal that the person who is suffering from depression is planning to end her or his life. A kind of manic episode."

"But she didn't seem depressed. Not in the time I knew her." Sophie gulped back her tears. "But then I really hadn't spent much time with her."

Faith said, "No guilt, Sophie. It's horrible, but this didn't happen because you didn't spend enough time with Ruth."

"She had just started a new relationship. She was so happy, she told me. And it had to have been someone in Savannah or nearby."

"Someone who may have ended things recently, which might have been enough to send her into a tailspin. The new year may not have looked very bright."

The call waiting beeped and Sophie said, "It's Will. I'll talk to you later."

"Any time. I love you, Sophie."

"Love you too—and thank you. I didn't know who else to call."

"I'm glad you did. Take the call and let me know if there's anything I can do. If Amy were better, I'd fly down right away."

Sophie pressed the key on her phone and Will said, "How are you doing, honey? I'll be home soon. We'll try to get some sleep, and then everyone is gathering for New Year's dinner out at Bells Mills as planned. That poor young woman. When Randy said he was concerned about her, he was obviously picking up on things others missed. Maybe some of the people she ran with did, too. She was a runner, right? That's what I've been hearing."

"She was," Sophie said, using the past tense with reluctance. "Did she leave a note? Have you reached her family?"

"No note, but the doctor said that's not unusual. Randy left word with her parents to give him a call. He'll let us know when he's spoken to them. I have to stop at the office and get the papers she filled out when she applied for the job. The only contact information in her purse was for her parents. There may be someone else."

"I'm all dressed. I'll run over. You won't know where to look anyway. Come home and get some sleep."

"I am so sorry, darling. I know how much you liked Ruth."

Sophie started to tear up again. "I'll miss her very much. We were just getting to know each other."

Faith hung up the phone and tried to turn her thoughts to the day ahead, but it was impossible. She did wish she could be with Sophie. It was obviously her first experience with the death of someone her own age, a friend, and the fact that it was suicide made it so much harder.

The last week had seen Amy improve to the point where Dr. Kane said she could return to school next Monday, starting with a half day the first week. Ben was leaving for France tomorrow evening, and Amy seemed to have accepted all their reassurances, although Faith suspected it was Daisy who had provided the most comfort. She'd overheard the girl tell Amy during one of their Skype sessions that Ben had greater odds of getting run over by a bus, particularly in Boston, where she understood they drove like lunatics. She'd added that since the French town was twinned with Aleford, Amy should just think of him as being home except with different food and "kids who drink wine like when they're ten." Amy had said "Yuck" and that she didn't think Ben would be drinking much wine because he was in training pretty much all year round with soccer and basketball.

Some years ago one of First Parish's parishioners had come up with the idea of a January 1 "First Day," inspired by Boston's First Night on New Year's Eve where the entire city became one large celebration— concerts of all sorts, art exhibits, dance, a parade, and fireworks over the harbor. First Day was in a more minor key, but the parish hall had been transformed by volunteers into a festive cabaret, and starting at two o'clock there would be a succession of local talent starting with a country music band called The Grits. Everyone signed up to bring finger food for the buffet. There were nonalcoholic hot and cold drinks.

Faith supplied a seasonal claret cup, a lovely, slightly fruity punch with red wine as a base to which Port, cassis, Grand Marnier, lemon juice, and club soda for fizz were added. (See recipe, page 236.) It was a Sibley family recipe that she had been given as a sacred trust from her father's sister, Aunt Chat, with instructions to be liberal with the Port. First Parish had two large punch bowls—this was New England, after all, where punch was a staple for celebrations—and an army of punch cups. Faith froze a small block of ice in a decorative French ice cream mold to keep the punch chilled and floated thin slices of navel oranges on top of the deep crimson brew. Eating the oranges that had been soaking in the punch after it was gone was one of her favorite treats.

Though Amy wasn't up to attending First Day, Faith felt comfortable leaving her. She would be next door, give or take a few tombstones to wend around.

The parish hall doors opened promptly at two when the band launched into their version of "Auld Lang Syne," starting with a banjo solo. While First Parish sponsored it, the event was open to the entire town. In no time, Faith was getting one of the reserve containers she'd brought to replenish the claret cup.

Pix came over for a cup, smiling mischievously. "I have a very nice New Year's gift for you. Call me when you get home, or better yet I'll come over. I also have something for Ben to take on his trip."

"Tell me!" Faith said. She had never been much for deferred gratification.

"Nope. Too juicy, and someone might overhear me."

Now Faith *really* wanted to know. "Okay. I'm on duty until four. Ben is at a last-minute meeting about the trip, and he'll be home around then, too. Can't you give me a little hint?"

"It will make Amy happy, too, although you won't be able to give her the particulars."

She gave Faith her empty cup to stash under the table with the other dirty ones. At this rate, Faith thought, she'd better run a load in the dishwasher right away. She was about to do so when a woman she vaguely recognized from the D.A.R. luncheon came over and said, "I had expected a wake here at First Parish, what with this being your husband's last First Day here." She gave a little laugh. "I think that's an oxymoron, but you know what I mean."

Unfortunately Faith did. Pix was looking puzzled and then the color drained from her face. "Faith, why would this be Tom's last First Day?"

The woman answered before Faith could. "Oh, me and my big mouth. He's going to announce it today, right?" She turned toward Pix. "I have a friend in the church on the South Shore where the Fairchilds are going. She's very excited."

"Please," Faith said anxiously, "I'd appreciate it if this went no further. Nothing has been decided, and there will definitely not be any kind of announcement today." *Or maybe ever.* The look on Pix's face was heartbreaking and she was tempted to grab Tom to see it.

The woman headed for the dessert table and Pix said, "It's true, isn't it? Sam and I have often thought Tom would outgrow us and want to move on." There was a catch in her throat as she said, "We've been lucky to have him, and you, this long."

Faith came around to the front of the table and hugged Pix hard. "Nothing, I repeat *nothing*, has been decided. Tom is going to be a guest preacher this month and then we'll see. The kids don't know any of this. *Nobody* was supposed to."

Pix managed a thin smile. "And you've lived here how long?"

She was right. Keeping a secret in Aleford, or any other small New England town, was like herding cats.

"See you later at the house," Faith said. "We'll talk more." She resumed her claret cup duties, pausing to drink one herself.

By four o'clock, Faith was exhausted, mentally and physically. She hadn't been sleeping well, one ear cocked to hear Amy, and she had also admitted to herself that she was a bit worried about Ben's trip. Not by the possibility of a terrorist attack, but simply by the notion of having her son an ocean away. It wasn't like going to camp.

She turned the punch ladle over to the parishioner who came to relieve her and put one more load of cups in the dishwasher before heading out. She stopped to give Tom a kiss, letting him know she was leaving. She did not tell him about the grapevine spreading its tendrils his way. He was having fun, and there was nothing he could do about it now. A bluegrass group was up now, playing a Fairchild favorite: "Roses Are Blooming." Faith left humming the lyric, "Come back to me, darling, and never more roam."

At the parsonage, Amy was watching one of her favorite Miyazaki DVDs, *My Neighbor Totoro*, and Ben wasn't back yet. Tom would have been grazing on the First Day food—Faith had observed this habit among other clergy. Their hours were irregular and they all seemed to have a talent for eating standing up and at any opportunity. She'd made a version of Hoppin' John for the kids and herself for supper, using the traditional black-eyed peas and rice, but with garlic chicken sausages instead of bacon or ham hocks.

Sophie would be out at Bells Mills sitting down to the New Year's dish and other traditional Southern fare about now. Faith doubted she, or the others, would have much appetite. There had been no word, so she assumed there was no further information about why Ruth had chosen to end her short life.

Pix knocked at the door, and Faith quickly waved her in. Worrying about the rumor that would certainly be all over town had not pushed Pix's tantalizing "gift" from Faith's mind. She was eager for her friend to spill the beans—and not the Hoppin' John kind.

"Coffee?" Faith asked. She'd learned early on as a suburban bride that this was the first question to ask anyone walking in your door.

"Thanks, but no. I had a cup of tea with Mother when I dropped her off at her house. Faith, let me tell you: keeping my mouth shut was one of the hardest things I've ever had to do. Her eagle eye was on me from the moment she got into the car until I left. She has always had an uncanny gift for knowing when I'm keeping something from her—or lying."

"I'm sorry," Faith said, also giving a passing thought to the impossibility of Pix telling a lie. Even a polite white one left her friend's face beet red. "So, what is this 'gift' you have for me? Quick. Ben will be home soon and the DVD Amy is watching is almost over."

"Mary Lou, one of the women in my yoga class, is Canadian."

So far, nothing special, Faith thought, although she loved Canadians. They were exceptionally nice, and their food was great, too. Even *poutine*—cheese curds and French fries, you had to give someone credit for imagination. She nodded at Pix, hoping to speed her up.

"Her son manages a ski resort in Quebec. They have all sorts of special contests during high season—ski races, fun obstacle courses—and one couple in particular was cleaning up the prizes, including the 'Significant Others Slalom.' The resort took photos, and when the manager heard that the couple was from Aleford, Massachusetts, he texted one to his mother."

"Still not getting this," Faith said, looking out the window for Ben. Aleford was big on winter sports. It went with the territory. Highly likely that a local couple would be the champion skiers.

"Oh, you will." Pix was grinning. "Mary Lou immediately corrected the names of the Aleford winners sent by her son. They'd checked in for the week between Christmas and New Year's as 'Mr. and Mrs. Anthony Frazer.' Amy's principal's significant pal was none other than his boss, Aleford's superintendent!"

Now Faith got it—and it was a gift! The superintendent wasn't married; the principal was. How could they have been so stupid?

"Mary Lou's son let them know what his mother had revealed, because he was pretty steamed that he'd posted a fake name on the Web site already. Maybe he even took the trophies back. Anyway, the pair checked out immediately. Looks like you have some leverage here to get Amy moved to the other middle school."

It was a delicious thought, but it was also blackmail, Faith promptly told Pix, who shook her head vehemently in disagreement. "They're the miscreants! Besides, you don't have to do a thing. The photo went viral, and they've both resigned for 'personal' reasons. In Tony's case, I'd say it's the fact that his wife, who was with her sick father in Florida, was taking it all *very* personally. Just sit tight. I hear that Amy's elementary school principal will be the acting superintendent. The assistant superintendent doesn't want the job."

This *was* good news. Faith was about to ask Pix whether she should try to get Amy moved before school started again when Ben rushed in. Like his father he never seemed to feel the cold and was wearing only a sweatshirt. For the short journey to the parish hall for First Day, Faith had put on one of Mr. Bean's long down coats, the extreme version used for arctic expeditions.

"*Bonjour, Maman et Madame Miller! Comment ça va?*"

"*Très bien,* and I have something for you." Pix smiled, getting up to give him an envelope. "Bon voyage from us."

"Wow, thank you so much!" Ben said, opening the envelope and discovering some euros.

"You've worked so hard to raise money for the whole group that we wanted you to have some cash that was just for you, but we expect a postcard!"

He gave her a big hug. "Don't worry. I have everybody's address."

Amy wandered in. The film was over. Ben showed her the euros. "They're so pretty," she said. "What's for dinner, Mom?"

Her daughter was on the mend, Faith thought happily, and the whole Mean Girl problem might be, too. Life was good.

Sophie slipped on a jacket and walked over to the office to see if she could find a hard copy of Ruth's application in one of the file cabinets behind the desk where Ruth had worked. They were wooden ones from Will's grandfather's day that Anson insisted they keep for hard copies, claiming he didn't trust computers when it came to saving records.

Letting herself in, Sophie was surprised to see her husband going through the file drawers. "Will, I thought you were going home to rest!" She went over and put her arms around him. It seemed ages since they'd received the call about Ruth's death.

He held her tight. "I'm so sorry," he said. "For us, but particularly for her family. To lose a child . . ."

She knew he was thinking of his mother and grandmother. Even though Amanda hadn't been Aurora's daughter in name, she was in spirit, and to have her predecease was against nature.

"Did you find Ruth's application?" she asked.

"No. Randy hired her, so it may be in his office, but his door is locked. Her computer is password protected. Maybe you can get in?"

As a partner, Sophie could, and while Will began searching, she had another thought. From the way they had greeted her that night at the Olde Pink House bar,

Ruth had obviously been close to her running mates. Sophie needed to let one of them know, and it was also possible that that person might have more information about the woman—a local emergency contact and others who should be notified. Maybe, even, why Ruth had resorted to such a desperate act. Sophie hated to give news like this over the phone, but it would be worse to hear it on the news or read it in the paper. She had no problem recalling the name of one friend—Esmeralda Higgins. Emmie.

Sophie found E. Higgins in Savannah on Switchboard, but would she be home on New Year's Day? The phone rang several times and Sophie was about to hang up when a breathless voice said, "Hello?"

"Hello. Is this Esmeralda, Emmie? I'm Sophie Maxwell. We met before Christmas at the Olde Pink House."

"Yes, of course I remember you. The carol singing! Sorry, I just came in from a run. Happy New Year."

Her tone of voice clearly indicated that she was wondering why Sophie was calling. Sophie took a deep breath.

"I'm afraid I have very bad news. Ruth Stafford died early this morning."

"What!" Emmie screeched. "No! No! That's impossible! I saw her yesterday. She's my running buddy.

Because we're both the same height, have the same stride. No! No! A drunk driver! She was hit?"

"I'm afraid Ruth took her own life."

There was complete silence on the other end of the line.

"I'm so sorry—" Sophie said at last, but Emmie cut her off.

"Maybe she didn't get along with her family all that well—they were total jerks, treated her like shit—but she was definitely not the suicidal type. It *must* have been an accident."

"It wasn't. Some of the people at the office thought she had seemed depressed. Maybe running was her way of coping and then she couldn't anymore."

"But we ran yesterday. She was ecstatic at our times! Best ever!"

Sophie didn't want to say anything more, but this fit with what Faith had said about a manic mood preceding a suicide in some cases.

"The only emergency contact information we have for her is her parents, and we haven't been able to reach them. I remembered you because of your unusual name, but are there others in the group we should notify?"

Emmie was sobbing quietly. "We were *all* her friends. I'll let people know. She got in touch with me about the club initially. I'm the secretary; I can check what she filled out when she joined. Now, if you want. The file is on my laptop."

"Thank you," Sophie said softly. She sensed that Emmie needed to get away from the phone.

While she waited, Sophie quickly told Will. He seemed intent on what he was doing and gave her a brief nod.

It didn't take long for Emmie to find the information. "Here it is," she said. "Ruth listed Mr. and Mrs. Randall Watson with a local address first and her parents second. Do you know who the Watsons are?"

"Yes, Randall Watson is a partner here. He hired Ruth."

Emmie seemed calmer. Resigned. "I'll call her friends. And let me give you my cell. Will there be a service here in Savannah, do you think? I know everyone will want to pay their last respects."

This hadn't occurred to Sophie, but of course they would. "I'll be in touch as soon as I know anything."

"Thank you." Emmie paused. "Would you like to get together sometime to talk? You seemed close to Ruth that night and she talked a lot about how much she enjoyed working for you . . ." Her voice trailed off.

"I would like that very much." Now Sophie started to choke up. "I'll call you soon." She hung up and felt hot tears start to stream down her face. Will was talking to someone on his phone and motioned her over, pulling her tight. She could hear Randy's voice, but not what he was saying.

"See you soon after we stop at home a minute," Will said and slipped the phone into his pocket. "Ruth's parents got back to Randy. We'll hear more out at Bells Mills. Randy said they'd been afraid of this. That she *had* suffered from depression, and this impulsive move away from their support had been worrying them. I want to get out of these clothes and then we'll head out there, okay?"

Sophie nodded, wishing she could crawl into bed and sleep for days, sleep with Will beside her.

It was a somber group gathered around the big dining room table. Anson said the blessing, adding a special prayer in memory of Ruth. The housekeeper, Blanche, had prepared a succulent pork roast to go with the Hoppin' John and other side dishes.

It wasn't long before Patty Sue broke the silence. "Well, I for one am starving and I'm sorry for the poor girl, but nobody knew her. I mean she wasn't even from here." She put a mouthful of peas in her mouth.

Sophie was having trouble even looking at the food and Patty Sue's words completely destroyed any appetite she might have been able to summon up. Remembering Emmie's question, she asked Randy,

"What arrangements are the family making? One of her friends from the running club wondered if there would be any kind of service in Savannah."

Randy shook his head. "She'll be cremated here and the service will be at the family's church in Illinois. The funeral home has set up a site for condolences. I have all the information, and I was wondering how to get it to these friends, so if you would do that, I'd be very grateful."

Sophie nodded. "Emmie—that was her closest friend in the club—was very shocked. None of them had seen any evidence of depression."

"Isn't that always the way?" Carlene said sadly. "I feel terrible. We should have done something. And if only we had gotten the message she left earlier." She put down her fork.

Randy, who was sitting next to his wife, put his arm around her. "Now, sugar, if it hadn't been last night, it would have been another time. Her family said there had been several serious attempts starting when she left high school. I want you to try to put this out of your mind, at least for the next week."

"Listen to him, Carlene. You two haven't been away for a dog's age and you'll love Nassau," Gloria said.

"I don't know that we should go tomorrow. It doesn't seem respectful," Carlene said.

Patty Sue jumped in. "Now that's just silly! Canceling your trip for someone you saw, what, five times? I'll go if you don't want to!"

"Carlene's going, sis," Randy said firmly. "Stop playing the field and find a good man like me to take you places." Sophie was surprised. For once he didn't sound as if he were teasing.

Anson spoke up. "We'll all miss Ruth. She was a lovely, bright young woman. But life goes on. Randall spoke to her parents about setting up some sort of scholarship at the high school she attended in her memory, and the firm will start the donations off."

If Anson had intended to change the topic, it worked, and the conversation turned to Carlene and Randy's upcoming trip. Sophie had never been to Nassau, so she concentrated on trying to swallow some of the peas and rice. Will had planned to leave tomorrow also, but on the drive out to Bells Mills, he'd told her he was staying until Monday.

After dinner, Will suggested a walk out to the dock. The late afternoon light was beautiful. Anson and Gloria said they'd join them.

"There won't be too many more days like this," Anson said. "You'll be surprised at how cold it can get here come February and March, Sophie."

She took his arm. "I believe I will. So far I haven't had to wear any winter clothes. I should pack them all up and send them to Maine. There's a group that distributes warm things to people in need."

"That is so sweet," Gloria said. "I swear you remind me of Will's mother more every day—so kind. When my late husband and I moved to Savannah from Atlanta, she and Anson took us under their wings. Introduced us to everyone, and the four of us just loved being together. My family was from here, of course—" She gestured at the house as they walked toward the water. "But I'd been gone awhile at school and then after I was married we were away for years. When Randy turned four, I put my foot down and said we had to come home. I didn't want him to grow up in a foreign place." She gave a little laugh. Somehow Sophie thought she wasn't kidding. Atlanta might as well have been on some other continent—or Mars.

They sat for a while in companionable silence on the same bench where Sophie and Will had sat after the Lowcountry boil. That evening seemed a very long time ago and recalling how miserable she had been, Sophie gave her husband's hand a squeeze. All was well now.

"You got yourself a pretty little house, Sophie, and I hear from my son that you are an excellent chef. I plan to be your first guest," Anson said. He stood up. "Now I want some of Blanche's coconut layer cake and after that a titch of something."

Inside, Sophie went to freshen up, making sure this doorknob functioned. She'd put that whole incident from her mind, but with the day's tragedy it had come back. She still needed to ask Will who'd said Sophie was feeling ill and had left.

Ask him when no one else was around.

Tom had been dismayed when Faith told him about the comment made in Pix's hearing at First Day, but not overly so.

"Actually we should consider it pretty amazing that it didn't happen sooner. I guess I'd better let the Vestry know."

"Know what?" Faith asked, startled. Tom hadn't even been inside the other church yet.

"That I've been asked to be a guest preacher and that they are looking to fill the position permanently."

She was surprised at how relieved she felt. He hadn't made his mind up.

"I'd like you to come," Tom added. "It's a week from Sunday. Ben will be gone, but Pix could look in on Amy if she still isn't a hundred percent."

"Of course." Faith wanted to see the church—and meet the congregation. Very much. She also realized she had forgotten to fill Tom in on the principal/superintendent scandal.

"And some people say there is no God!" he said. "She can surely go to the other school now."

"I thought I'd call the acting superintendent Monday."

The next afternoon Faith drove Ben to the home of one of the students whose parents had a minivan and were taking everyone to the airport. She wished it had been like the old days at airports and she could have walked down to the gate with him, waving good-bye from the big windows as the plane taxied off. Instead, she had to satisfy herself with a quick squeeze at the car door. Ben returned it even more quickly. He had been on his way in his own mind for days, maybe weeks.

Back home Amy was in the kitchen. "Finally! What took so long, Mom? I want to make cupcakes for you to drop off at Cindy's house. I know you'll say I can't go to the party, but this way I'll kinda be there."

"Cindy?"

Amy looked impatient. "From my English class. She called last week and wanted my cell so we could text. She's giving a surprise party for Isabel. We've been texting, too. She goes to Maine, but not as long a trip as Sanpere. Camden. But that's not all that far, right? And, Mom, I'm going back on Facebook, okay? A lot of people were mad about what Cassie did."

"Whoa. One thing at a time. Yes, you can make cupcakes and I'll help if you like. Camden is close by water, an hour and a half by land. And are you sure about Facebook?"

"I'm sure," Amy said. "If anything else mean happens I'm going to report her."

Well, this was one for the books, Faith said to herself. Now what? Move schools—or not?

The cupcakes were soon baking, and sending a rich chocolate fragrance all over the house while Amy made two kinds of frosting—mocha and peppermint. Tom came in and dipped his finger into the mocha.

"Dad! Stop it! I'll let you lick the bowl," Amy said.

Tom kissed the top of his daughter's head, meeting Faith's eyes. It wasn't hard to tell that his thoughts mirrored her own.

"Who was it on the phone?" Faith asked.

"Millicent. All very mysterious. I've been summoned to her house and she asked me to pick up Ursula. She said if Amy was well enough you could come, too."

Faith was under no illusions as to her status with Millicent but was happy to have been included. Maybe they would finally find out what had been going on all fall and winter with the woman.

"I have to drop these cupcakes off first. I'll meet you there. Amy, if you need us you'll call?"

"Duh! But I won't. Cindy, Isabel, and I are rereading all the Nancy Drews. They don't think they're stupid like Cassie said. They're classics! I'm starting with *The Hidden Staircase*. And, Mom, they think it's really cool that you solved some mysteries!"

Tom's face darkened. Faith knew her husband definitely did not think any of her involvements with murder and crime was "cool."

By the time she finished her errand and arrived at Millicent's, Ursula and Tom were sitting with cups of tea around Miss McKinley's formal dining room table. She was at the head, a stack of papers next to her.

"I am assuming that what I am about to divulge will stay in this room and go no further, although"— Millicent gave a gracious nod of the head much like royalty—"Ursula, you may tell your daughter in confidence. I would have invited her, but I didn't want a crowd." She looked at Faith. "Faith is here because I wanted to start by thanking both Fairchilds for the help their son has provided. Dare I say he saved my life—oh, not literally, but figuratively?"

Faith was stunned. What on earth could Ben have done?

"You may recall the speaker at the historical society last fall. A Harvard professor." Millicent's tone suggested another profession, something like "garbage collector." "I ventured to correct him on a point regarding the Rivoire family, the Revere's French antecedents."

"Yes, wasn't the talk called 'Paul Revere and the French Connection'?" Faith said.

"And a very silly, extremely inappropriate title it was. As if you have to pander to get individuals to listen to our nation's history." She gave Faith a look that clearly indicated there should be no further interruptions from her.

"Several weeks later the professor sent me a copy of a letter that he had come across in his research written by Paul Revere to a friend." Millicent passed a sheet of paper to each of them. "Since it is difficult to read the writing, I will summarize. The gist of the letter was that the silversmith was annoyed at one Ezekiel Revere— 'so called,' he notes—who was passing himself off as some sort of cousin in order to drum up business for his foundry. The significant sentence reads: 'Said Ezekiel is no relation whatsoever.'"

"Oh no," Ursula gasped. "This means . . ."

"Exactly," Millicent said. "It meant that I was not who I thought I was, nor were my parents, grandparents, and so forth. Frauds. All of us frauds who were living a lie."

Her words to Tom made sense to Faith now—"*She asked me what I would do if someone I respected had been lying to me for many years.*"

Tom was obviously recalling them as well. "But, Millicent, how could any of you have known? And I must say I think it was particularly mean-spirited of the professor to bring it to your attention."

Faith agreed—let sleeping Reveres lie, as they had been for a very long time.

"No, Reverend. He was merely doing what he thought was his duty. I despaired for a while. Perhaps you may have noticed that I was keeping to myself."

All three nodded, and Ursula was so bold as to pat Millicent's hand, receiving the hint of a smile in return.

"And then one day I was listening to an interesting piece on NPR about using the Web to research one's ancestry. I decided that I would find out just who I was—or more specifically, who Ezekiel had been." She patted a stack of papers. "Ben and I have been on a voyage of discovery together."

"We are happy he could help," Tom said.

"Oh, he more than helped! You will read all the results in a little monograph I am putting together on the subject. I do not wish to cast aspersions on Paul Revere. It could well be that he was ignorant of the facts, but more likely ashamed. I will explain. Ben was able to trace the foundry records. It was initially called the 'Hitchborn Works.' Deborah Hitchborn was Paul Revere's mother. She came from a large and well-connected family." There was a pause while Millicent preened, letting this fact sink in. "Ben and I began to suspect that Ezekiel was indeed a cousin of Paul's, but on the Hitchborn side—or possibly a brother of Paul's, born on the wrong side of the blanket."

All very interesting, but Faith was tempted to ask, "What's it all about, Alfie?"

Millicent pulled out a file with a flourish. "Ben urged me to have my DNA tested to see whether there might be a match with known Revere descendants."

Her son was a genius! And brave. Millicent would not have called them all here together were it not a happy issue out of all misfortune.

"I *am* a Revere. There is no doubt whatsoever."

Millicent stood up and went over to her sideboard. The framed mourning rings composed of the hair from those authenticated ancestors looked brighter than Faith had ever seen them.

"I believe this calls for a celebration. Sherry, anyone?"

Faith had the distinct feeling that the universe had settled back into place. No need to ask how or why Ezekiel had appropriated the name "Revere." It was in his blood, and Millicent's, too.

Monday morning arrived much too swiftly, but the weekend had been a time of healing and reflection. Ruth had been only a year younger than Sophie. Will pointed out that this made his wife's grief sharper, and it was true. She realized that her own happiness—her marriage, the new house, and the prospect of starting a family in the future, all things Ruth would never have— made her feel the loss more intensely. Saying good-bye to Will was eased by his promise to finish the job in Atlanta as soon as possible. "A few days more at most, darling, maybe sooner," he'd said, much to her joy.

Her phone was ringing as Sophie walked into her office. She answered it quickly.

"Hello, Mrs. Maxwell. It's Francis Whelan, and I know it's very short notice, but I'm hoping you'll have time today to go out to Bonaventure since I'll be departing at week's end to meet some friends in Venice. I am partial to the city in January."

Why not? Sophie thought. Things were slow in the office, and Will would be back soon. She'd want to be with him. Today was perfect.

"I am at your disposal." The courtly gentleman was influencing her choice of words. She added, "And please do call me Sophie."

"Meet me at the Mercer Williams House in an hour? It's on Monterey Square on Bull Street. I can give you a quick tour and then we can head out of town. We can take my car."

"That sounds wonderful, but are you sure you can spare the time if you are leaving so soon?"

"Time is what I most have to spare. Shall we say ten o'clock?"

Francis was waiting on the sidewalk in front of the house next to a bright red vintage sports car. "Bought it brand-new back in 1962. A Thunderbird Sports Roadster with Kelsey wire wheels, not that that means anything to you, I imagine, but it meant the world to me. Thought I was very hot stuff back then."

"And still are," Sophie said, thinking of Uncle Paul and his car, now theirs. Will would love to see this one.

Francis led her around the back of the house and inside through a gift shop. "I can be candid with you and not mince words as needs must with most of the people who come to visit the house. No Mercer ever lived here, particularly not Johnny, and no, I will not be discussing anything to do with the murder case involving my friend Jim Williams. As you will soon see, he was a true artist and a collector of all things beautiful."

Sophie smiled. "I regard The Book as 'faction'—a hybrid of fact and fiction—and would much rather hear what you can tell me about the house's true history."

"I knew you were my kind of girl from the moment I met you. So to start at the very beginning, the house was designed by John Norris. Construction was begun by Johnny's great-grandfather, General Hugh Weedon Mercer, in 1860. As it turned out, not the most auspicious time to embark upon a building project of this scope. The war interrupted things and the general had to sell it as it was. The house was completed in 1868."

As they wandered through the rooms, Francis pointed out the expert faux painting done by Jim Williams himself on baseboards and other areas to simulate wood and marble. "Jim bought this place in 1969 and restored it to more than its original glory. At a very young age, he was one of the pioneers in saving places from the wrecking ball all over the Lowcountry. And you can see from the paintings, furnishings, and everything else here that he had the 'eye'—that gift that enabled him to spot something all the rest of us would have walked by or thought was junk."

"It feels as though he just stepped out," Sophie said. "Not like a museum, but a place someone lived." She added, "Someone who loved it." The feeling was strongest in the drawing room, with its magnificent chandelier and portraits. The house on Habersham was on a different scale entirely, but she was longing for March and the chance to furnish her own nest.

Francis nodded. "Yes, Jim loved it. Many's the time I sat with him over a glass or two and he'd tell me about a recent find. Of course his big parties were something else altogether. We won't see their like again, not even in Savannah. Now, let's head out to Bonaventure. I've brought a picnic. Cemeteries make a wonderfully peaceful spot for an outdoor repast. I had Clary's do up some sandwiches and sides. Hope you don't mind."

"Mind? I'm delighted." Sophie linked her arm through Francis's as they left the house. She resolved to come back and take in the rooms again soon. Despite its notorious place in popular culture, she found it soothing, an oasis where one could lose oneself in the beauty of a bygone era. Will had been to the house many times, no doubt, but she wanted him to come with her, too. Wanted to go into all the house museums and everything else in Savannah with him. She almost laughed aloud. She was definitely becoming a native.

As soon as Francis had parked and they walked into the cemetery, Sophie knew she had been foolish in resisting a visit here. It was as if the cemetery had been staged by Edward Gorey. The sun filtered through more Spanish moss than she had seen anywhere else. The paths were a mix of sand and oyster shells.

"Come on," Francis said quietly. "Let's go visiting." He held a small cooler in one hand and took one of hers with the other.

They walked in silence past plots filled with marble statuary—Victorian angels, ornate crosses, weeping women with bowed heads, elaborate flowers that would never wilt. Sophie could hear birds far above and looked up at the sky through the canopy of live oak.

"Back in the day there were eagles. I'm talking way back in the seventeen hundreds when John Mullryne and his son-in-law Josiah Tattnall built their plantation here on the banks of the Wilmington River. *Bonaventure* means 'good fortune' in Italian, but their good fortune didn't last but a few years. They were Loyalists. The place was confiscated during the Revolutionary War and they were banished. Terrible fate for a Savannahian. Long story short—Tattnall's son bought it back, then sold it again. Every time it changed hands, keeping the family burial ground was a proviso. The graveyard expanded in time and finally the city bought it in the early nineteen hundreds as a public cemetery. You can buy a plot still, although the prices have gone up."

Sophie recognized the statue of Little Gracie from the myriad reproductions in Savannah's gift shops. She didn't see any tears on the child's face as Carlene had claimed, but there were bouquets of flowers and small toys at her feet.

"Here's the family plot where the Bird Girl statue used to stand. The original's in the Jepson now. Too many foolish people, no, worse—plain ignorant— would have their kids climb on it to take pictures and other appalling things. No respect." Francis shook his head.

There were still a few red camellias blooming, and Sophie thought once more that she didn't miss the bleak Northern winters at all. Noting her gaze, Francis said, "Get Will to bring you out when the azaleas are in season. Now, that's a rare sight."

A few minutes later, he turned right. "First stop, we'll visit the Aikens. I was only a little older than you when he came back to Savannah for their final years, but I had the pleasure of knowing him and his lovely wife well. Some were surprised that he wanted to return, but I wasn't."

"I think this must be another story," Sophie said. "I only know him as a poet and then his famous short story, 'Silent Snow, Secret Snow.'"

"Have a seat and I'll tell it. The bench is his tombstone, and later Mary's. Hoped people would come out and enjoy a martini while they sat surrounded by all this." Francis gestured elegantly at a particular stand of trees with lacelike moss so long it almost touched the ground. "Liked his martinis. I've brought a shaker from time to time, but today we're drinking sweet tea. Read the inscriptions before we sit."

The Aikens' names and dates were in the middle of the bench. On one side GIVE MY LOVE TO THE WORLD was inscribed and on the other: COSMOS MARINER DESTINATION UNKNOWN.

Francis took a Thermos and two crystal tumblers from the cooler. The tea tasted cool and delicious. Not too sweet—or maybe, Sophie thought, she had finally developed the right taste buds.

"What perfect epitaphs," she said.

"Yes—and especially when you know his story. He was born in Savannah, the oldest of four. His father was a doctor, and in his thirties he began to have fits of violence and other behavior that was out of character. No one has ever been sure why. When Conrad was eleven, he heard shots and discovered the bodies of his parents. His father had killed his wife, and then committed suicide. Their graves are over there. He was thirty-seven; she the same. Conrad was raised by an aunt in Massachusetts. You know what he accomplished, but because of the trauma he always feared for his own sanity. Coming back here made it all right. He was home, and boy did he enjoy it. He and his wife loved to entertain—and lived in the house next door to his boyhood one over on Oglethorpe."

It was an amazing story, Sophie thought, and as a tribute to Aiken's ultimate resilience of spirit, the bench was perfect. But the mention of suicide made her think of Ruth. Sophie wished she could have been buried in this lovely place. Maybe the family plot in Illinois was a nice one. But would she be permitted burial there? Ruth was Catholic, and suicide was considered to be a sin. Ruth had spoken of going to Mass again and becoming observant. One more thing that made her act so inexplicable, so hard to believe.

"Now, I hope I haven't depressed you. That's a very serious look."

Sophie smiled. "No, the opposite. I admire him all the more. I was just thinking about a friend of mine who died recently. A suicide."

Now his face grew serious. "I am sorry for your loss. The poor girl. I met her at your family's open house. So vibrant, so young. We never know."

He pulled Sophie to her feet. "Let's head over to Johnny's bench and have our lunch. Johnny Mercer, that is."

When they got there, he said, "Most people don't know that the caricature engraved on the bench is one Johnny drew as a self-portrait. That's his signature, too. Make yourself comfortable. Feel free to hum—or sing."

The names of some of Mercer's famous, and very singable, songs were engraved around the bench, and indeed Sophie did find herself humming "Ac-Cent-Tchu-Ate the Positive."

"Had to have Clary's shrimp salad once more before I take off, hope that's all right."

"Better than all right," Sophie said, taking a bite of the delicious overstuffed sandwich.

They ate in companionable silence. When they were done, Francis said, "Last stop. The Maxwells. Aurora and Amanda."

Sophie nodded. She very much wanted to visit the two women who had been so beloved by her husband—and so many others.

The headstones gleamed white in the afternoon sun, and there was a stone bench here, too, a simple slab mounted on upright scrolls with an inscription that read: "Cut them into stars and they will make the face of heaven so fine that all the world will be in love with night."

"*Romeo and Juliet,*" Sophie said, stroking the slightly altered words from the play.

"I'm going to put this cooler in the car. Would you like to sit here for a while?"

"Very much. Thank you. Thank you for everything, Francis."

He kissed her cheek. "You take your time, hear?"

Sophie watched him leave. There had been only a few other people in the cemetery today and none were near her now. She thought about the two women and wished for some images other than the portrait and photographs she had seen. She needed to ask Francis more of what he remembered and Will when the time felt right. Anson too. Gloria and her husband had been close friends, so she would help add to what Sophie so dearly wanted to know.

She looked about. A strong fragrance she had never smelled before was filling the air, but she hadn't seen any flowering shrubs on the plot. But there had to be. Such a powerful scent and it was making her eyelids heavy. She pictured a white trumpet-like flower. It was getting larger and larger. There were voices.

"*The doctor's on his way. More water? You've had so much, Gran!*"

"*More!*"

"*Mother, just tell us. What did you take? What was in the pillbox?*"

"*Dad, don't upset her. The doctor will be here. We should have called him last night. No, please stop crying! She'll be fine. I thought it was flu, too.*"

"*Moonflowers.*"

"*Did she say moonflowers or Moon River? Oh dear God, where is the doctor? I'll go wait in the street for him.*"

"*I knew she was taking Amanda's passing hard, but not this hard. I can never forgive myself.*"

"*Don't! She'll be fine! Look, she's saying something again. She's awake.*"

"*The seeds. Find the seeds. I'm coming. You find the seeds for me, Will. Anson can't.*"

The white flower grew larger and larger. Sophie felt as if she were burning up. The petals exploded and she heard a voice. A voice she knew.

"Sophie! Sophie! What's happening? Are you all right, child? Open your eyes!" She felt someone shake her gently and looked up into Francis's anxious face.

For a moment she could not remember where she was, and then it all rushed back. She jumped up. "The smell. It was the smell of the flowers. I must have fainted."

"Flowers?"

She looked around.

There were no flowers.

That night Will called to say good night and all sorts of other lovely things, promising to call again in the morning. But he must have had to be someplace very early, because there was no call, or even a text. On Wednesday morning, still not hearing from him, she assumed he must be having difficulty wrapping up the case. She reminded herself that she knew his job would mean an unpredictable schedule—and times when he'd be out of touch. She started to get concerned.

When she hadn't heard from him by early Friday morning, concern leaped to major worry. He had not answered any of her e-mails or texts and his phone went straight to voice mail. She didn't have any other way to reach him except through his secretary, Coralee Jones.

Will's office on Drayton Street was located near the studio apartment he'd been renting before his marriage, and Sophie had been in the apartment, but not the office. Coralee was part-time and Sophie hoped this was a day she was working.

Luck was with her, and Coralee answered the phone, "Tarkington Agency." Will had used his middle name to avoid confusion with the law firm.

"Hi, Coralee. It's Sophie. I'm wondering if you've heard from Will. I haven't been able to reach him this week."

There was a long pause. "When he's on a job, this happens sometimes; but I haven't been able to reach him, either, and he hasn't called in or gotten in touch any other way." Sophie was sure Coralee wanted to add that this was unusual, but she was a professional and Will's employee, not his wife's.

"Well, if you do hear, could you let me know?" Sophie gave her the landline at the house and her cell, besides the office phone. She hung up and her cell rang almost immediately. She grabbed it. Silly to worry!

Except it wasn't Will. "Hi, Sophie," Patrick Smith said. "I'm coming to Savannah in two weeks and wanted to go over some things with you. I'd also like to take you and your husband to dinner, although I must say he isn't very reliable in that department."

Ignoring the rest, Sophie asked quickly, "What do you mean?"

"Only that he stood me up Wednesday night. I had a delicious but lonely dinner at Miller Union, Steven Satterfield's great restaurant. Kind of surprised me that

Will didn't call. And I wasn't able to reach him to see if he wanted to make it another time."

Sophie quickly scheduled a meeting and assured Patrick that both she and Will would have dinner with him—their treat—then hung up and called Anson. She didn't want to alarm anyone, but this wasn't the Will she knew.

Gloria answered.

"Hi, Gloria. It's Sophie. How are you?"

"Just fine, thank you. Crazy busy, but I guess that must be how I like things, since it's like this all the time. Anson keeps telling me to slow down! And you? Will back from Atlanta?"

It was the opening Sophie needed. "No—and it's why I called. He was due back Wednesday, yesterday at the latest he said. I haven't heard from him. It's not like him. I wondered if maybe he's been in touch with you?"

"Oh, honey, it may not be like the Will you think you know, but it's exactly like the one we all do. He goes walkabout. Get used to it, darlin', and welcome to married life. You take care now."

Sophie hung up and tried to think whom else to call. Patty Sue would tell her the same thing, but snarkier. Sophie didn't want to give her the satisfaction. And she couldn't disturb Randy and Carlene's vacation. Should she call Laura? Miss Laura? She shuddered, thinking that she might know where Will was when Sophie didn't. But she'd known other things, like Will's having to go back to Atlanta. No, Sophie told herself firmly. There was no way Will would have been in touch with the woman who *aspired* to be his wife and not Sophie, his wife.

She tried to get some work done. Randy had advertised for a replacement for Ruth before he left and there were several applications to look at. Randy had also told Sophie that they all had to change their passwords. He was pretty sure they had been hacked. "You know about cyber security, but we had to educate Anson. He was using his birthday as a password." Sophie had been through a professional development course on the issue at her old firm and had immediately changed hers. She hadn't seen any evidence of hacking on her current account, but Randy was positive someone had been "roaming around in our business."

An hour later, after accomplishing nothing, she called Patrick Smith and asked him to get in touch if he heard from Will or saw him. He picked up on her distress immediately. "I'll ask around. From the questions he was putting to me earlier, I'm pretty sure he was investigating some kind of smuggling. He mentioned arms. But, Sophie, if anything has happened to Will—and he's a careful guy, so it hasn't—you would have heard."

Sophie thanked him and then made another call.

"Faith? Will has disappeared."

Chapter 10

Faith sat down hard, unnerved by the sheer panic in Sophie's voice.

"When did you last see or hear from him?" she asked, working to keep her voice steady and calm.

Sophie's wasn't, her words rushing into one another. "He left Monday morning, saying he would finally tie up the case and be back as soon as possible. A day or two with luck. He called Monday night and said things were looking good. I haven't heard from him since and neither has his secretary."

"Did he say anything about being hard to reach while he was finishing? No, of course he didn't, or you wouldn't be worrying."

"Just the opposite, in fact. He said we'd talk in the morning. I've called and texted him over and over. The

calls go right to his voice mail, and the texts go nowhere. They don't say 'delivered' or 'read.' No reply to
my e-mails, either."

"Is he good about keeping his phone charged? Wait,
he must. He's a detective. I was thinking of Tom." Her
husband still viewed his cell as a gadget he'd rather not
have to use. Besides not keeping it charged, he often
misplaced it. Last week Faith had found it in the refrigerator on a shelf by some leftover risotto, somewhat
diminished.

"Will loves his phone, upgrades every time there's
a new feature." Sophie gave a little sob. "Something's
happened to him. I know it has. Gloria said—I called
to see if they had heard from him—that this is what he
does. Goes 'walkabout.' But I *know* my own husband,
and if he says he'll call he will. When he left he made a
point of it. He knew how upset I was about Ruth. Oh,
and he didn't keep a dinner appointment with a contact
who is also a new client of mine."

"When was that?"

"Wednesday night. Patrick is based in Atlanta. He's
a reporter and Will had been in touch with him before
about a story Patrick did on various kinds of smuggling. Arms in particular."

Faith took a deep breath. She'd thought Will dealt
with cooking-the-books-type crime, not this sort.

"So the timeline is that Will set out for Atlanta Monday and we know he reached it, since he called you that night. He also set up a dinner date with this Patrick for Wednesday, so he was in touch with him Monday or Tuesday. Maybe give him a call to find out which day?"

"I will, and Patrick was also going to ask around."

"And how about calling the hotel, or wherever he was staying?" Faith suggested. She heard a very audible sigh.

"I never know ahead where Will is staying. It's been someplace different every time he goes to Atlanta, usually one of those chain residence-type places. He doesn't book ahead. Oh why did he have to be a PI? Why didn't he go into the firm with his father?"

"How about *your* week? Anything unusual? Anything that could be tied to Will?" When she didn't get a response, Faith said, "Sophie, what happened? Did you hear me?"

"Yes," Sophie said slowly. "Something did happen, but it's hard to describe, and while it has to do with Will, it doesn't have anything to do with him now. Or maybe it does. I don't know, Faith. Don't know a thing. . . ."

"Ben's still in France. Amy has gone back to school, not where her old friends are—her decision—and is fast becoming Miss Popular. Jet Blue flies nonstop to Savannah. I'll text you my flight."

"Really? You're coming?"

"Really. I'm very good at finding things."

Sophie hung up and immediately called Patrick, who did not have any news but confirmed that Will had called him on Tuesday to meet for dinner the following night.

"He wanted to eat early, darlin'. Should have remembered before. He said he was hoping to head back to Savannah after the meal or the next morning at the latest. He was just tying up some loose ends was how he put it."

Sophie thanked him and texted the information to Faith. The timeline was more complete now. Or less. No one had heard from Will or seen him since Tuesday. No one Sophie knew.

After speaking to Patrick, Sophie knew she couldn't stay in the office. Randy was still away, and Anson was out at Bells Mills. He had kept only a few of his longtime clients—those who had been with him since he joined the firm fresh out of law school—and he came in only when he was meeting with one of them, or happened to be walking by when he was in town.

There was a temp at reception, and Sophie knew some of the associates were in their offices, but the place felt very empty. She looked out the window at the magnolia that Will had climbed as a boy. The wave of fear that washed over her was so strong she thought she might be sick.

Faith would be here soon. She'd called to say she was going to be able to make an early flight. As Sophie gathered her things together, she concentrated on a to-do list. Get groceries. Make up one of the bedrooms for Faith. Find her husband.

Walking past Oglethorpe's statue as she cut across Chippewa Square, Sophie tried to think how to tell Faith what had happened this week. Out in Bonaventure Cemetery. She sat down on a bench under one of the oaks and went back over the experience. She almost felt herself slipping into a similar trance when she closed her eyes in order to recall it precisely. If she could get it right, her friend would come to the only conclusion that made sense. The conclusion Sophie had reached.

Aurora McAllister Maxwell hadn't committed suicide. She'd been poisoned.

The crew was back after the holidays at Gloria's spec house. They were still concentrating on the back garden space and hadn't been working on the house's interior—thoughtfully suspended so as not to interfere with the Maxwells' holiday. But Sophie knew there was still one bath to complete, and some of the bedrooms hadn't been painted.

She left to pick Faith up, locking the front door behind her, and saw that Lydia Scriven was walking Charlie in the square. Lydia! The woman had seen Will at times when Sophie had assumed he was still in Atlanta. Maybe she had seen him again. Sophie dashed over.

"Hi, a belated Happy New Year to you," Sophie called out, crossing the street.

"And to you, too. I hope the whole holiday was a good one for your first here in Savannah."

"It was, and Will surprised me with the house I'd fallen in love with over on Habersham. We can move in sometime in March."

Lydia gave her a hug. "I'm so glad—and glad for me. You won't be far away." She took a step back and looked at Sophie. "Is everything all right? You look a little peaked."

"Yes, or maybe no," Sophie blurted out. "Have you seen Will this week? Here in town? He left Monday to finish up his case in Atlanta and was supposed to be back by Wednesday. I haven't heard from him or been able to get in touch with him since Monday night."

"No," Lydia said slowly. "I haven't seen your husband since before Christmas."

Sophie felt her eyes fill with tears. "I'm sure it's all right. I'm just being silly. New bride syndrome or something."

"It isn't all right, and you're not being silly. Now, what are we going to do about it? Let me think."

"A friend is flying in from Massachusetts. I'm on my way to pick her up at the airport now."

"Good. I know you must have asked everyone you could think of—his family?"

"Yes, but they say he does this and I'll just have to get used to it."

"But he doesn't do this, does he? Not stay in touch."

Sophie shook her head, and Lydia added, "I'm a good Christian and don't believe in the supernatural, but I do believe in strong feelings. I have a strong feeling that Will is alive and well. We just have to find him. Now, you go get your friend and I'll ask around. What's your friend's name?"

"Faith."

"Well then, there you go."

Sophie was standing at the top of the corridor leading from the gates into the main part of the airport, which was a large town square with facades of old tyme buildings and rocking chairs as well as more conventional seating. A young man was playing show tunes on a piano in the center. Faith waved to her friend and was soon by her side. One look told her that Sophie hadn't heard from Will, or anything about him. "What a great airport," she enthused. "Are those real palms?"

"Yes, and wait until you see the outside. More palms and a big fountain. Did you check a bag?"

"Nope," said Faith. She had almost mastered packing light, and today in her haste to make the plane had managed with just a carry-on. The ultimate at this was Pix. Faith was helping her pack for a trip to Europe some years ago and only just managed to convince her friend that a spare set of shoes, not just the ones she was wearing, might be a good idea. And a few more changes of underwear. "But I can rinse things out," Pix had protested before giving in a little.

The warm air that greeted Faith as they headed for the car felt heavenly. She wasn't going to need the winter jacket she'd put on before leaving.

"Now, I want to get some food, preferably Southern. Someplace where we can talk and you can tell me what you didn't tell me on the phone."

"Was it that obvious?" Sophie asked.

"It was that obvious," Faith replied.

"We can drop your things at the house and walk over to a nice place that has a rooftop area. Very scenic—and very private."

Faith listened intently as Sophie described what she had experienced in the Bonaventure Cemetery. The container ships many city blocks long and as tall as many NYC buildings were making their way slowly down the Savannah River behind her, a curious backdrop for her tale. Sophie repeated the conversation she had "heard"—and then, at Faith's request, recited it again.

"The one voice sounded like Will's, a younger Will, and the other voice was definitely Anson."

"Moonflowers. I've heard of Moon Pennies, but not Moonflowers. Since she mentioned seeds, she must have been talking about a plant, however incoherently, rather than anything to do with the river."

"I thought so, too, and I looked the name up. It's *Datura stramonium,* also familiarly called jimsomweed. Faith, the photographs of the flower were *exactly* what I saw, and the description also mentioned the strong narcotic odor. The seeds and other parts of the plant are highly toxic. The symptoms include high fever, excessive thirst, amnesia, and hallucinations." She shuddered. "It would have been a horrific death.

I now know why Will was so upset seeing me in Aurora's wedding dress."

As a preacher's wife, Faith might have been supposed to treat Sophie's experience with skepticism, but she had heard other tales over the years that left her more than open-minded. She absolutely believed that Sophie had had some sort of vision, just as she believed the young woman had also found a body in the wardrobe weeks earlier.

A server came over. "May I start you on some drinks? And have you had a chance to look at our menu? Today's specials are listed on the back."

Faith suggested a sauvignon blanc. "Breakfast was a very, very long time ago," she said. "I'm hungry. Let's order a bunch of things." She scanned the menu. "The deconstructed shrimp salad, as well as crab spring rolls will go well with the wine. And the smoked salmon flat bread to continue the seafood theme?" She *was* hungry, but she was also pretty sure Sophie hadn't been eating.

When the wine arrived, Faith raised her glass. "To good fortune. After all, Bonaventure has given us the first solid clue."

As if in reply, Sophie's cell rang. She had set it down next to her and grabbed it. Her face immediately registered disappointment. It clearly wasn't Will.

"Hello?"

Hearing the voice, she put it on speaker and mouthed "Patrick Smith."

"Hi, Sophie. I haven't seen Will and don't have anything definite to tell you about his whereabouts, but I did get in touch with a source of mine who told me that Will had been in touch with him a few times, most recently Monday."

"What kind of a source? I mean, what was Will contacting him about?"

"It's as I suspected. Illegal arms smuggling. But he also added that Will had become involved in investigating it through tracing a money-laundering scheme. The guy said Will had told him the trail was leading him in a direction he was having trouble believing."

"What could that mean?"

"Possibly a legitimate business he wouldn't have predicted would be criminally connected. But, of course, that's the secret to a successful operation. Maybe a charity or something similar."

"Thank you, Patrick. This is a big help."

"I hope so, Sophie. And again, my gut tells me Will is all right. You take care now and call me any time, day or night."

They ate and went over the implications of what Sophie had experienced in the cemetery—what it could mean for Will, too. By the time they left the restaurant, dusk was falling. As they walked back to the house, Faith was charmed by the architecture, and the feel of the city—a slower paced way of life.

Crossing the square to the house, Faith realized she hadn't asked Sophie an important question surrounding the death of Will's grandmother. "Given that we now believe Aurora Maxwell's death wasn't suicide or a natural one, why would anyone have wanted her out of the way? What possible motive could there have been? From what Ursula said she was much loved."

"I know. It's been bothering me, too."

"Well, there's always the cui bono aspect. Who benefits? Was she a wealthy woman?"

"Judging from the jewelry in the safe-deposit box at the bank and the house—the furnishings alone must be worth a fortune—I'm sure Aurora left a substantial estate."

"And to whom?"

"Will. It all went to Will."

Back at the house they settled in front of Sophie's computer and began a search for more about *Datura stramonium*. There were further confirmations of what Sophie had already turned up. After that, Faith suggested they start investigating recent cases involving arms smuggling and/or money laundering in Georgia and South Carolina. Charleston was a huge container port as well, the tenth busiest in the United States. Savannah was the fourth.

While Sophie was doing this, Faith called Tom. She'd checked in with him when she'd arrived but thought she should let him know what was happening. He had been as worried as she was.

"Everything all right at home?" Sophie asked when Faith had finished talking.

"Yes. Amy was selected for one of the leads in the class play. *The Importance of Being Earnest.* Nice to know the classics aren't being ignored."

Sophie smiled. "Can you imagine what Oscar Wilde would have had to say about a bunch of middle schoolers uttering his lines?"

"And very funny they will be."

Faith pulled her chair back next to Sophie's and looked at the computer screen. "Tom thinks you should talk to the police."

"I've thought the same thing on and off." Sophie sighed. "But I think they would say what the family has been saying. Also, Will used to return on Fridays, which is only today. They'd think it was too soon to classify him as missing. Randy and Carlene get back tomorrow. If I haven't heard from Will, I'll call

Randy—and Anson, too. Gloria must have told him I was upset, and I'm surprised he hasn't called."

"He must agree with her—and Will has behaved pretty footloose in the past. But," Faith added hastily, "not once he met and married you."

A few hours later they decided to call it a day.

"Are you sure you don't mind sleeping in this room?" Sophie asked, opening the door to the room with the wardrobe.

"I wouldn't sleep anywhere else! Who knows, maybe the vibe will give me an idea of where Will could be. And besides, it's beautiful. Love the bed. Tom and I plus the kids could all fit in."

"It's an oversize king, and Gloria had the head and footboards copied from one at Winterthur."

"I wish I could get her to redo the parsonage—although given the Vestry it would be a *Design on a Dime* project." Faith laughed

"Good night. Wonderful that you're here." Sophie gave Faith a hug. "I'm just down the hall. Come get me if you need anything."

After Sophie left, closing the door behind her, Faith stood in front of the wardrobe. Faith was a believer in "cosmic coincidences," and the string of events that had begun with Will's reaction to Sophie's dress the night of the welcome party had been followed closely by Sophie's discovery of the disappearing corpse. The alarming anonymous letter. Getting locked in a box room on Christmas Eve. Her experience at Aurora's grave, and Will's disappearance. Coincidences? Faith didn't think so. Links.

The wardrobe didn't match any of the rest of the room's furnishings. It lacked elegance and seemed to have been a purely utilitarian piece. The drawer at the bottom had simple knobs straight from the cheap section of whatever hardware store had originally supplied them. Faith went over and tried to pull the drawer open. It stuck, and then she realized it wasn't a drawer at all, just a fake to finish off the piece that now didn't look all that old to her.

Faith opened the door and pushed the few things she'd hung up to one side. The interior was large enough for a good-size person, dead or alive. She stepped in and on impulse tapped on the back. It didn't open up into Narnia. It was very solid. She started to back out and stumbled over the boots she'd been wearing on the trip down, falling hard on one knee. The slight pain was overshadowed by what she'd noticed. There had definitely been a hollow sound. She moved completely out of the wardrobe and kneeled in front of it, first leaning in to examine where she'd hit. Then, using the heel of a shoe, she tapped. *Tap, tap.* She moved the heel, tapping across the floor of the wardrobe. The center sounded different, less solid. She stood up and got the penlight she always carried in her purse. When she shone it on that area she could make out lines—lines so faint as to appear almost invisible to the naked eye.

It was a trapdoor.

"Sophie, wake up!"

"I'm not sleeping. Come in."

The door opened and Faith said, "No, you come with me. I know how they got the body out so fast! Do you have a good flashlight?"

She did. After her experience she had gone and bought the equivalent of a handheld klieg light, which she kept by her bed.

Back in the front bedroom under the strong light it was easy to see the outline of the trapdoor.

"We'll have to find a way to pry it open," Faith said. "I felt around for a release—a catch—but it's completely smooth. Maybe there's a crowbar with the tools in the backyard."

Sophie trained the beam over the floor of the wardrobe. Faith had moved everything out.

"I don't think that will be necessary. See this dot? It looks like a wormhole in the wood, but it's placed exactly in the center of the line. I'm sure something screws in to pull it up." She rocked back on her heels and her eyes instantly zoomed in on the drawer knobs. She unscrewed one easily, muttering, "Righty tighty, lefty loosey."

It fit in just as easily, and she pulled the door open. "Bingo."

Faith looked over Sophie's shoulder. There was a folded-up wooden ladder like the kind used to access an attic or crawl space. Beyond their light, it was pitch-dark.

"All right," Faith said. "I'm going to change and go down. You stay here."

"As if," Sophie said firmly. "We'll both change, and I think there's another flashlight in the kitchen. Bring your phone. It may work. This could just be space that was created when they renovated years ago."

"And maybe not," Faith said.

Sophie dressed quickly, grabbed the other flashlight, and took two bottles of water. She wasn't sure why, but it seemed like a good idea.

Upstairs the ladder unfolded without a sound. The hinges had been oiled. It was a long way down and ended in a flat concrete-floored narrow passageway, barely tall enough for them to stand up. Soon they found themselves making a sharp turn.

"This doesn't feel old. The concrete is smooth, no cracks," Faith said.

"We must be under the garden by now. I wasn't crazy! The body was being removed while I was calling the police."

"I think we'd better be quiet," Faith said. She gasped aloud, however, when they came to the end of the recent work and the narrow underground structure gave way to a much larger brick-enclosed one that had to have been constructed many, many years ago.

"You go back, Sophie. One of us should stay in the house. If I'm not there in, say, an hour, call the police."

"No, *you* go back. It's my husband."

They both kept going.

"This must lead to the river," Sophie said softly in Faith's ear. "Yellow fever victims, rum, or other uses."

The floor was wet in spots, and every once in a while Sophie felt something crunch underfoot and gave a shudder. Eventually they came to another turn, and then two more.

"Shhh!" Listening hard, Sophie stopped—so abruptly Faith bumped into her.

"I hear something, turn off your light!" Sophie hissed.

They stood absolutely still. The sound was human and the human was moaning.

"It's Will!" Sophie shouted. "I know it is! That's exactly what he sounded like when he was sick! Will!

Will! Where are you?" She'd found him, but he was obviously hurt. Joy fought fear for the emotional upper hand.

They moved forward, following the sound, using only Faith's tiny flashlight.

"Slow down. He may not be alone—and if people *are* with him, they heard you," Faith said softly. They went a few more steps and Sophie felt Faith's hand on her arm. "You need to go back and call the police. This is too dangerous."

"*You* go. I'm not leaving Will."

They kept going.

After the next turn, the volume of his moans indicated that Will was close by. They couldn't hear any other voices. Sophie turned on her big flashlight. "Will! Darling! Where are you?"

"Oh God, Sophie! Are you really here? I'm at the bottom of some kind of cistern. Be careful!"

Faith turned her larger light on, too, and soon they saw Will's prison. He was alone—and unreachable at the bottom of a deep shaft.

"My ankle is broken and it hurts like hell, but I'm okay otherwise," he called up.

"But what happened? And where have you been all this time? Surely not here?" Sophie sobbed as she spoke. She needed to go back and get help, but she found herself rooted to the spot. She didn't want to leave him. Will started speaking before she could ask Faith to go without her.

The story was not a pretty one.

He had gone back to his room to pack, intending to leave Atlanta Tuesday night. "I was about to call Patrick Smith to cancel dinner and set a time to meet in Savannah when there was a knock. A female voice said it was the maid with clean towels. I wanted to tell her I was leaving and she could get the room ready for the next person, so I opened the door.

"There *were* towels, and the one thrown over my head was soaked with chloroform. I recognized the smell as I was blacking out. I think I was in some sort of truck, and then the next thing I knew I was here. They must have broken my ankle to keep me from trying to climb out, although without any light or a ladder I'm not sure I would have been able to.

"Someone—I can't see who—comes to check every once in a while and lowers some food and water. I could tell from the lights they shone when they came that I'm in one of the tunnels—from the damp smell, probably near the river. No one has come recently, so the plan now may be to leave me here to rot. I don't know why they didn't kill me right away."

"But why grab you at all?" Sophie shrieked. Faith put a cautionary arm out, and Sophie lowered her voice. "We found you because there's a ladder in the wardrobe leading down from the bedroom in the house, and I *did* find a body and—"

"Hush, darlin'. I know all that now. The whole thing is complicated. But right this minute I want you to leave fast. Later you can tell me what Faith is doing in Savannah. Hi, Faith."

"Hi, and we'll get you out of here soon," said Faith. "It won't take long to retrace our steps and call the police."

"No, I have to be here," Will said firmly. "I'll tell you exactly what to do. If I don't stay put a while longer some major crimes, including murder, will stay hidden."

Although their phones weren't getting a signal, Faith had power and was able to take down what Will dictated. Sophie tossed her phone to Will. If he was moved, he could be tracked. She tossed the bottles of water as well and considered tossing herself before good sense prevailed.

As they turned to go, Sophie said, "I can't understand why Gloria didn't know about the tunnel under the house. The contractors must have seen it."

"The contractors are part of the mob," Will said wearily, "and Gloria, too."

Although Faith wasn't on the scene when the sting took place—and the FBI, the Bureau of Alcohol, Tobacco, Firearms and Explosives, plus the Savannah police and Georgia State Police all lay in wait at various locations throughout the state, including the pit in which Will had been left—she and Sophie were getting a full description from Will.

Gloria's house was now a crime scene, so the three of them were in the library at the Monterey Square house. Sophie had described it to Faith, but it was even lovelier than she'd imagined. The library was cozier than the formal parlors, and the hot toddy she was sipping was adding to the warmth. Will had been treated and released at the hospital, having suffered no ill effects except for the ankle, now in a cast. He'd demanded a shower before they put it on.

Will and Sophie were sitting very close together on a large leather couch across from Faith with his foot on an ottoman. It was late, but no one had wanted to go to bed.

"I was in denial," Will said. "The job I was hired for seemed straightforward. Typical 'follow the money.' But the money kept coming back to Savannah. I was chasing leads all over the place, even out to Pin Point and a source there."

Faith looked at Sophie, who was blushing. She'd told Faith about tailing Will at Christmas. The blush confirmed that Sophie hadn't told Will.

"When I left after New Year's I knew I was close to a legitimate business that had been laundering money for a major arms smuggler. The shock was that it was Gloria's business and fake clients that Randy had created at the firm. I decided that I had to come home and confront them. I was positive Dad didn't know, but there was a tiny doubt. In any case, they were family. I owed it to them to ask them to explain. Instead, they blew the whistle to their associates, and I was a dead man."

Faith saw Sophie flinch and jumped in. "You must be relieved to know for sure your father was as ignorant of what was going on as everyone else."

Will nodded. "It was just Gloria and Randy. I knew my stepbrother had skirted a little close to the law when he was a teenager, but it never occurred to me that he would be engaging in criminal activity of this magnitude as an adult. Yet all the trails were leading to his mother and him—her very successful business for years and then, more recently, some of his activities at Maxwell and Maxwell."

He reached for his wife's hand. "I'm sorry, sweetheart, as I have said about a thousand times tonight, but yes, the body in the wardrobe *was* very real and intended as a warning to Gloria and Randy. The mob didn't know someone else was living there—they thought the place was empty, as it conveniently had been for a long time, enabling them to make, shall we say, 'modifications.' They got rid of the evidence fast, and we may never know how many others."

Sophie grimaced. "To be generous, I think his mother, Lady Macbeth, or whatever the equivalent is here, pressured Randy into it." She'd been fond of him.

Will's face looked stern. "You *are* too generous. It sickens me to think what the two did. And more will no doubt be coming out. They've turned on each other, and Randy has already said it was his mother who arranged Miss Sophronia's hit-and-run after she discovered the shadow clients and some of his dealings at the firm."

He did look sick, Faith thought—and should be in bed. "I think we should call it a night, quite a night, or rather day. I have an early flight tomorrow, so I'll say good-bye now. I've ordered a cab, so you're not to even think of getting up."

The house had a small elevator. Sophie helped Will in and before following him, gave Faith a tight hug. "You'll come in February? The school vacation?"

"Absolutely. And you, missy, call me with every detail as soon as you hear them."

Sophie gave her another hug. "I will—and Faith, I don't know what I would have done without you. You *are* good at finding things."

As each day revealed more of what had been going on, Sophie relayed the information to Faith, making good on her promise. "Carlene, who is the sweetest thing on two feet"—where was she getting these expressions?—"had no idea of any of it whatsoever and truly thought that Will was in Atlanta! Anyway, she's busy baking red-and-white cookies for her husband in prison. Although not for her mother-in-law. I'm glad Carlene was able to draw a line."

"Gloria puts new emphasis on the 'psycho' in 'psychopath.' It's horrifying—and frightening. She seems to have had no compunction at ordering a hit on her stepson, *and* the firm's treasured longtime employee, Miss Sophronia," Faith said.

There was a pause. "I haven't told you the worst." Sophie drew a deep breath. "Gloria faked Ruth Stafford's suicide. She came over to wish her a happy New Year with a bottle of champagne, lethally spiking Ruth's drink and then setting the stage, even making the 'drunken' slurred call. Randy had told her that

Ruth was pregnant by him and he intended to do right by her. That he would support the child. Ruth apparently didn't want him to divorce Carlene and was looking forward to being a single mom. She'd always wanted children."

"Oh, Sophie, this is beyond belief. Why would Gloria have to get Ruth out of the way? She didn't know anything about the money laundering, did she?"

"No. I think Gloria may not have trusted Ruth to keep quiet about whose baby she was having and thought she would also blackmail Randy for more money."

"As in what she would have done?"

"Got it. Besides, she has a thing about her family, and introducing a Northern strain into the mix couldn't be tolerated. Carlene and Randy's children were going to be the only grandchildren so far as she was concerned."

"Poor Ruth," Faith said. "Wrong place, wrong time, and most assuredly wrong man."

"She really did love him, I think—and maybe the same. He was devastated by her death, and I don't think he could have faked it. Although he was the one with all the prior suggestions that she was depressed."

"Think Carlene knows about the pregnancy?"

"I doubt it." Sophie laughed a little. "Otherwise those red-and-white cookies would be laced with rat poison."

When Faith, and family, returned to Savannah in February, they happily stepped into balmy sunshine. Will had somehow managed to get the Habersham house owners to find other accommodations, and the Maxwells had been in their new house for almost a month. Faith and Sophie were sitting in the small garden of the new house while Will was giving Tom, Ben, and Amy his own special Savannah tour. Faith was basking not just in the warmth, but also in the growing things all around. Leafy growing things. About the only good thing she could think of when contemplating an empty nest in not too many years was being able to take time off other than school vacations to go someplace tropical. Though, they'd always be tied to a parish or something similarly clerical—and for the foreseeable future it was still going to be in Aleford.

The word did get out. Not from the woman Faith had encountered on First Day, but a distant cousin of Tom's father who was in the new parish and present when the Reverend Thomas Fairchild (possible candidate, word had it) guest preached—an event Faith made by the skin of her teeth, arriving from the airport just before the eleven o'clock service. Marian called Ursula and the two women confronted the reverend in much the same way they would have confronted a child filching a penny from his mother's purse without asking. Ursula made it clear that she did not intend to go to her Maker with anyone other than Tom by her side, and Marian chimed in, equally firm, that she preferred the distance for now. "You have your turf, I have mine," she'd said.

Tom had admitted to misgivings once Amy was settled in school and contemplated the difficulty of wrenching Ben from his. And Faith from Have Faith. And the parish.

"But that doesn't mean a change at some point," he'd said to Faith.

"I certainly hope so," she'd replied. Okay, Aleford for now, but life was long. . . .

Sophie had gone into the house to get them some iced tea. "It might could be too sweet for you," she said, returning. She placed a tray with the glasses and a plate of praline cookies on a small Victorian wrought iron table.

"You are going native fast, darlin'," Faith teased. "But while the others are away, fill in the gaps. I know that Patty Sue was the merry prankster, penning the anonymous letter, which she got Laura to deliver after she deliberately kept you at The Pirates' House until dusk—wearing her hooded cape. But have you turned up any proof that it was Patty Sue who locked you in Christmas Eve?"

"First, to her dubious credit, Laura Belvedere had no idea what was in the letter, and when I finally did tell Will about it and he confronted Patty Sue, she said the same thing. Laura had been upset when Will announced our betrothal, but Patty Sue took it way worse."

"But she hadn't even met you!" Faith took a swig of tea. It wasn't at all sweet. Sophie hadn't strayed that far from her roots.

"It had nothing to do with me. Or maybe a little. She feared a Yankee bride would mean the end of Will's largess—think credit card bills—and besides; he was *supposed* to marry Laura. Neither woman had ever not gotten her own way. But nothing Patty Sue did was illegal. She had a mother and brother for that. As for the 'Incident of the Doorknob That Didn't Turn in the Night,' I have no proof, but who else could have done it?"

Ben and Amy took that moment to come running into the garden. "You have got to come see the square with the turtles holding up a kind of globe! It's not far, Mom. We know the way," Amy said.

"It won't take long," Ben added.

"Go," Sophie said to Faith. "The piece is in Troup Square—very close—and it is special. My father-in-law won't be here for a while. He's out on Skidaway playing golf. I think I told you he's buying a place at The Landings. He has a lot of friends there."

Bells Mills was on the market. Anson and Will had decided to turn the Monterey Square house into a house museum, and Francis Whelan was helping with the particulars. Maxwell & Maxwell had not gone under—the hacking was not bad hats but part of Will's investigation. And Patrick Smith's film was optioned in a bidding war, which satisfied him he'd made the right choice with Sophie. Anson might still get his cameo.

The back garden was suddenly empty. Will and Tom were inside watching a game. She should bring the tray into the kitchen and check on the roast for dinner, but Sophie's mind was on something that had not been solved. Would never be.

A week after Will's rescue, late in the day, she had driven out alone to Bells Mills and gone into Gloria's garden behind the house. It wasn't hard to spot the moonflowers, even though they weren't in bloom. The leaves were distinctive.

Aurora had been the obstacle in Gloria's plan to marry Anson. His mother would have sized up the woman. So Aurora had to go.

Sophie sat, lost in her thoughts, until the night sky was overhead.

" 'Cut them into stars and they will make the face of heaven so fine that all the world will be in love with night,' " Sophie had murmured gazing up.

The air was suddenly suffused with a fragrance that she had not wanted to shake off then—or ever. It wasn't one she recognized—magnolia, gardenia, definitely not moonflower.

What she did recognize was that she was no longer alone. There were three in the garden.

Author's Note

"I Fall in Love Too Easily." It's a favorite song composed in 1944 by the great Jule Styne, lyrics by the great Sammy Cahn, recorded with piercing emotion first by Sinatra and notably followed over the years by Miles Davis, Dionne Warwick, Linda Ronstadt, Chet Baker, Tony Bennett, and many others. The sentiment is bittersweet, but when I hum it to myself, I'm not feeling sad. It's always been a characteristic. (Oh yes, I'm talking about you, Barry Z., third-grade crush.) I *do* fall in love easily, maybe too easily, and am glad for it.

While writing *The Body in the Birches*, I fell in love with the character Sophie Maxwell, and while visiting a friend several years ago who had moved to Savannah, I fell in love with the city. This book is the result.

First Sophie. In the last book, she personifies the song lyrics, appearing in chapter one with a broken heart after falling in love disastrously fast. At the end, she is in much better shape. I found as I created her that I was thinking of Faith Fairchild as she was in the early books of the series, and the notion of pairing the two women again here in *Wardrobe*, a kind of sequel, was hard to resist. Both were outsiders as new brides—one in the North, one in the South—but their experiences are much the same. They have to learn what is essentially a new vocabulary, and since this is a murder mystery, the process is complicated by a body or two—or three. Both have husbands with jobs involving secrets they can't share with their wives—a member of the clergy and a private investigator have to be tight-lipped. Both have in-law issues. Faith's sister-in-law causes major problems for her before and after the nuptials. Sophie faces more serious in-law troubles. Unlike Faith, however, Sophie has someone to turn to for help—and it's Faith. It was a pleasure to write about their friendship, celebrating the bonds between women, and men, too, no matter what age, truly one of life's great joys.

And it was friendship that took me to Savannah. I had been to Virginia, the Carolinas, Louisiana, and other parts of the South, but never Georgia, specifically

Savannah. Then Meg moved there, so three of us started going down to see her—no chore to leave winter behind, never a chore to be with Meg. That first trip, the four of us explored Savannah as newcomers with our hostess, a newly seasoned guide. Savannah is a very walkable city, and we walked. I picked out the house I wanted, not unlike the one Sophie gets for Christmas, and learned which square had which statue. We spent many hours in Bonaventure, and it would not be a trip to Savannah without going out to Tybee. Each time in the city has been just as special as the first. Going back to a place one loves is always a treat—checking out the familiar, finding the new. It has the same feel as rereading favorite books.

When it comes to Savannah, subsequent visits meant eating all the delicious food described in these pages—and discovering more dishes. On my last trip, the culinary highlight was attending Chef Joe Randall's "The Dinner Party, A Southern Cooking Class Lecture & Demonstration." Go to his Web site: www.chefjoerandall.com and be amazed at his credentials—and his food! We sat back, sipped wine, and watched the chef and his wife, Barbara, prepare shrimp cakes with herb mustard sauce; a salad of beets, Smithfield ham, Bermuda onions, and Georgia peanuts on Bibb lettuce; Southern-fried quail with gravy, mashed potatoes, and green beans; and finally sweet potato pie with praline sauce. We had been warned to eat lightly during the day and come hungry. With such a long growing season, all the places where we ate showcased the chef's regard for fresh, local ingredients. And at the cooking school, you also get a running commentary that is both an education and theater.

One trip to Savannah was marked by an evening at the Jepson Center for the Arts, part of the Telfair Museums, with John Berendt, author of *Midnight in the Garden of Good and Evil.* It was a party and a chance to watch Savannahians doing what comes naturally. The food was catered by Clary's Café, and the music— Johnny Mercer of course—was provided by Jeremy Davis and the Equinox Trio (thank you for the dance, Archie!). It was an extraordinary experience to look out architect Moshe Safdie's soaring wall of glass and watch Telfair Square move from dusk to dark while the inside glowed.

In all my books, place is almost as important as character and plot. I am in love with all of them—the fictitious town of Aleford somewhere west of Boston that came to mind so many years ago; always Manhattan; Sanpere, the beloved made-up island off the coast of Maine; Rome, the Eternal City; and now Savannah. Yes, I fall in love too easily—thank goodness.

Excerpts from

Have Faith in Your Kitchen

by Faith Sibley Fairchild with Katherine Hall Page

PIMENTO CHEESE

1 cup (8 ounces) grated white cheddar cheese

1 cup (8 ounces) grated sharp yellow cheddar cheese

1 jar (4 ounces) sliced pimentos, drained

1 cup mayonnaise (Duke's if you live where it's sold, otherwise Hellmann's)

1 tablespoon chopped chives

Salt and freshly ground black pepper to taste

Pinch (or more) cayenne

This is a very easy, highly addictive dish. Simply mix all the ingredients together and it will keep in an airtight container in the refrigerator for up to a week. As mentioned in the book, it makes delicious grilled cheese; but it is also great for other sandwiches, on crackers—traditionally the Keebler Club type—and stuffed into celery or other veggies. One of the cheeses has to be orange in order for it to be the real deal.

Makes 3 generous cups.

Mrs. Eugenia Duke of Greenville, South Carolina, created Duke's Mayonnaise in 1917. It has more egg yolks and less sugar than other brands, which makes it tangier (it's the South after all).

Some pimento cheese recipes call for Worcestershire sauce, Old Bay, and a favorite adds roasted garlic powder, available from Penzey Spices. Hard to go wrong with any combination.

If you look up "pimento cheese," you will find the claim (probably true) that it started in the North, but it is truly the caviar of the South now.

Pimentos, as Ben Fairchild notes, are those little red things in olives—*Pimiento* is the Spanish name for these cherry peppers, a variety of the chili pepper.

SAVANNAH RED RICE

4 strips bacon or 1 cup
   diced smoked sausage

1 cup diced yellow onion

1 cup diced red bell pepper

1 cup diced green bell pepper

1 clove garlic, minced

2 (14 1/2 ounce) cans diced
   tomatoes with juice

1/2 cup water

1 cup uncooked Carolina
   long-grain rice

1 teaspoon salt

1 teaspoon freshly ground
   black pepper

1 tablespoon hot sauce such
   as Tabasco, or to taste

Butter to prepare casserole
   dish

Fry the bacon in a large skillet until crisp and remove from the pan. Drain on a paper towel and crumble. Set aside.

Preheat the oven to 350 degrees.

Reusing the large skillet, over medium heat sauté the onions, peppers, and garlic in the bacon grease until soft. Add the tomatoes, water, rice, salt and pepper, hot sauce, and the crumbled bacon and stir for about ten more minutes.

Pour the mixture into a buttered casserole dish and bake until the liquid is absorbed, approximately 30 minutes.

Serves 6 generously.

Red rice comes to us from the Carolina and Georgia coastal Gullah or Geechee people from West Africa. There are many variations. Some recipes call for smoked sausage instead of bacon and add celery. Chef Joe Randall adds tomato paste and cooks the mixture on the stove top. Other recipes cook the rice first, adding it to the pan and then baking it.

The greatest variation comes in taste buds—the heat will increase the farther south one goes! A versatile side or main dish, Savannah red rice is a treasured part of Southern culinary heritage.

CHEESE GRITS

4 cups water

1 1/2 cups milk

1/2 cup half-and-half

1 1/2 cups long-cooking grits

1 tablespoon unsalted butter, plus more for preparing the casserole dish

1/4 teaspoon salt

1/4 teaspoon freshly ground black pepper

2 large eggs, beaten

1 1/2 cups grated cheddar cheese, preferably sharp

Combine the water, milk, and half-and-half in a heavy saucepan. Stir the grits into the combined liquids and bring to a boil, stirring occasionally.

Add the butter, salt, and pepper and immediately turn down to low. Keep a sharp eye on the grits, stirring as they thicken. This will take about 30 to 40 minutes.

Preheat the oven to 350 degrees. Once the grits have thickened, add the eggs and cheese, stirring until the cheese is melted. The grits should appear a bit fluffy.

Pour the grits into a buttered 1- to 1 1/2-quart casserole dish and bake for 40 minutes.

Serves 6, with leftovers.

Leftover grits, or hominy as true Southerners call them, are not just for breakfast (although there is nothing better than a couple of eggs over easy, thick country bacon, and creamy grits straight from the saucepan). Cut into squares and fried, the above recipe is equally delicious the next day as a substitute for a starch.

Instead of cheese, or in addition, chopped greens such as kale or collards may be stirred into the grits. Shrimp 'n' grits is just plain heaven.

Grits, preferably stone ground, are ground hominy kernels—white or yellow corn—that have been then passed through a screen. Quick grits are grits that have had the germ and hull removed. If you use them, you need to stir more frequently since they cook faster. When using long-cooking grits, follow the package instructions for rinsing them. Places like Anson Mills in South Carolina sell their products online now: www.ansonmills.com.

SWEET POTATO PIE WITH CARAMEL PECAN SAUCE (OPTIONAL)

1 pound sweet potatoes, peeled and quartered

5 tablespoons unsalted butter, softened

3/4 cup light or dark brown sugar

1/4 teaspoon ground nutmeg

3/4 teaspoon cinnamon

Pinch of salt

2 large eggs, beaten

1 cup half-and-half

1 teaspoon vanilla extract

An unbaked pie shell

Preheat the oven to 350 degrees.

Steam or boil the peeled potatoes until soft. Drain and puree using a food mill (sweet potatoes can be stringy). Set aside.

Cream the butter, sugar, spices, and salt by hand or with a hand mixer until light and fluffy. Beat in the eggs, half-and-half, and vanilla extract. Add the potatoes and beat until smooth.

Pour the mixture into the unbaked pie shell and bake for 40 to 50 minutes. A thin knife or skewer inserted in the middle of the pie should come out clean.

Serves 8.

Faith's favorite pie shell recipe may be made in your food processor or by hand:

PIE SHELL

1 1/2 cups all-purpose flour	1/2 cup cold unsalted
Pinch of salt	butter in pieces
Pinch of baking powder	1/4 cup ice water

If using a food processor, put all the ingredients in the processor, with the regular blade attached, and slowly add the ice water with the motor running until you have a nice ball of dough. If mixing by hand, cut the butter into the dry ingredients and then slowly add the ice water, mixing until the dough holds together.

Tightly wrap the ball of dough in plastic wrap and refrigerate for 1 hour.

On a floured work surface, roll out the chilled dough into a 14-inch round.

Press the rolled-out dough into a 9-inch pie pan, crimping the edges.

CARAMEL PECAN SAUCE

The caramel pecan sauce is listed as optional, because to many adding anything to a treasured sweet potato pie recipe is not only gilding the lily, but also downright blasphemous. However, this sauce is delicious on ice cream, pancakes, waffles, and all sorts of other concoctions. Plus, every once in a while, too much is just fine, and you may want to spoon it over your pie.

1/4 cup unsalted butter
1/2 cup light brown sugar
1 tablespoon half-and-half

2 tablespoons dark corn syrup
1/2 teaspoon vanilla extract
1/4 cup chopped pecans

Combine the butter, brown sugar, half-and-half, and corn syrup in a small saucepan and cook over low heat, stirring until it is smooth—approximately 5 minutes.

Remove from the heat. Add the vanilla extract and pecans. Stir and spoon over each serving, if desired.

The sauce will keep in the refrigerator for up to a week.

CLARET CUP

2 tablespoons sugar

1/4 cup water

2 bottles dry red wine

1/2 cup Grand Marnier, or
a similar orange-flavored
liqueur

1/2 cup crème de cassis

1/3 cup Port or Madeira

1/4 cup freshly squeezed
lemon juice

1 (1-liter) bottle chilled club
soda

1 (1-pint) block of ice (in
a decorative mold, if
available)

1 large naval orange, sliced

Make a sugar syrup by combining the sugar and water in a small saucepan over low heat until the sugar has dissolved completely. Cool.

Place all the remaining ingredients, except for the soda and ice, in a large punch bowl and stir. Chill, covered, until cold. Before serving, add the soda, ice, and decorative orange slices.

Makes approximately 12 cups.

The beauty of this punch is that the recipe may be doubled or tripled, depending on the crowd. Make it up ahead (except for the soda, ice, and oranges), storing it in empty liter soda bottles in the refrigerator—easy to replenish the punch as the party goes on. The orange slices left at the end in the empty bowl are delicious.

"Claret" is the British way of referring to red wines from the Bordeaux region of France, a term going back many centuries. Claret Cup has a nice elegant sound for the holidays.

About the Author

Katherine Hall Page is the author of twenty-two previous Faith Fairchild mysteries, the first of which received the Agatha Award for best first mystery. *The Body in the Snowdrift* was honored with the Agatha Award for best novel of 2006. Page also won an Agatha for her short story "The Would-Be Widower." The recipient of the Malice Domestic Award for Lifetime Achievement, she has also been nominated for the Edgar, the Mary Higgins Clark, the Maine Literary, and the Macavity Awards. She lives in Massachusetts and Maine with her husband.